*Incubus*

**RAY RUSSELL**

SPHERE BOOKS LIMITED
30-32 Gray's Inn Road. London WC1X 8JL

First published in Great Britain by Sphere Books Ltd 1977
Reprinted 1977 (three times), 1979, 1980 (twice), 1981, 1983

TRADE
MARK

Set in Intertype Baskerville

Printed and bound in Great Britain by
Collins, Glasgow

# Incubus

GALEN is an imaginary composite of several California towns and is not meant to portray any actual community.

# ONE

# THE TERROR

We are all of us creatures of manifold appetite. We hunger for food, water, sex, power, praise. We differ from each other only in the proportions of these hungers. Some of us yearn inordinately for food, and other hungers pale beside that one, though they are never entirely absent. Some of us yearn chiefly for sex; others for power; the saints among us hunger for grace; but not to the exclusion of other hungers. And yet testimony exists to tell of one whose appetites are not multiple; who burns with just a single hunger; whose every moment is ruled by it; whose whole life is obsessively directed toward one, and only one, purpose.

Henryk Stefanski
*Studies in Paranormality*
(Translated by Witold Tomaszewski)

# I

I WAS BORN TONIGHT.

How good I feel!

How fine it is to be born out of darkness and know at once the reason one was born.

How blessed to be formed into a state of strength, of power, of might, of blood that hums along the veins, of flesh as hard as oak.

How wonderful to sniff the air and smell the scents and seek them out and do the thing that I was meant to do.

Sublime to feel the lusciousness, the sweet shrill marvelous delight, the bliss, the heaven, the fulfillment, and the sure and certain knowing that one's birth has been a blaze of meaning.

I think that I was born before this night, as well, born long ago, born and born again on many nights, in other places far from here, but of that I am not sure, it does not matter.

All that matters is that I was born tonight, and I have done the thing, and it was good to do, and I will do the thing again.

# 2

FAR OUTNUMBERING all other names of California towns and cities are those derived from the Spanish, often beginning with San or Santa to denote, respectively, a male or female saint, like Saint Didacus (San Diego) or Saint Barbara. Some

13

of these have been whittled down from lengthy originals, the most famous being The Village of Our Lady the Queen of the Angels of Porciúncula, or, in Spanish, El Pueblo de Nuestra Señora la Reina de los Angeles de Porciúncula, better known today as L.A.

Some place names that might seem to be Spanish are actually Indian, like Sonoma. Other Indian names on the California map are Napa, Shasta, Modoc, Yolo, Lompoc, Yuba. There are many more.

You may have heard that the name Azusa was fabricated by a subdivider out of the slogan, 'From A to Z, the best in the USA.' But that's not true. It's an Indian name, too, corrupted from Asuka-gna, which, in the language of the Gabrielino Indians, means Skunk Hill.

Not all the cities and towns of California have Spanish or Indian names, however. There are the purely descriptive names, like Long Beach or Thousand Oaks. There's the occasional bilingual example, such as Anaheim, that thriving community basking in the reflected glory of Disneyland: founded and named by Germans, the first half of the name honors the Santa Ana River that flows beside the town, and the second half is the German word for 'home'.

Tarzana may be the only town in the world named after a fictional character: Edgar Rice Burroughs' ape man.

Some names have been borrowed from other regions – Ontario, Venice, Naples, Inglewood, Monmouth. The last wasn't named after Monmouth, Wales, as you might think, but Monmouth, Illinois, by a settler who hailed from there.

One California town was founded by a man named H. H. Wilcox, but it had no name until his wife, on a train trip, met a lady in the dining car who kept up a running monolog about her country estate in the east, called Hollywood. Mrs Wilcox thought that would be a nice name for her husband's new town.

There are the colorful old mining community names, of course – Mad Mule Gulch, Mosquito Valley, Chicken Flat, Pinch-em-Tight. But most of them are gone now.

And there are always the towns and cities named after

men. Sometimes the man's name becomes fancified, the way the name of the pioneer railroad builder, William Newton Monroe, became Monrovia. And sometimes people think a town is named after someone quite other than the man it's actually named for. Burbank is a good example. Most people assume it's named after Luther Burbank, the botanist. Not so. It's named after David Burbank, a dentist. Halfway between Los Angeles and San Francisco is another one named after a man, the placid little town of Galen, not to be confused with Galena. No, it's not named after the famous Greek physician of the second century.

It's on the coast, and if you didn't know you were in California, you'd swear that the ocean that licked the toes of the town was the Atlantic, not the Pacific. That's because Galen is the most New Englandish town you've ever seen outside of New England. It's something about the way the piers look, and the fishermen with their nets. Something about the red barns, and the way the houses are built, as if to stand against the snows of winter storms. Of course, the people don't say 'Ayeh', or any of those other Pa Kettle things, but they're a tight-lipped, narrow-eyed lot, for the most part, and in a pinch they could pose for a package of Oysterette crackers. When a heavy fog moves in from the sea and hangs over the town, chilling your bones and blurring the clear California outlines of things, then you're on the Eastern seaboard and no mistake. They say some of the movie companies have made films there, stories with New England settings, and the audiences were none the wiser.

The way they tell it, the town was started back in the middle 1800s by a man named Calvin Galen who had come out to California and brought his New England ways with him. Some say he was from New Hampshire, others claim he was from Maine. Nobody seems to know for sure. Might have been Massachusetts.

There are still some Galens in Galen. Two of them. But they're nowhere near as important as they used to be. One of them is Agatha Galen. She's in her seventies now. Lives in the old Galen mansion at the north edge of town – a grand place in its time, but pretty much gone to seed these days.

Her nephew, Tim, lives with her. Tim's father was Agatha's brother, Matthew. His mother was the former Kate Dover. They're both dead now. And they're all the Galens that are left. Agatha is a pillar of the church – that's the little white-washed frame structure that you might notice as you approach the town from the south. The most picturesque church you're ever likely to see outside of a Grandma Moses painting. Steeple and all. The pastor is the Reverend Francis Keaton: married, no children. The handful of Catholics and Jews in Galen have to drive into the nearest town, Midvale, for worship. Galen is hardcore WASP.

The town boasts a little two-year college, the full nomen-clature of which is the Edmund Jabez Galen Memorial College, the name being bigger than the school itself (isn't that often the way?). It exists mainly on a private endow-ment originally established by Tim's great-grandfather, Edmund, in honor of himself. Probably because nobody else volunteered to honor him.

The way it's worked with the mayoral office is like this: every four years a town council of four members is elected. And each of these people takes turn being mayor for one year. Even had a woman mayor once. This year it's Joe Prescott (widower; one son, Charley). Joe owns the town's only movie theater, the Paradise.

There's a newspaper, *The Galen Signal*, printed on an old flat-bed press. The editor is something else again. Her name is Laura Kincaid, and she's a full-bodied beauty in her late twenties. Dark brown hair, brown eyes, a real looker. A lot of the men in town including some of the married ones, have tried to make time with her, but she hasn't given them much in the way of encouragement. Her father has been dead a few years now. He owned and edited the paper, and Laura took it over when he died. She does a good job of it, too. The folks in Galen are awful gossips, a regular bunch of old hens the way they cackle, men and women alike, but there's never been any gossip about Laura. Bill Carter, he's about sixty, used to work for her father, and he still handles the printing chores.

The town has more than one doctor, but the main medical

16

man, the one people trust most, is Dr Sam Jenkins. Naturally, he's known as Doc. He's in his mid-fifties now, tall, gangling, with bristly iron-gray hair and a perpetually ironic expression. About six or seven years ago, the county lost its coroner, Maynard Andrews, when he died at the age of eighty-four. Doc Jenkins grudgingly accepted the temporary chore of acting coroner until a replacement could be found, and to this day he's still the acting coroner. He and his wife, Martha, have a teenage daughter, Jennie. All the boys are crazy about her. She's just about the cutest girl in town.

But Galen has a lot of pretty girls and women. There's little Mary Lou Grant, who sells popcorn and candy at the Paradise, and her mother, Anita: a nice-looking woman, but an invalid now. There's Prue Keaton, the Reverend's niece. Her mother, Helen, a schoolteacher, isn't exactly hard on the eyes, either. Even Belinda Fellowes, who sells tickets in the Paradise box office, although she's got to be crowding fifty, is a fine figure of a woman, if you like them on the hefty side. Joe Prescott does. And, of course, there was Melanie Saunders. Galen seems to have more than its share of attractive females. Maybe that's how all the trouble started.

Any trouble that does start up is handled by the county Sheriff, Hank Walden. Hank and his wife, Sarah, live in Galen, and that's where he makes his headquarters. Hank's totally bald, built like a barrel, and has a bullfrog voice. He's got a young deputy, Clem Conklin, who's his exact opposite: skinny, soft-spoken, all hair.

There's a small hospital, hardly more than a clinic, nothing fancy (for fancy medical treatment you have to go into Midvale), and there's a cozy, old-fashioned inn, owned and operated by Jed Purdy and his wife, Ruth. Melanie Saunders used to work for them as a waitress. Good-looking girl with the kind of figure that made the fellows say she was built like a brick firehouse, only they didn't exactly say firehouse. A little 'fast', some of the older folks called her, and maybe she was, but of course they don't talk that way about her anymore. Folks in Galen aren't ones to speak ill of the dead. Particularly when they die in such a terrible way.

*

Melanie was enjoying a moonlight swim with Tim Galen that night, diving off the edge of the old pier. They were naked, what folks used to call skinny-dipping (maybe they still do), but there wasn't anything skinny about Melanie. Tim, yes, he was always a slender boy, but Melanie really must have been something to write home about when seen in a state of nature, as they say.

The way Tim told it later, he'd been having a cup of coffee at the inn that evening, getting on to closing time, and it was Melanie who waited on him. 'Soon as we close up,' she told him, 'I'm going for a dip in the ocean. Want to come along?' He told her he didn't have his swimtrunks with him, but she just laughed and called him chicken, so he took her up on it.

It was foggy that night – it's often foggy this time of the year – and it must have been hard for them to see each other down by the ocean except when they were close up. It gets quiet at the beach at such times. The fog is like a furry blanket, soaking up the sound, cushioning the spoken word, or even the shouted word, soft-pedalling the steady rhythm of the waves. The muted sound and fog-thick air make an aura of the unreal hang over the beach, as if you're on some strange planet where natural laws aren't the same as they are here. You feel like you're in slow-motion, moving through an atmosphere of damp gray cotton. And you're cold, particularly if you don't have a stitch of clothing on.

But Tim and Melanie, being young and high-spirited and full of fun, probably didn't feel the cold. The pair of them were splashing around, making noise, laughing, frolicking. Tim made a grab for her and tried to kiss her. She pretended to be alarmed at this and squealed and pulled away from him, pushing his head under the water playfully, and then swam away from him, toward shore.

His head bobbed up, he blinked, spouted water, looked around, couldn't see much in the fog and dark and with the salt water in his eyes, and he called out: 'Melanie! Hey, Mel?'

He couldn't see her, but he heard her: 'Come and get me!'

18

'Don't think I won't!' he shouted, and began to swim back to shore.

Under the pier, Melanie emerged nude and dripping from the sea and hid from Tim among the old rotted pilings. She could hear the sound of his splashing approach, and his voice, promising, 'I'll get you!'

When he reached the shore, he couldn't see her, but she was nearby, behind one of the pilings, trying hard not to giggle at him. He probably looked kind of comical, what she could see of him, that buck-naked skinny young fellow, shivering, hair all wet and plastered down. And then he must have stepped into shadow, or behind another piling, because she couldn't see him anymore.

She couldn't see who was standing behind her, either.

But just a second or two later, she surely felt him. She knew it was a him because the hands that gripped her were strong and bruising. As she turned and tried to fight him off, there was no doubt at all it was a him, even though she still couldn't see him clearly.

Melanie was 'fast', as they say, and she'd gone with a lot of the men of the town. The male animal couldn't have held many surprises for her. But the attacker who seized her under the pier that night must have been like nothing she'd ever experienced before. That's why she screamed so loud and long.

It didn't do her any good. He threw her down on the wet sand and covered her with his dark shape, and to her it must have been an agony beyond all imagining.

After a while, she stopped screaming.

Who knows how long after that it was when Tim found her, and kneeled naked beside her, saying, 'Mel . . . what is it? . . . what happened?'

Her eyes were open, but they were blank, not seeing anything. Her face was dead, without expression.

Tim tried to get her to move. He kept talking to her. 'Come on, we've got to get you out of here. What's *wrong*? We've got to get our clothes on and –'

He touched her. Melanie's face split in two as her mouth

19

stretched wide in a scream that never stopped.

It stopped later, much later, at the hospital, but only after Doc Jenkins injected a massive dose of sedative into her bloodstream. 'She'll be quiet for a while,' he told the nurse. 'If she wakes up and starts screaming again,' he added, 'give her another shot, the same dosage, then call me. I'll be at home.' The two of them lifted the now-limp body of the sedated girl onto a bed.

In the corridor outside the private room, Sheriff Hank Walden was waiting, with Tim Galen. Tim had dressed by this time, of course, but his hair was still damp and lank from his midnight swim. He was the first to address the doctor: 'How is she?'

'Under sedation,' was all Doc said.

The sheriff asked, 'Did she say anything?'

'No,' said Doc. 'But she remembered. That's what triggered the hysteria.'

'Remembered who, I wonder?' said the sheriff, as the three men left the hospital.

Tim immediately said, 'It wasn't me, Sheriff – you've got to believe that!'

Hank Walden was non-committal. 'No one's accusing you yet, son. You just stay put for a minute.'

The sheriff walked Doc Jenkins to his car, outside in the hospital parking lot.

'Poor girl's not much older than my Jennie,' said Doc, more to himself than to Hank.

'What do you make of it?' the sheriff asked.

Dr Jenkins shook his head. 'I didn't want to say in front of Tim Galen,' he replied, 'but this case is just like that college girl last month . . .'

'Gwen Morrissey?'

'Yes. That was the most vicious case of rape I'd ever seen or heard of – until this one.'

Gwen Morrissey was a Galen College co-ed. She had been brutally raped and killed in Galen Park the previous month, just before the end of term. Not a clue had been found as to the identity of the attacker.

Doc opened the door of his big Buick convertible, but he didn't get in. He stood there, shaking his head, searching for words.

'Whoever did it,' he said finally, 'was . . . not normal.'

'Understatement of the year, Doc.' said Hank. 'Any fool knows a man who would do a thing like that isn't right in the head.'

Doc seemed about to respond to this, but he remained silent.

'That *is* what you meant, isn't it?' Hank asked.

The doctor hesitated before replying. 'I haven't had time to do a complete examination of Melanie yet. I'm going to see her again in the morning. Then I'll drop by your office.' He got into his car and closed the door.

'Now, hold on, Doc,' said the sheriff, leaning into the car window. 'You're not telling me everything, and I don't like that. I have a right to know. It may be a clue.'

'Tomorrow, Hank.'

'Damn it, Doc, that son of a bitch is loose out there somewhere. I need all the help I can get.'

'But I don't *know* anything yet!'

'All right,' said Hank, 'all right. You come see me tomorrow, after you examine Melanie. And in the meantime I'm locking up Tim Galen. So far he's our only suspect.'

'No,' said Doc Jenkins. 'Not Tim.'

'What do you mean, not Tim? They were swimming bareass together! *Who*, then?'

'I don't know who,' replied the doctor. 'But it wasn't Tim.'

Sheriff Walden stood speechless with frustration as he watched Doc Jenkins drive out of the hospital parking lot.

The car radio was proffering a melancholy passage of a Mahler symphony as the black Porsche two-seater made its way up the California coast. It was a clear sunny day, but the driver's mood was somber, and the music complemented his feelings perfectly. He was a man in his early forties, with straight, jet-black hair of an almost Oriental density, relieved at the temples with a beginning hint of gray. His jaw was

21

strong, his mouth a gash, his eyes as hard as carborundum. He had started early in the morning from his home on the campus of a small San Diego college, and he was now approaching Santa Monica. He felt hungry, so he turned off the coast highway into town.

He parked half a block from the beach, bought an hour of time from the meter, and walked down to the ocean front. The promenade was shabby, but the sun-warmed air was like a golden broth, rich and restorative.

He strolled past an old hotel, with peeling pink plaster. Everything was sunwashed, seaswept, windbroomed, clean, bright, light. Sand and water. Sailboats on the sea. Lavender mountains in the distance. Kids on bikes. Barefoot girls and long-haired boys. Wizened winos talking to themselves, giving their alter egos hell.

He stopped for a moment to watch a fat middle-aged homosexual, in denims and a big straw hat, choreographing a young swimsuited couple dancing on a patch of grass. They pirouetted and posed. The girl was wearing an ultra-scanty string bikini. The Porsche driver watched her admiringly, then he walked on.

Pigeons strutted boldly right up to his feet. Predatory seagulls swooped. Two sparrows fought, chirping fiercely. He watched old men playing chess and checkers at long wooden tables. He saw a group of half-naked girls, stewardesses he surmised, chattering in French as they sunned themselves on the sand under AIR CANADA towels.

'Normalcy,' he thought to himself, smiling inwardly at the convenient illiteracy of Warren G. Harding's famous coinage. The Known World.

His hunger pangs grew sharper, and he began to look around for an eating place. BEACHWARE, said one sign. SOFT ICE CREAM, said another. A third offered HOT DOG ON A STICK, a repulsive suggestion, but he was too hungry to care. He bought one, and ate it on the way back to his car. Soon, he was on the coast highway again, driving north. The car radio had deserted Mahler for Sibelius. He switched it off.

'Julian Trask, fortyish, divorced, is a saturninely hand-

22

some man in vigorous maturity. His manner is as dry and cool as a ten-to-one martini. His speech has not completely lost the crisp accent he brought from England when he settled in the U.S. almost two decades ago. He is serious, seldom smiles, and his relentless dark eyes seem able to pierce any mystery. They may, indeed, hold mysteries of their own.' That was how a newsmagazine had described him a couple of years before, in a short piece in the Science section. He considered the description to be somewhat swashbuckling, but not too inaccurate.

As he stopped for a moment, somewhere in Malibu, at one of the few traffic lights on the highway, he saw a blonde girl standing at the side of the road, lyrically thumbing, a tote bag in her other hand, eyes hopeful, teeth flashing, brash navel staring directly at him.

He shrugged at her in rueful apology, and drove on as the light turned green. Under other circumstances, he might have picked her up. But not today. He had more important things to think about, and to do, and many miles to drive before he would reach Galen.


# 3


*... a little thing she is younger than twenty and more than usually pleasing to behold her face is pale in sharp contrast to the sunset blaze of her unbound hair she wears a single garment of coarse fabric it is too large for her hanging loosely about her body and reaching down to her unshod feet her stomach growls with emptiness for she has been given nothing but water for two days and little of that she sits on a hard wooden chair*

*ill-smelling torches are set in walls of blackened stone they give off more smoke than light greasy smoke that stings her eyes and nostrils it makes her cough the three men in the*

*chamber with her do not appear to be so troubled they are*
*accustomed to it creatures of half-light that they are stale*
*air and torch smoke is their natural element*

*one of the men is stripped to the waist showing wide*
*bands of muscle and a barrel chest covered with sweat and*
*dark bristles he stands alongside her his flesh exudes a chok-*
*ing animal stink*

*the second man sits at a simple desk a sharpened quill*
*in his hand ink and paper ready he looks bored*

*it is the third man who frightens her most and yet he is*
*the gentlest seeming of them all elderly tall with white hair*
*and deep set eyes he was obviously handsome in his youth*
*he wears magisterial garb of utmost austerity his voice when*
*he speaks is soft cultivated assured . . .*

# 4

BILL CARTER was always first at the *Signal* office, every morning. He unlocked the door, his hand a bit shaky, vision a
mite blurred, and walked straight to the old press he'd been
nursemaiding half his life. It was one of the original Miehle
two-revolution flat-beds, a relic from the turn of the century,
but it had been kept in good condition through the years,
and met the *Signal*'s modest needs more than adequately.
He would reach under the press to a special hiding place and,
as his hand closed around the familiar gin bottle, a sense of
well-being would spread from his fingertips and radiate
through his whole body. With the first gulp of the day, his
hand would steady and his sight sharpen into clear focus.
He'd be ready for work, raring to go. Bill was a man of strict
discipline. He never drank off the job.

This day was no different from any other. As he was
beginning to set type from the pages of copy left for him
by Laura the evening before, Laura herself would arrive –
and arrive she did, right on time. She looked good, but then

she always looked good. A cheerful smile, bright yes, and those full curves under her simple dress – Bill wasn't too old to appreciate them, not by a long shot.

'Morning, Bill,' she said briskly.

'Morning, Miss Kincaid.'

As usual, Laura had a few last-minute copy changes that had occurred to her upon awakening. 'Bill, second graph of the property tax story, change "equitable" to "fair".'

Bill nodded. 'Yes, ma'am. Just like your dad used to say – why use a four-cylinder word when one will do? But this tax story is pretty long – you aim to chop it down some?'

'No. If you need more column space, jump to page three and drop the movie review.'

'Joe Prescott won't like that none. Took out a big ad for his Paradise Theater today.'

'He won't mind. We roasted the picture.'


Nearby, a little later that morning, Julian Trask's shiny black Porsche pulled up in front of The Galen Inn. Julian got out and stood for a moment, looking at the quaint colonial exterior of the building. He smiled. It hadn't changed. Lifting a single large suitcase from the trunk, he entered the inn.

The interior hadn't changed much, either, nor had the proprietor. He remembered Jed Purdy as a man of middle years, and he still fit the description, although he had been fifty then, and now was a shade past sixty. Jed, doing his accounts behind the desk, looked up over his glasses as Julian approached.

'Yes, sir? Help you?'

He didn't remember Julian, but that wasn't surprising. Julian had never stayed at the inn as a guest, just dined here a few times in the old days.

'A room, please,' he said, setting down his suitcase.

'Certainly. Be staying in town long?'

'I'm not sure.'

'That's all right. Take all the time you want. Just sign here, please.'

The room into which Julian was ushered a few moments

25

later was as charming as he expected it to be. Lace curtains. The smell of wood. Hand-rubbed chairs. A big soft four-poster bed. Like something out of another century. It was a welcome change from the plastic-and-chromium motel rooms to which he had almost resigned himself.

He felt seedy from the long drive. A shower was the first order of business. Heaving his suitcase onto the bed, he unlocked it and took out his shaving kit. Packed next to it was a book, an immense and ancient volume, bound in tough brown parchment. He locked the suitcase again before stepping into the bathroom.

It was close to noon when Julian strolled over to the *Signal* office. The noise of the press was deafening. Laura, busily correcting proof at her desk, didn't even notice him enter. He leaned over the desk and shouted over the racket: 'Can I get some business cards printed?'

'Embossed or regular?' Laura started to ask, and then she looked up. 'Julian!'

'Hello, Laura.'

She yelled over the din to Bill: 'Time for lunch, isn't it?'

Bill nodded, stopped the ear-stunning machine, and diplomatically left the premises.

Alone together, in relative silence, Laura said, 'It's been a long time.'

'Too long,' he agreed.

'What brings you back to Galen?'

'Would you believe: lust?'

She laughed. 'Little me? Or do you have some other lady hidden away in Galen?'

'You're the only one.'

The playful banter masked a passionate but unconsummated attraction both of them had felt eleven years before. Julian had taught a course at Galen College and Laura had been a seventeen-year-old student of his who precociously had graduated from high school a year prior to the customary age. She'd had a schoolgirl crush on the dynamic young Briton, and he had been powerfully drawn to her. But Julian was scrupulously ethical, and there was a little legal tech-

26

nicality called statutory rape to be wary of, as well. If it had not been for those two strong deterrents, Julian could have had her for the asking.

'Well,' Laura said brightly, 'this calls for an exclusive interview, at the very least. When our little town is honored by a visit from the famous Julian Trask, that's news.'

'Good news or bad news? Anyway, a couple of esoteric books and a squib in *Time* don't exactly make me famous.'

'Maybe not,' she said, 'but you've done pretty well since the days you taught anthropology here. Cup of coffee?' She got up and moved toward a hot plate where a globe of inky-black brew was bubbling.

'Thanks. Cream, no sugar.'

'You'll be sorry.'

'You've done all right yourself, Laura,' he said. 'The *Signal* compares favorably with the Emporia *Gazette* in its heyday. And you're a lot prettier than William Allen White.'

'Why, thank you, Julian.'

'Of course,' he added, 'that's only one man's opinion.'

'You're no gallant!'

'Not at all. Just paying well-earned respect to Galen's Fighting Newswoman.'

'News*person*,' she responded as she handed him a steaming cup.

'Right. I apologize. But you don't mind if I continue to think of you as a woman?'

'I'd kill you if you didn't.'

He cautiously tasted the coffee, and winced. 'Wow. I will have some sugar, after all.'

'Told you so.' She spooned a heaping mound into his cup. 'Yes, the paper has kept me busy since Dad died. I enjoy it. It's an awful lot of work, of course.'

'You're not married?'

'With my deadlines? I have enough trouble just getting the *paper* to bed – let alone anybody else.'

Julian laughed, and tried another sip of his coffee. 'Ah. Much better. But you do take time for lunch, don't you?'

'Are you buying?'

'If I may.'

27

'You may. I'm not *that* liberated. Just give me a minute to powder my nose.'

The dining room of the inn was precisely as Julian had remembered it. Hurricane lamps, barometers, fishing nets, miscellaneous nautical decor. Corny, but nice. Everything gave the appearance of being gently aged, softly worn, smoothed by the comings and goings of countless hands and feet. Tablecloths! Julian was sick to death of formica. Soon after he and Laura had been seated, she said. 'I skipped breakfast this morning. I wanted to get some corrections to Bill before he locked up the front page. I'm famished.'

'Fine,' said Julian. 'What will you have?'

'As long as you're treating, I'll go off my diet. Eggs Benedict. To hell with the calories.'

'On you, the calories all seem to go to the right places.' When the waitress appeared, Julian said, 'Two orders of Eggs Benedict and coffee.'

When the waitress had left, he said, 'The Saunders girl works here, doesn't she?'

'Until recently, yes,' said Laura. 'I hope she'll be well enough to return to work soon. But how do you know about her? She wasn't working here eleven years ago.'

'No,' he said. 'Since the end of term, I've been in Mexico, living among the Indians, doing research for a paper I'm writing. The ritual and religious connotations of the *Psilocybe mexicana.*'

'*Psil —* '

'It's sometimes called the magic mushroom. I studied under a very wise old *curandero*, sort of an unofficial priest of the cult. Learned a lot from him. Anyway, when I got back to San Diego, there was a lot of mail waiting for me at the college. And among it was a pile of back issues of *The Galen Signal.*'

'What?' said Laura in surprise. 'You're a subscriber?'

'For the past eleven years. Didn't you know?'

She shook her head. 'I farm out things like that.'

'Yes, I've had a soft spot in my heart for Galen ever since I taught here, and I wanted to keep in touch. But, as I started to say, I was *out* of touch for several weeks when I was down in Mexico. That's why I didn't see these stories until just recently.'

He reached into the inside pocket of his jacket and took out a couple of *Signal* clippings, which he unfolded and placed on the table. One, a story about Gwen Morrissey, was headlined, COLLEGE GIRL RAPED, KILLED. The second bore the headline, WAITRESS SECOND RAPE VICTIM, with a subhead reading, MELANIE SAUNDERS IN SHOCK; ATTACKER UNKNOWN.

Laura glanced at the clippings and handed them back to him. 'Yes,' she said, 'that's the *Signal* brand of yellow journalism, all right, but what does it have to do with anthropology?'

Julian toyed with a breadstick for a moment before replying. 'Well, I've drifted away from pure anthropology, you know. I've created what amounts to a whole new field of study.'

'Even so,' said Laura, 'how does it concern a couple of rape victims?'

'I think we'd better save that until after the Eggs Benedict. It might spoil your appetite.' He snapped the breadstick in two. 'Laura,' he said, 'what are my chances, d'you think, of seeing Melanie Saunders?'

Laura shrugged. 'You have to clear it with Doc Jenkins.'

'I remember him,' said Julian, 'but I doubt that he'd remember me. Could The Fighting Newsperson pave the way for me with an introduction?'

'She might,' said Laura, 'if you didn't keep evading her questions.'

Julian smiled. 'Later,' he said. 'In my room. I have something up there that might help explain.'

As Julian closed and locked the door of his room, Laura said, 'I can't stay long. And I'm not being coy. It's just that this *is* a small town, and it's broad daylight . . . '

'And you're a respectable unmarried business woman. Business *person*. I understand. That's not the reason I locked the door.'

He pulled his suitcase from under the bed, unlocked it with a key from his pocket, and said, 'Sit down. I want to show you something.'

She sat at the foot of the four-poster bed as he lifted from the suitcase the enormous parchment-bound book. 'What *is* that, the Gutenberg Bible?' she asked.

'Hardly. An it's even older than the Gutenberg.'

'It must be valuable.'

'Beyond price,' said Julian. 'Extremely rare. This may be the only copy in the United States.'

As he held the closed volume before her, Laura traced the title with her fingertips. It was printed in old Gothic lettering. The second word of the title contained an 'i' with a hole for a dot, a puckered indentation almost like a bullet hole. *'Artes Perditae,'* she read aloud. *'Lost Arts?'*

'You remember your Latin.'

'Well, that much, anyway.'

She opened the book at random – the brown parchment binding crackled as she did so – and began turning the pages slowly, with great absorption. Columns of dense Latin, printed in the spiky old Gothic typeface, met her gaze. The impenetrable mass of type was occasionally relieved by small engravings, crude old drawings of wizards, witches, demons.

She turned a page. 'What's this?' she asked. 'It's not Latin,' Before Julian could reply, she had begun to form the words with her own lips: *'Oreela boganna . . .'*

'No!' cried Julian, closing the book with a sharp clap.

They heard a low, deep rumble, as if a subterranean railroad train were passing under the inn. The drinking glass on the bedside table clinked and chattered against the water carafe. Frightened, Laura sprang to her feet and clung to Julian. Then the sound passed.

'It's all right,' Julian said with relief. 'No harm done.'

Laura was shamefaced and said, with some embarrassment, 'Don't know why I can't get used to those little California tremors. Lived here all my life.'

Julian squeezed her reassuringly in his arms. 'Yes,' he said. 'That may be all it was.'

'Of course. What else could it have been?'

'Nothing. You're right. A little quake.'

She was puzzled to see him lock the old book into his suitcase again. 'What was it you were going to show me?' she asked.

'Show you?' he said, with false heartiness. 'That was just an excuse to entice you up here to my den of iniquity.' He took her easily into his arms. 'Stay,' he said.

'I really can't.' In a lower voice, she added, 'Not now.'

She gently extricated herself from his embrace and walked to the door. 'I'll set it up for you with Doc Jenkins,' she said. 'Maybe he can see you this afternoon.'

'Thanks.'

She smiled. 'And can I have a raincheck?'

He pantomimed elaborate indifference. 'Well, I'll think about it.'

Laughing, she left. Julian patted his suddenly damp brow with a pocket handkerchief. 'That was close,' he muttered to himself, and was interested to note that his hands were shaking.

## 5

*... his voice when he speaks is soft cultivated assured*

*thou hast naught to tell me he asks for what is far from the first time*

*she shakes her head*

*her interrogator sighs and turns to his scribe*

*set it down thus he says the accused having failed to respond to merciful questioning was on this date put to the torture*

*she stiffens at the dreadful word the half naked man at her side suppresses a smile the quill of the scribe scratches against the paper*

*art ready rackmaster the interrogator asks the sweating man the rackmaster nods*

*then do thou make a beginning of this business but with lesser measures now and let us pray she will speak ere other methods are required*

*the man called rackmaster is already binding her tightly to the chair with leathern straps from a table in a dark corner he selects a small metal instrument of which the principal feature is a screw deferentially he asks the interrogator fingers or toes my lord*

*the interrogator shrugs delegating this minor decision*

*shaking with fear she watches the rackmaster kneel before her and take her foot in his hand like a fairy tale prince with a dainty shoe but his fingers are rough and calloused against the skin of her bare foot she tries to pull away but he holds her foot fast in his grip he forces one of her toes into the icy screw and slowly . . .*

# 6

DR SAMUEL JENKINS nursed one frustrated ambition. He saw himself as a cracker barrel wit of the Mark Twain or Will Rogers variety. It was an ambition not entirely frustrated, because for some time now he had been contributing an every-so-often column to *The Galen Signal*, under the pseudonym 'Will Clemens', in homage to his two favorite humorists. Laura was only too happy to publish his little pieces – they helped fill her pages and cost her nothing – and she conspired with Doc to keep his deep dark secret. Despite their conspiracy, most of the *Signal*'s readers had a pretty good idea who Will Clemens was. They recognized Doc's style.

Later that afternoon, as he sat in his office waiting for Julian to arrive, he read over his latest opus and made a few pencil changes:

Among the more militant young women of my acquaintance, including the charming editor of this paper, there is a growing preference to be addressed as 'Ms' (pronounced 'Mizz'), rather than 'Miss' or 'Mrs' (pronounced 'Miss' or 'Missus'). The idea, as I understand it, is that 'Ms' does not reveal the woman's marital status, which they consider to be nobody's business but their own. After all, they argue, men have never suffered the indignity of having a marital-status label attached to their names for all to see – 'Mr' (pronounced 'Mister') is used for bachelors and benedicts alike.

They have a point, and I'm more than willing to oblige them, but the prefix does present problems. For one thing, 'MS' has had only three meanings for me all my life. One of them is the abbreviation of the word 'manuscript'. Another means Multiple Sclerosis. And another is the initials of Minnie Sawyer, who, when we were both in first year high school . . . but that's *really* nobody's business.

The other problem is that pesky pronunciation, 'Mizz'. To my ears – too long in city pent, perhaps – it is redolent of mint juleps, crinoline, and banjo music. It conjures up visions of those sugar plums Scarlett O'Hara and Butterfly McQueen and even Little Eva. These damyankee lips of mine, their habits formed early by the harsh argot of the Deep North, would feel uncomfortable saying 'Mizz'.

Still, I aim to please, so I've tried other pronunciations of 'Ms'. The best of these is 'Mzzzzz', which sounds like a large and very upset horsefly, and therefore cannot be wholeheartedly recommended.

I've really gone out of my way to be nice. but I just can't hack it. The best I can do is try to make a deal with the wimmin-folk (see? I *told* you how 'Mizz' transports me instantly to the old plantation). The deal I offer is this:

I'll agree to use 'Ms' – pronounced any way they like, including 'Mess', 'Muss', or 'Moose' – if they will agree to at least *try* a prefix of my coinage, to be applied indiscriminately to men *and* women, married or single.

Because, now that I think about it, I feel it's nobody's business what sex I am. Why should I be saddled with a label – the odious and discriminatory 'Mr' – which clearly stamps me as a male? This relic of the repressive past reveals entirely too much intimate information about me, without my consent. Every letter I receive bears the hated 'Mr' in front of my name, right out there on the envelope. It blatantly announces to my mailman that the addressee is of the male sex. This is downright indecent – especially when you consider the fact that my mailman is a mailwoman. Why should this naked masculinity be thrust in her face, six days a week?

I therefore came to the conclusion that all human beings, regardless of sex, age, or marital status, should be addressed by a common prefix. The first one I thought of was simply 'M.' (pronounced 'Mmmmmm'), but I immediately realized that this would too easily be confused with the French 'Monsieur'. My next candidate was 'M?' (pronounced 'Mmmmmm?'). The upward lilt at the end has a happy aptness, indicating that the whole subject of gender is open to question, which is exactly what we want it to be, right? Still, there's something awkward about 'Mmmmmm?'. I said it aloud to myself, several times, sitting in the local inn sipping Scotch, and it sounded like a constant request for information – precisely the thing we want to avoid. Also, Jed Purdy refused to serve me any more Scotch. He said I'd had enough. My next idea was the single character '?'. But I had great difficulty pronouncing this. Most of my attempts sounded like wind whistling down the chimney. Or worse. Jed escorted me bodily to the door.

The only solution, I finally decided, is to eliminate *all* such troublesome prefixes and use unadorned names.

Then it dawned upon me that *names* are the most outrageous invaders of privacy the world has ever known! Our given names reveal our sex. Our last names disclose our ethnic origins. Obviously intolerable – probably unconstitutional.

We are left with one hope. I respectfully suggest that all of us, whatever our sex, abandon our names, as well as our prefixes, and address each other by our Social Security Numbers.

On second thought, Doc decided to delete the reference to the mailman being a mailwoman. Galen had never had a distaff mail carrier, although Doc knew they were becoming familiar sights in some of the bigger cities. It would be a false note in the *Signal*. With a flourish of his pencil, he struck out the passage. He sat back, pleased with his creative powers. A moment later, Julian knocked on his office door.

Doc had a surprisingly clear memory of his visitor from the days when Julian had taught at Galen College. As he motioned him into his office, he peered at him with scientific scrutiny, and said, 'Kidney stone, wasn't it?'

That's *right*,' Julian answered with amazement. 'What a memory!'

'High uric acid level, over seven point two. Still on the same medication, Zyloprim?' Julian nodded. 'Good. Drink plenty of water, at least two quarts a day, don't let yourself get dehydrated. Pass any stones since that last time?'

'No stones. I've been flamboyantly healthy'

'You're looking good. Sit down.'

Julian sank into a deep chair, upholstered in old brown leather, as the doctor settled himself behind his desk. 'I didn't think you'd remember me,' said Julian. 'That's why I asked Laura Kincaid to arrange an introduction.'

Doc Jenkins smiled. 'I'd do anything for Laura. Her father was one of my closest friends. And she's a fine gal. Smart as a whip. And good-looking as they come. Ought to get herself a husband. If I weren't a married man myself, and a bit long in the tooth . . . But what did you want to see me about?'

'Melanie Saunders.'

'What about her?'

'I'm interested in her.'

Doc snorted. 'Somebody else was interested in her, too, the other night – so interested he damn near killed her.'

'I know,' said Julian. 'That's why I'm here. I'd like to see her, talk to her if I can.'

The doctor shook his head. 'The girl's in shock. Severe catatonia. I don't want her upset. She couldn't tell you anything, anyway. Won't say a word. Once in a while she snaps out of it long enough to scream, so we keep her sedated most of the time.'

Julian leaned forward in the chair. 'If I could talk to her, I might be able to get through to her, find out who attacked her . . .'

'Getting through to her,' said Dr Jenkins brusquely, 'just might push her completely over the edge. You represent yourself as a scientist, Mr Trask, but you're not a psychiatrist, you're not even a pill pusher like me, you're some kind of anthropologist or whatever. I can't let you meddle in

35

matters you're obviously not qualified to handle.'

'Doctor,' Julian inquired, 'isn't there something about this case that didn't get into the paper? Something about Melanie's condition?'

'How could you possibly know that?'

'Just a guess,' said Julian. 'An educated guess. The other girl, Gwen Morrissey, died – but there were no reports of her being beaten or stabbed. Apparently, she wasn't assaulted in any way – except sexually. Does a woman usually die from sexual intercourse, even rape? And, just a moment ago, you said Melanie Saunders was nearly killed. How?'

Doc Jenkins rose from behind his desk and walked over to the window. After staring outside, unseeing, for several moments, he returned to the desk, picked up his pipe, and began to fill it from a humidor of strong tobacco. 'Mr Trask,' he said, 'you have to realize that Miss Saunders is my patient. Her privacy has to be respected. I can't go around telling intimate details of her medical condition.'

Julian changed tactics. 'Why wasn't Tim Galen arrested?'

'Ask the Sheriff.'

'Tim Galen was with Melanie that night, wasn't he? Why isn't he the prime suspect?'

'Because,' said the doctor, 'he couldn't have been the rapist.'

'Why not?' Julian asked. 'He's a man, isn't he? Sexually mature, developed?' Doc Jenkins said nothing. 'Or,' pursued Julian, 'is he inadequate? Impotent?'

'Tim's a patient of mine, too,' said the doctor, 'and his medical condition is just as confidential as Melanie's.'

Julian sighed. 'All I really want from you,' he said, 'is one minute with Melanie Saunders. Is that really such an unreasonable request?'

'One minute?'

'That's all I ask.'

'Not alone with her.'

'In your presence.'

Doc had forgotten to light his pipe. Now he did, sucking and smacking until he got it going. 'I still don't know what

36

business it is of yours,' he said, 'but Laura vouches for you . . . ' He puffed at his pipe. The fumes hung in the air of his little office. He walked over to the clothestree where his hat was perched. Plucking it off and jamming it squarely on his head, he said, 'All right. Let's go.'

As they drove to the hospital in the doctor's Buick, Julian asked, 'What made you change your mind?'

Doc Jenkins did not answer immediately. When he did, he said, 'Your educated guess was pretty accurate. So you just might be onto something. And if you are, I'm not going to get in your way. I've got a daughter just a couple of years younger than Melanie, and –'

With a screech of brakes, he brought the car to a jolting stop. He had missed by mere inches an amiably homely young man in his late teens who grinned with embarrassment at the doctor. The lad was big, chubby, apple-cheeked, with a generous sprinkling of freckles and a wild shock of bright red hair.

Doc Jenkins yelled angrily at him out the car window. 'Damn it, Charley! You could land in the hospital dashing across the street like that!'

'Sorry, Doc,' said the young man, 'but think of all the bread you'd make, patching me up!'

'Very funny!'

The doctor started the car again and drove on. 'Charley Prescott,' he informed Julian. 'Father owns the movie theater and is acting as Mayor this year. Quite an intelligent lad, actually, when he's not behaving like the village idiot.'

'Patient of yours?' Julian asked.

Doc nodded.

'And do you feel the same about him as you do about Tim Galen? That he's not the rapist?'

'I do. Charley's not our man. And I'll tell you something else. I don't think the culprit is a Galenite at all. I think he's got to be an out-of-towner.'

'I wonder,' said Julian, half to himself.

'Look, Trask, why don't you come right out and put your

cards on the table? Why do you, a total stranger, suspect Tim and Charley even after I tell you I'm sure it wasn't either of them? I've known those two boys ever since they were born.'

'Doctor,' said Julian, evenly, 'I'll put my cards on the table, tell you everything I know, everything I suspect, even the wildest hunches that flicker across my mind – after I talk to Melanie Saunders.'

'Fair enough,' said Doc, as he turned in to the hospital parking lot.

'How is she today?' Dr Jenkins asked the nurse at the desk.

'Doing nicely, Doctor,' she replied. 'Very quiet. For the past few hours she hasn't even required any sedation. Not a sound out of her.'

'Good, good.' Doc Jenkins walked past the desk and down the corridor, Julian following.

The doctor stopped outside Melanie's room. 'I'll go in first, and have a look at her. If I still think it's advisable for you to talk to her, I'll let you in. But just for one minute, that's all. Wait out here.'

Doc Jenkins entered the room. Julian's thoughts flew at once to the two words Laura had read aloud in his room earlier that day. It had been a mistake, he realized now, to be so free with that book. And as for his theories and suspicions, he no longer planned to share them with Laura. Why frighten her?

He dwelt on these thoughts for only seconds when the door to the hospital room opened again and Dr Jenkins appeared. He leaned against the door jamb. His face was gray. 'Dear God,' he whispered.

Julian pushed past him, into the room.

He almost walked right into a pair of bare feet. They floated in mid-air, exactly at his eye level. He looked up. A naked girl was suspended from the ceiling by her neck. The young body turned slowly, first this way, then that. The face was purpled, the eyes bulging, the tongue obscenely lolling from the mouth. With the aid of her torn hospital

gown, an overturned chair, and a heating pipe on the ceiling,
Melanie Saunders had taken her leave of this world.

Incongruously, through his shock, Julian's mind recorded
the absurd note that her toenails were painted bright red.

# 7

. . . he forces one of her toes into the icy screw and slowly
tightens it

lightning bolts of agony shoot upward from her toe to the
very roots of her hair and she screams

tell me says the interrogator

she shakes her head teeth clenched

the rackmaster tightens the screw again

shrieking and twisting in the chair she feels and hears a
tiny bone break

tell me the interrogator repeats seductively

she says nothing her foot is slick with blood

from his kneeling position the rackmaster turns and speaks

by thy leave my lord these women do oft have about them
such evil charms and trinkets that deaden god's good pain
wilt thou still not permit her to be searched

her cries were most piteous and real says the interrogator

playacting sir they are dissemblers by nature these
wenches

the interrogator looks at him sternly and says dost talk of
searching for what pleasure 'twill afford thee

nay i warrant thee my lord

the interrogator indicates assent with a weary flutter of
his hand

at this the zealous rackmaster strips her naked with one
quick rending of cloth the coarse shift that has been her only
covering he throws contemptuously to the floor she cowers

*in shame on the chair pressing her knees close together*
   *loosening only those straps necessary for the search the*
*rackmaster forces her head down to her knees and . . .*

# 8

THAT NIGHT, following a grueling afternoon with Sheriff
Walden and the cadaver of Melanie Saunders, Dr Jenkins
received Julian into his home 'for a drink and a talk'.

It was after eleven when Julian arrived at the attractive
two-storey house. The doctor answered the door. He was
relaxing in a sweater and slacks, with a pair of old carpet
slippers on his feet and a glass already in his hand. 'I'm a
couple of drinks ahead of you,' he said. 'You have some
catching up to do.'

'Several years ago you told me to avoid that stuff,' Julian
reminded him. 'Bad for my uric acid condition.'

'Tonight, it may be just what the doctor ordered. Come
into the living room and meet my wife.'

Martha Jenkins, a woman of about fifty, had never been
a beauty, and might have been thought of as plain if it had
not been for the glow of kindliness that mollified her features.
Middle age had made her better-looking than she had been
in youth, rounding out and softening what had been a somewhat angular face and body. In the last decade or so, her
husband had taken to describing her fondly with a line from
*Pinafore*, 'plump and pleasing person.'

After introductions, the doctor said, 'I'd present you to my
daughter, but she happens to be out.'

'With Tim Galen,' said his wife, disapproval in her voice.

'Now, Martha, Jennie's perfectly safe with Tim. How
many times do I have to tell you that? Why don't you be a
good hostess and build Mr Trask a drink?' He turned to
Julian. 'Scotch and soda all right?'

'Perfect.'

'Make me another while you're at it, will you, dear?' said Jenkins.

When she handed the men their drinks, her husband proposed no toast. He simply lifted the glass to his lips and half-emptied it with a long swallow.

Martha Jenkins, smiling at Julian, said, 'I'll leave the two of you to your man-talk,' and discreetly left the living room.

The doctor lowered his body into a commodious easy chair. 'Man-talk,' he said. 'Yes, I suppose it is. Rape, murder, suicide. Hardly topics for family conversation . . . ' He shuddered. 'Poor Melanie. She couldn't bear to live with the memory of that experience. Well, she might have died anyway. She was very badly ruptured. And even if she had lived, she never could have had children. Maybe she's better off.'

'Maybe,' said Julian. 'But I wish I could have learned something from her first. Just a word or two might have been enough.'

'Enough for what? Why should an anthropologist be interested in this at all?'

'Strictly speaking, I'm not an anthropologist anymore. I've become a maverick. My field is called Exotic Cultures.'

Doc grunted. 'Fancy name.'

Julian smiled apologetically. 'That's the public relations term for it. A more accurate one would be Extranatural Cultures.'

'Even fancier,' said Doc. 'But . . . *extra*-natural?' He frowned. 'Beyond Nature? There isn't anything beyond Nature. Nature is the whole show – that's all there is, there isn't anymore.'

'Not beyond Nature, exactly,' said Julian. 'Beyond the laws of Nature as we happen to understand them now.'

'That's an awfully delicate distinction,' said Doc Jenkins. 'Don't you think it's dangerously close to double-talk?'

'Not really. After all, the superstition of yesterday often becomes the science of today – or tomorrow. Astrology becomes astronomy. Alchemy becomes chemistry. Take your own field. The herbal cures of primitive peoples, folk medicine, witch doctors' antics, acupuncture – many of them are accepted, sooner or later, by medical science.'

Doc Jenkins said, 'You'll have to admit that your field does smack of charlatanry, just a bit.'

'Correction,' said Julian, '*quite* a bit. That's one of my biggest problems. Getting people to take it seriously, stop their laughing long enough to listen. That's why I gave my studies that euphemistic name. Sometimes it all depends on what you call a thing, you know. Call it a ghost, for instance, and everybody laughs at you. But call that same thing a manifestation of persistent energy, continuing after the event of physical death – in other words, give it what you call a fancy name – and they just might listen.'

'Mr Trask,' said the doctor, 'I certainly hope you're not suggesting those girls were raped by a ghost?'

'No. Something a good deal more solid and more dangerous.'

'And what,' asked Doc Jenkins, 'might that something be?'

Julian was about to reply when they heard the front door open and close. 'That'll be Jennie,' said the doctor. A moment later, his daughter entered the room.

She was an uncommonly pretty girl of about eighteen, with hair like cornsilk. She kissed her father and turned her blue eyes with bright curiosity upon Julian, who had risen to his feet.

'Dear,' said the doctor, 'this is Mr Trask, an old patient of mine, who used to teach here at the college. My daughter Jennifer.'

The girl shook Julian's hand. 'Just Jennie, please, Mr Trask. Nobody calls me Jennifer except Dad, when he's had a few drinks. Liquor makes him terribly formal.'

'How do you do.'

'Have a good time?' asked her father.

She shook her head. 'Tim's very down tonight.'

'We all are, honey.'

Smiling at Julian, she said, 'Well, I'm off to bed. Nice meeting you, Mr Trask.'

'Good night.'

She cantered quickly upstairs.

'Lovely girl,' said Julian.

The doctor nodded. 'Even prettier than the Morrissey and Saunders girls,' he said, quietly. 'Now, where were we?'

Julian sipped his Scotch and soda. 'There's a book called *Artes Perditae*,' he said, 'but I think I ought to begin with easy stages, and cite a book you're more familiar with. Do you have a Bible in the house, Doctor?'

'Sure,' replied Jenkins. 'I have several reference works. Encyclopedias, dictionaries, Bartlett's *Quotations*, *The Guinness Book of World Records*, the Bible . . .'

'I see. Then I take it you're not a religious man?'

'I'm religiously skeptical,' said Doc. 'To me, every statement is a lie until proven true.'

'Good,' said Julian. 'We're two of a kind. I'm a very hard sell myself. Do you mind if we consult your Bible? Purely as a reference work?'

'Why not?' said the doctor, rising and striding over to his bookshelves. Selecting a black leather volume, he returned to Julian. 'King James all right?'

'Turn to the Book of Genesis,' said Julian, 'Chapter Six.'

The doctor flipped the pages. 'Got it.'

'Would you start reading, please? From the top?'

Doc Jenkins read aloud: ' "And it came to pass, when men began to multiply on the face of the earth, and daughters were born unto them — " ' He stopped reading and looked up at Julian. 'This is thirsty work,' he said, and placed the Bible on the coffee table. Lifting the Scotch decanter, he said, 'Freshen your drink?'

'No, thanks.'

'I'll just darken mine a bit, if you don't mind. This has been a hell of a day.' He poured until his drink was a deep amber of undiluted whisky. Holding it up to the light, he said, 'Now that's what I call a pip of a urine specimen.'

Returning to his chair, he took a long gulp from his glass, and said, 'Sorry to break off abruptly like that, but I don't think you're going to find The Galen Molester by looking in the Bible or in any other musty old tomes. With all due respect to your so-called science, I think it's a lot of rubbish, eyewash, hogwash, poppycock, balderdash, and, not

43

to mince words, bullshit.' He set down his glass. 'Sorry, shouldn't have said that. Rude. It's the Scotch talking.'

Julian waved an indulgent hand, saying, 'I'm used to it. Ninety percent of my time is devoted to letting people get all the intolerance and prejudice out of their systems.'

'Intolerant?' said the doctor. 'Prejudiced? Is that what you think I am?'

'What do *you* call it when a person shuts his mind and refuses to listen?'

Doc Jenkins nodded in agreement. 'Good point. It's just that I think we're wasting precious time by these side trips into Fantasyland. While we're sitting here amusing ourselves with Bible readings, some Galen woman may be in the process of being raped by a madman.'

Julian said, 'Do you have a better idea? Do you really think you and I should be out there beating the bushes?'

'No,' said the doctor, shaking his head. 'I'm just upset and stymied and tired and scared and a little drunk.'

'It *is* getting late,' said Julian, 'and my theories are admittedly a bit hard to accept at the best of times. What do you say we continue this discussion tomorrow?'

'With that,' said Doc, 'I completely concur – provided you have one more drink with me tonight.'

'Sorry, this is my limit,' said Julian, and added with a smile, 'My condition, you know.'


Upstairs in her bedroom, Jennie prepared to retire. The window was open, admitting cool air, pungently spiced with the fragrance of a sturdy Brazilian pepper tree that grew near the house. A stout limb of the tree reached almost to her window.

Crouched on that limb, hidden by leaves and darkness, a Shape was watching her every movement. It squatted on bulging haunches of pure muscle, toes securely hooked into the rough bark. The eyes never blinked.

Jennie slipped her dress over her blonde head and placed it, for the moment, on the bed. She wore a brassiere and pantyhose. Reaching behind her, she unhooked the bra and dropped it also on the bed. Her breasts were small but perfectly formed, with tea-rose tips youthfully tilted

The Shape in the tree gripped the limb more t
its toes.

In her bedroom, Jennie coaxed the pantyhose d ... over
the slight swell of her hips. Sitting on the bed, she peeled
them the rest of the way, off her slender legs. She got up
again with a bounce. Her lower hair was a blur of floss, not
much darker than the gleaming gold of her head.

Her female musk hit the Shape in the tree like a blow. Its
nostrils dilated as it sucked in the intoxicating essence, growing dizzy with it. A tongue darted out to lick dry lips. In its
mind, no thoughts moved, only feelings, urges, needs. And
these roared like a blast furnace, scorching its nerves.

Not bothering to don a robe in what she assumed was the
privacy of her bedroom, Jennie sat down nude before her
dressing table mirror, and began to brush her hair. With
each each lively stroke, her breasts trembled like flowers in a
light breeze.

In the tree, the Shape felt its maleness fill with rushing
blood and hunger.

Jennie continued to brush her hair. Her naked back was
like satin, her spine a subtle straight long crease from the
nape of her neck to the deeper crease below.

Drunk with her aroma, the Shape on the tree limb moved
nearer to the window.

Jennie stood up. Two of her, one in the mirror, front,
back, breasts, belly, buttocks, fleecy nest, all seen at once.

A wave of her delicious odor pummeled the Shape. It
moved closer and closer to the open window.

A knock at her door. 'Just a minute,' she called, running
lightly, on the balls of her feet, to the closet for a robe.

The Shape retreated a bit, skittering swiftly backward on
the limb, into the safety of the leaves.

Jennie slipped into the robe and opened the bedroom
door. 'Oh, hi, Dad.'

The Shape climbed quickly and effortlessly down the
trunk of the tree, touched ground, and ran off into the dark.

'Time you were in bed, isn't it?' said Doc Jenkins.

'Just about to,' replied Jennie. 'Did your guest leave?'

'Yes. Sleep well, honey.'
'You too.'

Outside, somewhere in the slumbering town, the Shape was blending invisibly with the neutral and anonymous night.

# 9

... *the rackmaster forces her head down to her knees and deftly plunges his hand between her buttocks an expert index finger trained by long usage to the task probes her crooking and searching she cries out more in humiliation than in pain next he savagely spreads apart her primly held knees and slides two fingers into her kneading and pinching as they penetrate deeper and deeper into the warm interior of her body*

*'tis clear thou'rt no maiden he mutters*

*enough the interrogator snaps didst find no charms*

*naught sir says the rackmaster*

*turning to the patient scribe still sitting with poised pen the interrogator speaks*

*the accused having been stripped was subjected to the most diligent search of her body cavities no charms or tokens having been found there of any sort and in particular of that sort said to make the flesh insensible to pain she was remanded again to the care of the rackmaster who was required to administer the extremity of torture*

*the rackmaster's face brightens at this oh she will prove most rackworthy my lord he says and eagerly begins to unstrap her from the chair...*

*the old magistrate walks nearer to her and speaks velvetly...*

## 10

'SHE'S DEAD.'

The words were spoken in a voice dry, cold, without timbre or tone, colorless, pitchless, almost sexless. The voice, in fact, of Agatha Galen. Oldest surviving member of the family that built and named the town, she was now past seventy, and fashioned out of flint. It was not age that made her flinty: Miss Galen had always been forbidding, formidable, even in her youth. Photographs of her taken at the age of twenty showed the same gaunt face, severe coiffure, unsmiling mouth, and basilisk stare.

She had lived all her life in this house, like her parents before her. It had been built, at the north edge of Galen, probably less than a hundred years before, but it looked older because its style harked back to a Jacobean design heavy with medieval influences. The steep gabled roof, leaded casement windows, high chimney clusters, and overhanging upper storey all spoke of a bygone time. And for several decades, its stern grandeur had not been maintained. It had fallen into disrepair; not exactly an eyesore; a shabby landmark and grim, gray monument to outworn ways.

Morning sunlight slanted into Agatha Galen's dining room, as she put down her copy of the *Signal* and looked across the table at her nephew. He had not touched his eggs and bacon, and was silently sipping his coffee.

Tim Galen was a thin but well-built young man of twenty. Under a helmet of thick brown hair was a face of exceptional beauty. High cheekbones gave his amber eyes a faun-like tilt, a pagan flair. His lips were full and sensuous. He was said to resemble his mother.

'Did you hear me, Timothy?' said his aunt. 'That girl friend of yours killed herself in the hospital.'

'I know,' was all he said, not looking at her.

Agatha carefully folded the newspaper. 'And you feel nothing?'

He looked into her pale eyes. 'Of course I do. But why do you keep calling her my girl friend? Jennie Jenkins is my girl friend. Mel and I just went for that one swim.'

'A fatal swim for her, as it's turned out.'

'Aunt Agatha,' he said with a sigh, 'I feel terrible about it, but it wasn't my fault.'

'I pray to God it wasn't.'

Tim looked at her, dumbfounded. 'You think I did it, don't you?' he said. She looked away. *'Don't you?'*

She did not answer him.

He threw down his napkin and rose from the table, abruptly.

'Perhaps,' said Agatha, 'you can't be blamed . . . '

This stopped Tim in his tracks. He echoed her words: ' "Can't be blamed." Oh yes. "In my blood," is that it? Am I going to hear all about my "evil forebears" again?'

'Your father was a fine man,' she insisted.

'Yes, your brother could do no wrong, I know. He was a Galen. His ancestors built this town. But then this "hussy" threw herself at him . . . '

'Kate Dover was a loose woman,' said Agatha.

'She was my mother. And her name was Galen. Please remember that. My father gave her his name, your name, my name – Galen.'

'She was never a Galen,' said Agatha, her eyes glinting. 'I never accepted her. A woman like that. Without shame. With disgusting habits. Whose ancestors were burned as witches.'

'That old wives' tale . . . '

'It's true.'

'I doubt it,' said Tim, 'but what if it is? What if her ancestors – my ancestors – were burned at the stake? Who burned them? *Your* ancestors.'

'Yes,' said Agatha, proudly. 'We Galens punished the unholy. We were never ashamed of it.'

'Not ashamed? Of killing, torturing?'

48

'For God—'

'*They* were the godly ones — the poor women you Galens burned alive.'

He turned and strode angrily out of the dining room. 'Timothy!' she called. 'Come back!' But his only answer was to slam the front door on his way out of the house.

Agatha sat at the table for several minutes, her spine ramrod-straight as always, then she got up and walked calmly out of the dining room, to the door which led to her cellar. She opened it onto darkness. After groping for a light switch, she snapped it on, and a naked bulb cast a feeble, cheerless glare upon a rickety staircase that led into the depths of the old house. Cobwebs and thick layers of dust were testimony to long disuse. Carefully, Agatha began to descend the creaking stairs.

At the foot of the staircase, she pushed aside a number of old cardboard boxes, looking for the one she wanted. A small spider and a shiny black beetle skittered away, frightened at her sudden intrusion. At length, she found what she was searching for. A box like the others. She opened it. Methodically, she began to take out its contents: an empty picture frame, an old knife, a piece of worthless crockery. Now, her lips pressed tightly together, she lifted out of the box an enormous book, bound in age-darkened parchment.

Galen Park was sparsely populated at this time of morning. A few pre-school children and their mothers. Some old folks. The occasional dog. And today, sitting alone on a bench, Jennie Jenkins. The sun was warm and brilliant, the air 'clear as gin', as Bill Carter was fond of saying. Jennie was obviously waiting for someone, and now he appeared.

'Hello, Jennie.'

'Tim!' she said, rising. 'I've been waiting and waiting!'

'Sorry,' he said. 'Got into another hassle with my aunt.' They began to stroll along the path. 'Do you know she actually thinks I'm the one who attacked Melanie?'

'She can't!' said Jennie, incredulous. 'The sheriff let you go. Nobody's accused you.'

49

'She has,' he said bitterly. 'How about you? Feel safe with the town sex fiend?'

'Oh, Tim!' Now coyness colored her voice. 'But I *should* be very angry with you.'

Tim knew what she meant. 'Because I was with another girl. But it wasn't a real date. Just a swim.'

'Just a naked swim. At midnight.'

'She dared me.'

Jennie took his arm. 'Well, it's all over now.'

'Is it?'

'I just meant—'

'I know,' said Tim. He stopped walking, and disengaged her arm from his. 'Look, Jen,' he said, 'I've got to run. Have to find a job and earn some bread – damned if I'll freeload off my aunt anymore. I want to get away from her, out of that house.' He kissed her lightly. 'I'll call you.' He turned and walked away, leaving the park.

As he passed the whitewashed Church of Christ, Tim nodded briefly to Reverend Keaton, who was standing outside, and quickly walked on. He was in no mood to hear the Reverend's arch reminders about his not attending services for quite some time. Reverend Keaton returned his nod and watched Tim until he walked out of sight. The Reverend was a tall man with lank, graying hair and a face that was skull-like in its leanness and asceticism. He turned and entered his church.

In the *Signal* office, Laura Kincaid was at her desk, correcting galley proofs. As Tim walked in, she looked up and smiled at him. 'Hello, Tim. How are you?'

Tim shrugged. 'I'm all right.'

'I suppose you heard about Melanie.' He nodded. 'I'm sorry, Tim. It must have been horrible for you.'

'A lot worse for her, Miss Kincaid.'

'Of course.' Brightening, Laura said, 'Now then, what can I do for you?'

'Well, I'm looking for a job.'

'For the summer?'

'I was thinking of something more permanent. Thought you might have an opening here at the paper.'

'Could be,' said Laura. 'We're a very small staff, of course, but if you don't mind doing a bit of everything – messenger, window washer, proofreader – '

'Fine.'

'You're hired,' she said. 'We'll negotiate your salary later, all right? These galleys won't wait. Bill Carter will show you the ropes.' She called across the office. 'Bill? Put this fellow to work, will you?'

Bill looked up from his composing stick. 'Sure thing,' he said. 'Plenty to do.'

Later that afternoon, as Tim was sweeping up in the *Signal*'s storeroom, his thoughts crept through dank underground caves of doubt and melancholy:

*All this terrible shit that's been coming down . . . the Morrissey girl killed . . . Melanie blowing herself away like that . . . could Aunt Agatha be right about me? . . . is it something in my blood like she says? . . . can I be the one and not even know it? . . .*

Night.

Like a meticulously scored crescendo and crash of brazen cymbals, occurring again and again with symphonic precision and regularity, the waves of the Pacific approached the shore, and grandly broke, and retreated, and approached to break again.

The moon could not pierce the heavy veils of fog. The old rotted pilings of the Galen pier were invisible ten inches from the eye. Nor could the ear detect any sound save that of the brassy crashing waves.

It was not a place or time for any man to be; no man or woman or child. And yet a figure walked here, upright, no dog or cat, walked slowly and with care, in the fog, the spray, the ever-recurring climax of water smiting shore.

Now the figure crouched, bent down, as if looking for something in the unseeable wet sand. A hand reached out

51

to touch the sand, almost tenderly, as if fingertips would tell what eyes could not.

Suddenly, the figure froze, stiffly alert and unmoving, apprehensive, still crouching, muscles tensed for instant violent action, if needed.

For another figure had silently, stealthily drawn close to the first. The dark and the fog canceled out all details of their species or sex; both were no more than shapeless masses of potential threat; but, in those intervals when the waves were gathering their forces for another explosion, in those few moments of relative quiet, each could hear the other's breathing. And it could hear, too, the beating of its own heart.

A spear of light stabbed the dark, and the fog swirled milkily in its beam.

'Oh, it's you, Mr Trask.'

Julian, shielding his eyes from the blinding ray of Hank Walden's powerful flashlight, stood up from his crouching position.

'Sheriff? You gave me quite a start.'

'What are you doing out here?' Hank asked. 'Hell of a time of night.'

'I couldn't sleep,' said Julian, 'and I got to thinking about the Saunders girl. This is where she was attacked, wasn't it?'

'Just about.'

'So I thought I'd look around, maybe find some hint, some clue . . . '

'In this damn fog?'

'I know,' Julian admitted. 'Foolish of me. Can't see your hand in front of your face out here tonight.'

'Even if you could,' said the sheriff, 'you'd be out of luck. Tide washed everything out to sea long ago.'

'Of course,' said Julian. 'There weren't any tracks?'

'Tracks?' said Hank. 'You mean footprints?'

'Well . . . yes.'

'No. Not a one. Not even Melanie's or Tim's, by the time we got here. The tide just erased everything. Mr Trask, it's not too safe out here in the fog. You'd best come back with me and Clem. We've got the car over yonder.'

'Good idea,' said Julian. 'Thanks.'

Clem Conklin's voice cut through the fog: *'Sheriff?'*

'We're coming, Clem, keep your pants on,' called Hank.

*'Hurry up,'* the deputy shouted.

Julian and the sheriff walked as quickly as they could in the direction of the car. Clem turned on the headlights to guide them

'All right,' said Hank when they reached the car, 'what are you fussing about?'

'Doc Jenkins,' said Clem.

'What about him?'

'They patched him through to the car radio. He's over to the *Signal* office. Wants us to get there right away.'

'What happened?' asked Julian.

'It's Laura Kincaid,' said Clem. 'Doc's with her now. That crazy rapist bastard broke into her office and attacked her, not twenty minutes ago.'

## II

*... the old magistrate walks nearer to her and speaks velvetly my child do not force us to this the pangs thou hast felt already are but play the rack will stretch thee limbs from trunk thou wilt be dismembered like a sow on the butcher's block but thou wilt be less fortunate than the sow for thou wilt be butchered whilst yet alive this good man is not named rackmaster for no cause he is indeed a master and he will keep thee quite alive until thou art a thing of bleeding pieces why shouldst thou suffer that wretch thy lover hath betrayed thee confess the sinful congress thou hast enjoyed with him tell us the way of it describe the manner of his lust the look of him the name by which thou called him o child full well we knoweth by other testimony what thou hast lain with but thou must needs now tell us of it with thine own tongue why*

53

*suffer for a vile creature who used thee as his leman for his
pleasure and then abandoned thee speak now whilst yet thou
art unbroken*

*she sits silent*

*speak snarls the rackmaster playfully tweaking her
mangled toe and sending a flash of pain forking through her
foot*

*she shakes her head*

*rack her says the interrogator*

*she struggles but in vain against her tormentor's strength
as he drags her naked body by the hair off the chair across
the floor to . . .*

## 12

THE DOCTOR'S CAR stood in the middle of the street outside
the *Signal* office, headlights still on, the driver's door wide
open. Almost colliding with it in the fog, Clem braked the
patrol car to a screeching stop, and sprang out, simultaneously with Julian and the sheriff. All three men sprinted
through the open *Signal* door.

Chaos.

The rear window of the office was smashed. Desk lamps
had fallen to the floor, their bulbs shattered. Chairs were
overturned, desks stood at uncustomary angles. Broken glass
crunched underfoot, and the pungent smell of gunpowder
was unmistakable in the air.

'Laura!' cried Julian.

She was propped up in a chair, Doc Jenkins busily tending
to her injuries. Her dress was in shreds, torn half off her
body. One brassiere strap was broken. Her shoulders and
upper arms were red with gashes, as if they had been raked
by sharp claws. Her hair was awry and she was drenched in

sweat. 'I'm *all right*, Doc, really,' she was saying as the other men ran in. 'Just a little shaken up.'

Doc Jenkins quietly continued bandaging her wounds.

'Laura, what happened?' said Julian, kneeling beside her chair.

Between shuddering and unsteady breaths, she said, 'I was working late. Double-checking the arithmetic in my follow-up to the property tax story. The door was locked, windows too. There was this crash – someone just erupted through that rear window over there – scared me out of my wits –'

'Who was it?' asked Sheriff Walden.

Laura shook her head. 'Too dark, couldn't see. The only light burning in the whole office was my desk lamp, that gooseneck thing on the floor near your feet, and it was shining in my eyes when I looked up. Whoever it was made it to my desk in about two steps and just swept the lamp to the floor, broke it, and then it was pitch dark. He . . . grabbed me . . . ripped my dress . . . ' Her voice faltered, the last reserves of her strength drained away, and she began to weep.

'She's done enough talking for now,' said Doc. 'I'm going to take her home and tuck her into bed and give her a good strong sedative. And, Hank, you better put a guard on her house.'

'I'm all right,' Laura insisted, wiping her eyes with the back of her hand.

Julian gave her his handkerchief. 'Laura, dear. Did he . . . ?'

She shook her head. 'My virtue's intact, thanks to Dad's old service revolver in the desk drawer.'

'I was driving by,' said Doc Jenkins, 'on my way home from the hospital, and I heard the shots. Six of them. But by the time I got in here, he was gone.'

Laura frowned, puzzled. 'I can't understand why I didn't kill him. I emptied the gun into him – point blank – and yet he got away.'

The sheriff turned to Clem. 'Shouldn't be too hard finding a man with six bullets in him.'

'Probably lying dead someplace by now,' said Clem.

'That would suit me just fine,' said the sheriff, 'although killing's too good for him.' He addressed the doctor and Julian: 'If you two fellows will see that she gets home, Clem and I will start smoking out that son of a bitch.'

'We'll see her home,' Julian assured him.

The sheriff and his deputy left the newspaper office. In a moment, they had driven away.

Laura had been put to bed and sedated by Doc Jenkins, and was now sound asleep in her modest single-storey house. Doc and Julian were sitting in her living room, sampling her sherry, having failed to find anything stronger.

'I guess it's all over,' said Doc, 'and not soon enough to suit me. Two girls dead and another escaped by the skin of her teeth. That maniac must be either dead or dying. And even if he isn't, he won't be hard to spot. We'll soon know who he is. And, mark my words, he won't be a Galen man. He'll be someone we've never seen before. Someone from out of town. A total stranger.'

Julian did not appear to be listening. When he spoke, he was reconstructing the events of the night. 'You were driving by the *Signal* office, you say, and you heard the shots . . .'

'That's right.'

Julian pondered that for a moment, then shook his head emphatically. 'It couldn't have been you,' he said. 'No way you could have broken in that rear window, attacked Laura, then escaped through the window again and made it to your car and driven it around to the front of the office in time . . .'

'You think *I* might have attacked her?'

'No, Doctor,' said Julian patiently. 'I've just explained how you couldn't possibly have been the one. How did you get into the office, by the way? Laura said the door was locked.'

'She opened it for me. She wasn't unconscious, you know.'

'Yes, I see, of course.'

'Besides,' said Doc, 'if I had six slugs in me, do you think I'd be sitting here calmly sipping Laura's sherry?'

'No, but her attacker might.'

56

'What?'

Julian hurried on to another question. 'How did you get through to the patrol car radio? Laura's phone?'

'Yes.'

'Immediately?'

'No. My first thought was to take care of her. I went out to the car to fetch my bag, then I cleaned and disinfected those gashes of hers first.'

'How long between the time you heard the shots and the time you phoned?'

'Five or ten minutes. No more than ten. But Hank wasn't in the office, neither was Clem, and I had to untangle some red tape before the operator would patch me through to the patrol car. Even when she did, it was a while before anybody answered. I guess they weren't in the car. Finally, I got through to Clem.'

'How long, all together? Fifteen minutes?'

'Could have been.'

'Twenty?'

'Possibly.'

Julian put down his wine glass. 'Time enough for Clem, or the sheriff – or me, for that matter – to escape from the *Signal* office and make it to the beach.'

'Trask, are you crazy?' said Doc.

'You're in the clear,' Julian said, 'but we three are prime suspects.'

Doc drained his glass. 'Christ, I wish this were whisky,' he said. 'You keep forgetting one little thing, my friend. Or, rather, six little things, fired at point blank range. Are you suggesting they were blanks?'

'No. But it doesn't prove a thing.'

'You amaze me,' said Doc Jenkins. 'You positively baffle and amaze me.'

With perfect steadiness, Julian replied, 'I haven't even begun to baffle and amaze you, Doctor.'

It was not only the oldest house in town, it was also the most uninviting. Literally, for no one could remember when any but a member of the Galen family had ever been invited

57

within those walls, and figuratively as well, for its austere design, gaunt enough by day, imparted positive uneasiness at night, in fog and silence. More than one generation of the town's children had called it The Haunted House, and had looked with big-eyed awe and distrust on any person going in or out of it. If such qualities as guilt, or grief, or regret could be made tangible and solid, they might take the form of the glowering structure wherein Agatha Galen and her nephew lived.

'It's only a house,' said Sheriff Walden, as he and his deputy climbed out of the patrol car and stood in front of the Galen home. 'Nothing to be scared of.'

'Hell, I'm not scared!' said Clem.

'Glad to hear it,' replied the sheriff with a grunt, 'because *I'm* sure scared of any man who can live with half a dozen slugs in him. But come on, let's get this over with.'

Clem followed the sheriff as he walked through the fog up the brick-paved path to the front door. A gigantic brass knocker was affixed to it. Taking hold of it, the sheriff rapped three times. The sounds echoed inside the cavernous old house. They waited. There was no response.

Clem said, 'Nobody home, I guess,' and turned to go.

Wearily, the sheriff dropped a detaining hand on the deputy's shoulder, and with his other hand, reached for the brass knocker again. Before he could touch it, the door was opened by Agatha Galen.

'Evening, Miss Galen,' said Hank Walden.

'Do you have any idea of the hour, Sheriff?' she said, aloofly.

'I'm sorry to disturb you, ma'am, and I wouldn't do it if it weren't important. We'd like to see your nephew.'

'Timothy is asleep.'

'We'd still like to see him. I'm afraid.'

'I shall ask my nephew in the morning to pay you a visit at your office.'

At that moment, Tim's voice said, 'Let them in, Aunt Agatha.'

Grudgingly, she opened the door wider and stood aside to let the two men enter. Tim was standing at the cold fire-

58

place, in his pajamas. 'Hello, Sheriff. Clem. What is it?'

'I understand you're working for Laura Kincaid,' said Walden.

'That's right. I just started today. What about it?'

'She was attacked tonight in the newsaper office.'

'*What?*'

'But she's all right – managed to put six bullets into the man.'

'He didn't . . . do anything to her?'

The sheriff shook his head. 'Just a few scratches, and badly shaken up. The office is a mess.'

'Who is the man?'

'We don't know. We're looking for him.'

Tim smiled grimly. 'Oh, I see. You didn't drop by just to tell me about my employer. I'm the first name on your list of suspects. Because I was with Melanie that night.'

'You do work for Miss Kincaid,' said the sheriff. With a smile, he added, 'But you obviously didn't take six slugs tonight.'

Agatha stepped forward and said, 'Then I suggest you continue your search elsewhere, Sheriff.'

'We will, ma'am,' he replied. 'Sorry to have troubled you. Good night.' He and his deputy left the house.

When she heard the patrol car drive away, Agatha turned to her nephew and said, 'It's very chilly tonight. Please build a fire, Timothy.'

Tim rekindled the embers in the fireplace, and soon had a cheery blaze going.

'You returned home less than an hour ago, didn't you?' she said. 'I was awake. I heard you come in.'

'That's right,' he said.

'Where were you?'

'*Out*, Aunt Agatha, minding my own business. I wish you'd do the same.'

'And what exactly *is* your . . . business, Timothy?'

He looked at her, studying her face. 'I don't believe it,' he said at last. 'I'm hearing it but I don't believe it. You still think I'm the one. Gwen Morrissey, Melanie Saunders, and now Laura Kincaid. I did it all – right?'

' "Thou hast said it." '

'Don't quote Scripture at me!' Tim shouted. 'I've had it up to *here* with that stuff! Tell me: where in the Bible does it say you have to suspect your own brother's son of being an insane rapist and murderer? Even when the sheriff knows better!'

'The sheriff is a fool.'

'No,' said Tim, 'Hank Walden is no fool. He believes the evidence of his eyes and his own good sense. He looks at me and he *knows* I can't be the man he's looking for because that man had six bullets fired into him tonight. Six bullets! Do I look like I had six bullets in me? *Look* at me, damn it! Do I?'

He yanked off his pajama top and threw it on the floor. His lean torso was unmarred.

Agatha said, 'I have no wish to see your nakedness.'

' "Nakedness!" ' Tim laughed joylessly. 'Look at me – even Doubting Thomas did *that* much. I can spout Scripture too! Do you see any bullet holes? Any blood?'

'Of course not.'

'Well then!'

'I didn't expect to,' said Agatha.

'Thanks,' Tim said sourly. 'Is that your way of finally admitting that I'm innocent?'

'Not at all,' answered Agatha. 'It merely means that I am not ignorant. Most people are. Ignorant of the infinite possibilities of evil. True, raw, original evil. It is entirely possible for someone – a particular sort of someone – to take six deadly bullets into his body and yet not show the slightest sign.'

## 13

*... her tormentor drags her naked body by the hair off the chair across the floor to the rack*

*it stands in a shadowed alcove of the chamber it is of spare design purely utilitarian a marvel of simplicity the epitome of the efficient in its way it has a modest beauty an engineer could admire it as an unassuming ode to function this homely mechanism of good wood and metal and leather is honestly and stoutly built this bedlike frame these straps this crank this windlass these chains and manacles all serve allotted purposes and serve them well here the ankles of the accused are to be shackled there the wrists when this crank is turned the flesh and bones will straighten then slowly stretch the body will resist at first the finer the body the longer the resistance but in time it will appear to flatten and grow tenuous tissues will be pulled to the tearing point the skin will split at many places muscles and tendons will rupture bones will crack joints will sever and snap asunder a fountain of sweat blood urine faeces will flow from the assaulted body*

*the rackmaster throws her on the machine face up and quickly shackles her hands and feet spreadeagled she is a gleaming white x of flesh firm flesh and young it will defy the rack for a time before tearing apart shackles secured on her thin wrists and ankles the rackmaster takes a moment to study his subject with arms and legs pulled in opposite directions her body is taut and rigid her ribs sharply etched her belly a flat drum around her navel her veins and muscles clearly outlined under the creamy flesh the fiery tangle of her hair hangs down almost to the floor of the chamber her skin made tight and glossy by the strained position seems to glow like a soft lamp in the half dark her lower hair is a bright coppery triangle gooseflesh evoked by both cold and fear prickles the whole length of her body her nipples are erect and hard as she lies nude panting with fright belly fluttering she is a kind of bride on a dark parody of the nuptial couch anxiously awaiting the intense and ardent rhythms of her spouse whose name is pain*

*a quarter turn to start my lord asks the rackmaster . . .*

# 14

JULIAN WAS AWAKENED by the throb of a stiff neck. The skin of his entire body felt like sandpaper. He opened one eye cautiously and saw an unfamiliar wall. Then he remembered. He had spent the night in a chair in Laura's living room.

Groaning, he straightened his arms and legs, and rubbed a hand over his bristly face. His clothes were corrugated with wrinkles. He peered at his wristwatch. It had stopped at 4.17. An electric clock on a nearby table told him it was almost 6.30. He slowly rose from the chair and walked into Laura's bedroom.

She was still deep in drugged sleep, breathing evenly and heavily. One foot protruded from under the coverlet. Her vulnerability was effectively symbolized by its delicate and unprotected bareness. Julian stroked it affectionately before covering it.

As he returned to the living room, he saw Doc Jenkins drive up and park in front of the house. Julian met him at the door. 'Right on time, Doc,' he said.

'I can't stay long,' said the doctor. 'Patients to visit.'

'Just give me a chance to get back to the inn for a shower and a shave and a change of clothes. I won't stop for breakfast. I'll raid Laura's kitchen when I get back here.'

'Fair enough,' said Doc. 'But I still can't see why you don't trust Hank or Clem.'

'It's as I told you last night,' Julian said. 'I trust you because of the time involved. I trust myself because I *know* I didn't do it – even though nobody else knows it. But those other two fellows are still possibles.' Julian nodded toward the bedroom. 'She's still dead to the world. I'll be back soon.'

He left the house.

The doctor walked briskly into the bedroom. Carefully, so as not to waken her, he pulled the coverlet off the upper half of her body. She wore a nightgown sheer as gauze; the deep brown discs of her aureoles were clearly visible. He looked at them with admiration. He pulled the coverlet down further. Her nightgown had crept up around her waist and her curl-crowned cleft returned his stare. He fought and conquered a sudden fierce desire to touch it.

'Dirty old man,' he muttered. He replaced the coverlet, then dutifully examined the bandages and checked her pulse.

With a long sigh, he returned to the living room to wait for Julian.

After he had shaved and showered, Julian strolled naked from his bathroom, toweling his body, deep in thought. The coarse dark hair of his torso was roughly cruciform, the crossing bar traversing his broad chest from nipple to nipple, the vertical beam extending from the hollow of his throat down to the dense ebony thicket of his loins.

He sat, nude, on the edge of the bed and picked up the phone. It was three hours later in Boston; not too early to call Professor Stefanski. He gave the inn's switchboard operator the number and hung up. While she placed the call, he quickly dressed.

When the phone rang, he grabbed it immediately, and was soon hearing, for the first time in several years, the dense Slavic accent of his old teacher: 'Julian? It is you?'

'Yes, Professor. How are you?'

'Old, Julian. I am now old. You are calling from where?'

'Galen, a little town in California.'

'The climate is good, yes?'

'Very nice.'

'Here it is raining since three days dogs and cats.'

'Professor, I need your help. Quotations from some of those old books in your personal library.'

'Yes, go on.'

'It won't be too much trouble for you?'

'No, I am glad. Tell me the books, I will write down.'

'First, please write down a telephone number – I'll be at

that number in a few minutes. Phone me there when you have the books on your desk.' He gave him Laura's number. 'Now, first of all, the book by Boguet . . .'

'Boguet, yes, I am writing, go on.'

'And the Remy book. And the Billuart. And who wrote the one with the long title?'

'De Lancre?'

'Yes, Pierre de Lancre. And I almost forgot – I'll want Benedict's treatise, too.'

'Benedict. That is all?'

'I think that's all I need.'

'I will call you at this number I have written. But Julian . . .'

'Yes, sir?'

'What now are you investigating? These books . . . these authors . . . is it possible you have found –'

'Not on the phone, Professor. This is a hotel switchboard. Yes: it's possible. At last.'

'My God. My God.'

'I'll hang up now, sir. Please call me as soon as you can.'

'I will. And Julian, my boy, so you should live to be as old as me, you will please, please, so *carefully* proceed . . . yes?'


Doc Jenkins was feeling thoroughly ashamed of himself as he sat in Laura's living room. He searched his mind and could find no excuse for his curious behaviour. Some men perhaps could rationalize it by telling themselves their interest was purely medical; a physical examination; but Jenkins took pride in never kidding himself. There was no medical necessity involved in uncovering her completely. It was lechery, nothing more. Taking advantage of a drugged woman, a woman he had drugged himself. Unworthy of a gentleman, unforgivable in a physician. Male menopause? The last flaring-up of virility's candle flame just before it sputtered into senility? Probably. But still no excuse. No excuse, either, that for years he had found Laura powerfully attractive. He began to feel a strange kinship with the rapist, in the sense that he now understood him. For one moment,

Doc had stood on the brink of doing a vile thing. If the urge had been just a little stronger, or his will a little weaker, he would have gone over the edge, slaked his lust on a helpless woman. He, good husband and father, respected member of the medical profession, pillar of the community. Good old Doc.

Julian's car pulled up outside. The doctor got to his feet. He'd be glad to leave this house. Could he ever face Laura Kincaid again without suffering a twinge? Could he ever treat her, examine her, touch her body? Could he trust himself?

He opened the door and let Julian in.

'Is she still asleep?' asked Julian.

'Last time I checked, she was.'

'Thanks for spelling me, Doc.' The telephone rang. 'That may be for me,' said Julian, and walked to the phone as Doc left the house.

Outside, on the porch, Doc felt a stab of fear. Was it possible he himself was the rapist . . . periods of blackout . . . no memory . . . schizophrenia? As he walked to his car, these misgivings prodded him.

In the car, as he turned on the ignition, he answered himself: No. He might be a dirty old man, but he wasn't the rapist. There were too many hard physical facts to refute it. Those bullets. And Julian's point about the time element the night before. And at least one other.

He drove away from Laura Kincaid's house.

Inside, Julian was cradling the phone, having scribbled copiously in his pocket notebook, transcribing the passages read to him by his old teacher in Boston. He studied these notes now, with a mixture of uneasiness and elation. They told him nothing new, nothing he had not previously known or suspected, but they served to confirm a hypothesis that was swiftly congealing into fact in his mind.

'What time is it?' Laura asked, drowsily, behind him.

He turned and saw her standing in the doorway, her eyes heavy with sleep. She was dressed only in her nightgown.

'Time for breakfast,' Julian replied cheerily, slipping the

notebook quickly into his pocket. 'I'm hungry, how about you?'

She shook her head. 'Did I hear the phone?'

'Just a call for me.' He walked over to her. 'How are you feeling?'

'All right . . . have to get to the office . . .'

'Absolutely not. Doctor's orders. Keep her quiet, he said.'

'The afternoon edition . . .'

'Bill Carter will have to get along without you for once.' Indicating her attire, he added, 'Aren't you cold?'

She nodded, hugging her arms, which were bare except for the bandages. 'Yes, cold,' she said. She looked up at him, into his eyes, for what seemed a very long time. 'Warm me, Julian. Make me warm.' She stepped closer, her body touching his, never taking her eyes from his.

Desire kindled in him and spread like brushfire, consuming and possessing him completely as he seized her face in his hands and devoured her mouth with his. Urgently, without words, without tenderness, they clawed and kneaded each other with sudden hunger and were in the bedroom unaware of walking there, on the bed and nude without recalling undressing, swept along by the pounding and inexorable tide of their blood.

They were both, later, ravenous for breakfast. Laura, wrapping a robe around her, asked him, 'Can you scramble eggs?'

'If I have to.'

'You have to. I have to phone in today's front page story to Bill Carter.'

'A blow-by-blow account of our title bout?'

She threw a pillow at him. 'Last night's brutal attack on The Editorial We. That ought to sell a few more copies.'

'You're a tough lady.'

'Let's hope those eggs of yours aren't tough.'

'Eggs Julian? Tough? As gossamer as your nightie.' He lifted it, with one finger, from the bedroom floor where it had fallen. He was surprised to see that it was ripped along the seam, from top to bottom. In the frenzy and impatience

66

of his passion, he had literally torn it from her body. She laughed at his surprise.

The afternoon's *Signal* was read avidly by the people of Galen, even though the news of Laura's ordeal was already old, and had been the subject of shocked gossip all day. Laura had allowed herself a few indignant journalistic admonitions about the ineffectual nature of the sheriff's office, and these were not received with open arms by Hank Walden, although he realized there was some justice to them. He also realized that Laura Kincaid was in the business of selling papers.

Possibly the most worried man in town was Doc Jenkins. When he got home that night, exhausted from his after-dinner rounds, his thoughts were black. As the only person who had thoroughly examined the attacked women, he alone knew the extent of the attacker's incredible and violent lust. And he was worried about his own lust, too; the fleeting episode with Laura continued to nag his conscience as a thing unspeakably shameful. Glowing coldly like the moon through mist was his fear for the safety of his daughter, a magnetic target for the rapist.

If, as he settled wearily into bed beside his sleeping wife, he had been able to see outside Jennie's room, he would have been even more worried. At that moment, someone was climbing the pepper tree and making his way slowly and stealthily to her window.

## 15

*. . . a quarter turn to start my lord asks the rackmaster*
*the interrogator nods*
*the torturer grips the crank and turns it with artful slow-*
*ness letting the awful creaking assail the victim's hearing*

*it is no lack of oil that causes the sound the crank is delib-
erately made to spur an agony of the mind rivaling that of
the body*

*she feels it first at ankles and wrists the fearful tug of
war that promises solemnly to wrench her feet from her legs
her hands from her arms and in that molten instant sweat
springs from every pore of her naked skin she feels it ooze
all up and down the length of her stretched body scalp and
palms and soles and small of back threads of sweat between
her buttocks and her breasts a trickle that teases its way
down past her navel to the ruddy fur below she yowls with
wide distended mouth gone dry as sand from loss of moisture
and the craftsman at the crank wisely tilts a dipper of water
past her lips it is not mercy but its opposite in his novice
days desiccation robbed him of some subjects prematurely*

*drink deep girl drink all thou wilt he says we must not
let thee sweat and piss thyself to a death too soon*

*the interrogator having waited until the first shock of
the rack has passed now stands over her and says spare thyself confirm for us those certain tales that hath been told
by other women thy lover did he do sodomy upon thee as
well or didst receive him into thy ...*

# 16

SILHOUETTED AGAINST THE MOON, a lithe form crouched on
the limb of the tree just outside Jennie's window.

From her bed, Jennie saw it, gasped, and clutched the
bedclothes around her. The window was closed and locked,
but didn't the paper say Laura's attacker had crashed right
through a locked window?

Now the shadowy form extended a hand and tapped
against the glass. Jennie was petrified, unable to move, unable to scream. After a moment, another tap, more insistent.

'Jennie?'

She recognized the tapper's voice. 'Tim?'

With a sigh of relief, followed instantly by a frown of curiosity, she swung her bare legs out of the bed and tiptoed to the window in her shortie nightgown. 'What on earth,' she said, unlocking the window and opening it. 'Tim –'

'Shhhh,' he cautioned.

She whispered, 'This is hardly the time to pay a visit. Climbing the tree like a monkey?'

'I had to talk to someone,' he said, his voice low. 'There's nobody else. I think I'm going crazy. Can I come in?'

Sympathy flooded her. 'Oh, Tim ... sure ...'

He scrambled in the window. 'Sorry about the cat burglar stuff,' he said, 'but I knew your folks would be sleeping, and I just didn't want to see them tonight anyway. I only wanted to see you.'

'What happened to your arm?'

'It's nothing,' he said. 'I'll tell you later.'

They embraced and kissed. Without further ceremony, Jennie pulled her nightgown over her head and dropped it on a nearby chair. Taking him by the hand, she led him to her bed.


'I'm *glad* you climbed the tree like a monkey,' she said, somewhat later. They were lying side by side under the sheet, talking softly.

'Me, too,' said Tim. 'But, honest, I didn't come over for this. I mean, it was great, it gets better every time, but I really did come over just to talk.'

'So talk,' said Jennie.

'How can I, when you're doing that?'

'One-track mind? Okay, I'll be good. There.'

He began to tell her of the sheriff's visit, and of the strange thing his aunt had said to him after Hank and Clem had left.

'But that doesn't make any sense, Tim,' Jennie said. 'Someone can be shot six times and not show it?'

' "A particular sort of someone" – her words.'

69

'It's not you who's crazy, it's your aunt.'

'The only thing is,' said Tim, 'she's almost made me believe her crazy talk. When I asked her what she meant by that, she said ...'

'Timothy, go into the study and open the old escritoire. Here is the key. You will find some old family relics there. An old knife and a book, a large book. Bring them to me here.'

Tim took the key from his aunt and, still in only his pajama bottoms, padded into the study of the Galen house and opened the dark mahogany escritoire that stood there. The knife was light, but the book was large and heavy. He carried them back to the living room.

'Put them down, Timothy.'

He placed them on a coffee table. 'What are they?' he asked.

'I suppose they're part of your legacy,' said Agatha. 'From your mother's side of the family.'

'That book,' he said. 'It's familiar. I seem to remember leafing through it for hours, when I was very little, looking at the pictures. One time when you locked me down in the cellar to punish me for something. And the dagger, I think I remember that, too ...'

'No doubt you do. I'm sure you were told not to look into those old cartons and trunks in the cellar, and I'm also sure you disobeyed. You always disobeyed.'

'What is the book? What are you trying to tell me?'

'The book is very old,' she said, 'no one knows how old. I have heard it is valuable, perhaps as valuable as a Shakespeare first folio. It was your mother's. Passed down to her by *her* mother, and her mother before her. Most of it is in Latin. Some of it is in another language, the language of the dawn gods. Your mother could read it.'

Tim touched the parchment of the book's binding. It felt cold and smooth and like nothing else he had ever touched before.

'Human skin,' said Agatha. 'At least that's what your mother claimed.' Tim pulled his hand away as if burned.

70

'A woman's skin,' she added. 'Executed as a witch, somewhere in Europe, back in medieval times. That's the hide of her back and belly, carefully peeled from her body while she was still alive to appreciate it. There were six of them, your mother said. One by one, they were broken on the rack to make them confess, and confess they did. They would have been better off remaining silent and dying on the rack. Their confessions condemned them to even worse deaths. Each woman was publicly skinned from top to bottom like an eel, flayed from her scalp to the soles of her feet, then all six were crowded into an enormous vat of brine up to their necks. You know how salt water hurts if you have just a small scratch – imagine what it was to them, with no skins at all. Like acid. Fnally, a fire was built under the vat and they were slowly boiled until they were dead. The screams of those boiling witches could be heard a mile away. Not very pleasant, but no doubt they all deserved it. There was a seventh witch, the story goes, but she escaped, she was rescued from the rack . . .'

Tim interrupted her: 'You said something about, what was it, "dawn gods"?'

'So your mother called them,' said Agatha. 'Creatures older than the human race. Scoffed at by Darwinians, of course, but those heretics scoff at many things. Your mother used to recite a verse, translated from the old tongue . . .'

Agatha closed her eyes to prod memory, and chanted in a slow monotone:

> *They were unholy, dark and cold,*
> *The gods who ruled the dawn,*
> *When Man was young and They were old,*
> *They and their hellish spawn.*

She opened her eyes. 'It's somewhere in that book, in the original language,' she said.

Tim conquered his repugnance at the human parchment and picked up the massive volume. He opened it at random, finding several places where the leaves had been ripped savagely away, leaving only ragged margins, and this too he remembered from his childhood, these strange gaps.

'Your father did that,' said Agatha. 'He said they contained things no human eye should see.'

'If he believed that,' said Tim, 'why didn't he just burn the book?'

'Burn it?' echoed Agatha. And she actually laughed: a dry cackle. 'Don't you think he tried?' She touched the parchment. 'The skins of the witches were given to their families, as reminders and warnings. But the families used them to make new bindings for their copies of an accursed book that was old even then. Six copies, each bound in the skin of a witch. Falsely accused, your mother said, but of course she would say that. If they weren't witches, why did their families have this evil book? Do you see the way the 'i' is dotted in the title – with a hole?' Tim's finger probed it. 'All six of the books are said to be like that. The holes are the witches' navels.'

He withdrew his finger instantly. He felt fascinated by these horrors, in spite of himself, but he also felt impatient with his aunt's meandering narrative. He said, 'Does all this have anything to do with bullets?'

'You were a poor student in Latin, as I seem to recall,' said Agatha, 'so I suppose I shall have to translate for you. Give me the book.'

He handed the heavy tome to her. She turned the pages, then read aloud:

*'For no weapon will prevail against the dawn gods. Strike them with axes of bronze and their flesh will consume it; smite them with sword of iron and their bodies will devour the blade.'*

She looked up at him. 'If bronze and iron,' she asked, 'why not lead?'

Tim smiled bitterly. 'That's it, then? The prosecution rests? I'm the man Laura Kincaid shot, but my body "devoured" the bullets? They just dissolved inside me? Let's get the sheriff back here, Aunt Agatha, and you can make the accusation here and now. Then I'll sit back and laugh when they drag you off to the mental hospital where you belong!'

'Accuse you?' said Agatha. 'No. There is Galen blood in your veins, tainted but Galen blood. This family does not

72

betray its own. I want you to understand yourself, control yourself if you can, for your own good, your own safety. And for the honor of the Galen name. Yes, that too. I'm not ashamed to admit it. Despite what you are, you are my brother's son, and I love you.'

'*Love?*' said Tim, the word snapping from his mouth like profanity. 'You never had any love for me or for anyone else. You're all hate. If you love anything, it's death and torture. I wish you could have seen your face when you were telling me what they did to those witches. It was almost alive.'

'Timothy, I know you think me a foolish old woman, but – '

'Yes, I do,' he said, 'foolish and vicious and nasty-minded. But I'm going to do both of us a favor. I'm going to get rid of this superstitious nonsense . . . '

Yanking the book from her hands, he threw it into the crackling fireplace.

'*No!*' she shouted, terrified.

Before she could reach it to spare it from the flames, the book somehow had fallen from the fireplace of its own accord, landing on the carpet unharmed. Tim picked it up and was about to toss it into the fire again, but Agatha seized his arm to restrain him.

'It's no use!' she said. 'Your father tried that. Earthly fire cannot burn the unholy words.'

'We'll see about that,' he said, and moved to the fireplace, shaking off her hand.

'Please, Timothy, I beg you!' she said. 'You will offend Them – They will strike back!' She pointed to the floor. 'It's too late – They've already struck back!'

A spark had leaped from the fireplace to the carpet, a bright scintilla of heat. It was followed by a second, and a sizzling third, and the dry old fibres of the carpet began to burn.

Tim stamped on them, but without visible effect. 'Get some water, quick!' he said.

'No use,' she responded. 'Water would be powerless. You must make amends to Them.'

In one rapid movement, she seized the heirloom dagger

73

from the coffee table and slashed Tim's bare arm. He cried out in pain and outrage; blood streamed from his arm; the blade was smeared with it. Agatha plunged the bloodied blade into the floor, in the center of the small but quickly growing pool of fire. It stood upright, its point imbedded deep. The fire flickered out, leaving behind only a tendril of smoke.

Tim clutched at his wounded arm. 'Why the hell did you do that?' he shouted.

Agatha replied, 'Only the blood of one of Their own can quench the unholy fire.'

'You really *are* crazy,' he said. 'Sparks have burned carpets before.'

'And the book? The way it leaped from the fire?'

'*Leaped* . . . that's ridiculous. It fell out, bounced out, I didn't throw it right, that's all.'

'Do you really believe that, Timothy?'

'I believe this,' he said. 'All that stuff about swords and axes and bullets having no effect is just so much garbage. If it were true, then how the hell did you slice my arm?'

She smiled thinly. 'Look closely at your mother's blade,' she said, as she tugged at it and pulled it from the floor. 'What does it look like to you?'

It was certainly no ordinary knife or dagger. Its blade was curved, making it somewhat resemble a small scimitar, except that the cutting edge was on the inner curve, rather than the outer.

But all Tim said was, 'A knife. An antique knife.'

'Antique, yes,' said Agatha, 'but what kind of knife?'

'How should I know?'

She ran her finger along the dull edge of the blade, with a sensuousness Tim had never seen in her before. 'It's a skinning knife,' she said. 'The very knife they used to peel the skin from those witches. You will call it superstition, but in those times, God-fearing people believed that ordinary metal could never cut the skin of a person descended from the dawn gods, a person with that pre-human blood in his veins.'

She twirled the handle in her fingers and the blade flashed

74

with reflected firelight. 'So they made a special knife to skin them with. While the metal was still molten, they added blood from the ruptured hymen of a nun, a bride of Christ who willingly sacrificed her maidenhead for the triumph of God. And when it came time to temper the blade, it was plunged not into ordinary water, but into holy water. A unique knife. One of a kind. A knife to skin witches.'

## 17

*. . . thy lover did he do sodomy upon thee as well or didst receive him into thy mouth speak*

   *silence*

   *speak child or be racked again*

   *rack and be damned she shouts*

   *another quarter turn my lord*

   *two quarters says the interrogator his face livid with anger and venom in his voice for the first time ay two quarters and then two more and then a half turn and then a full turn and then another and another until this bitch of hell doth speak*

   *hell then indeed the chamber soon becomes a grotto of excruciation an orgy of mounting vaulting pain of eyes rolling in wild disbelief frenzied head tossing from side to side shackled hands closing and opening in spasms toes curling and writhing like plump little worms thighs twitching like a mare's flanks belly undulating breasts quivering nipples jutting buttocks tensing every inch of her flesh protesting straining fighting and the rack methodically dispassionately continuing to destroy her while its placid stinking master smiles benignly as he works and the noises are flung from wall to wall the interrogator's shouts and her slaughterhouse screams and the endless croaking of the crank that turns again again again as she with horror feels her knees begin to*

*separate at their joints her shoulders start to leave their
sockets her spine become a column of white fire her flesh sur-
render mindlessly its steaming store of sweat and blood and
sundry other substances in a series of spurts and gushings
and still the screeching crank continues to turn propelling
her toward that peak of pain where hope says all must end
but when that peak is reached another peak appears above it
high and hot and blinding bright and so the pain keeps rising
rising higher higher climbing into dizzy airless regions and
approaching now the tallest peak the peak past which no
higher pain is possible not possible impossible for human
flesh and bone to feel a greater pain than this but now that
peak has been attained and yet another peak arises beyond
until at last two soul deep words come bleating from her
mouth . . .*

# 18

TIM AND JENNIE were lying side by side in her bed. 'I know
one thing for sure,' said Jennie. 'If you stay in that house any
longer your aunt will drive you even crazier than she is.'

'But maybe there's something to it,' he said, his voice
troubled. 'A lot of people believe in that occult stuff. They
can't all be crazy.'

'Maybe not,' said Jennie, 'but if you look real close at
what she says, you'll see it's full of holes.'

'She keeps plugging up those holes,' he reminded her.

'Sure she does – by making things up as she goes along. A
person can be clever and crazy at the same time, you know.
Look – ' She drew her hands out from under the sheet and
methodically counted on her fingers. 'First you prove your
innocence by showing her you don't have any bullets in you,
right? So she reads something about bronze axes from a silly
old book, and maybe it's not even *in* the book, maybe she

76

wasn't translating, just making it all up, but even if it is in the book, what does that prove? Then, when she slips up and forgets her own lies and cuts your arm, and you call her on it, she makes up another fairy tale about a special knife. Don't you see?'

Tim thought about it, and felt partly reassured. 'What about the book, though, and the fireplace, and the fire?'

'It's just as you told her, Tim – sparks have caused fires before, things have fallen out of fireplaces before . . .'

'Why did the fire go out?'

'It probably would have gone out anyway, by itself.'

Tim nodded. 'I suppose so.' He stared at the moonlit ceiling. 'Jen . . .' he said, after a time.

'Yes?'

'What if I *am* that rapist?'

She caressed him, under the sheet. 'You don't have to rape anybody,' she said fondly.

'No, seriously. Forgetting all that witchcraft stuff, what if I'm some kind of nut? What if I black out and don't remember what I did?'

'I don't believe that for a minute,' she said firmly, 'and you mustn't believe it, either. Stop brooding about it, Tim. It's terrible about Melanie and the others, horrible, but you didn't do it.'

Again he was silent for long moments; then he said, 'I keep thinking about that book, bound in human skin . . .'

'Want to bet? It's probably plain old everyday sheepskin.' She stifled a yawn.

'And that hole over the "i" in *Perditae* . . .'

She looked at him. 'What was that word?'

'Part of the title, *Artes Perditae*.'

Jennie frowned. 'That's funny.'

'What's funny?'

'There was a man here, visiting my father. His name was Trask. I met him, just for a minute. But when I was on my way upstairs, I swear I heard him mention that title to Dad . . .'

Tim sat up. 'Are you sure?'

'No, not sure . . .'

'He must be that fellow from out of town who's staying at the inn.'

'Probably . . . Hey, where are you going?'

Tim had thrown off the sheet and left the bed. As he hastily dressed, he said, 'I'm going to see him.'

'Now?'

'Why not? It's not that late. And if he knows anything about that book, by God he's going to tell me.'

Julian was not asleep. He was sitting at the desk in his room, studying the notes he had jotted down during his second phone conversation with Stefanski.

No man in the world knew more about parahuman behavior, about the hairline boundary between fact and fantasy, science and superstition, than old Henryk Stefanski. In the first half of his life, he had studied the lore on the spot, as it were, at its European origins, first in his native Poland, then in Russia, Germany, Transylvania, France, England. Everywhere he traveled, he had made remarkable discoveries, created new links, drawn audacious and perceptive conclusions. And from almost every city and town, he had carried away with him a bit of valuable documentation, a book here, a letter there, usually purchased, sometimes freely given to him, occasionally (he had admitted privately to Julian) stolen. By now, his library was the most complete and comprehensive in the field, and contained many items of legendary fame and priceless rarity.

The copy of the *Artes Perditae* now in Julian's care was Stefanski's. The old man had never completely revealed, even to Julian, how he had come to be its owner. 'Enough to say that at a time when a loaf of bread was worth more than gold, I traded the last remaining bread in a certain place for a rusty key and a map drawn in my own blood on a scrap of envelope by a starving man. By another starving man, I should say, because I too was starving.' Julian had often wondered about that 'certain place' – a famine-blighted town, a Communist prison, a Nazi concentration camp? Stefanski had never said anything more on the subject. In later years, he had journeyed to the United States to study Salem at first hand, and had eventually settled in Boston.

As he studied his notes and occasionally referred to the Gideon Bible in the desk drawer and the *Artes Perditae* lying open before him, Julian often felt a strong impulse to phone Stefanski again to double-check or discuss a detail. But the three-hour time differential made that impractical. The old man was not well; he needed his sleep.

So did Julian. It was late, even here in California. He allowed himself the luxury of a long, wide, yawn, and was about to switch off the desk lamp when he heard a knock at his door.

He got up from the desk, his legs stiff from long inactivity, and walked over to the door. Leaving the chain bolt securely fastened, he opened the door an inch and saw a young man.

'Mr Trask?'

'Yes.'

'Can I talk to you? My name is Tim Galen.'

All thought of sleep fled from Julian when he heard the name. Tim Galen, the man who had been with Melanie when she was attacked; the man Doc Jenkins insisted could not possibly be the culprit; Tim Galen, descendant of the town's founding fathers.

'Just a moment,' said Julian, temporarily closing the door again. Quickly crossing to the desk, he swept his notebook and the *Artes Perditae* into the drawer. Then he unfastened the chain bolt and opened the door to admit his visitor.

An hour later, having listened attentively to Tim and asked a series of pointed questions, Julian sat back in his chair, steepled his fingers, and silently sorted the new information in his mind.

Finally, he said, 'The first thing I want you to understand, Mr – okay if I call you Tim?' Tim nodded. 'Please understand that I'm not a psychic or a medium or anything of that sort. I'm not a superstitious person, like your aunt. In my approach to the supernatural, I'm a confirmed agnostic. And a scientist. I require proof. Nothing you've told me so far is proof. It could all be explained as coincidence, or invention,

79

or natural causes. Your friend, Jennie – a very lovely young lady, by the way – is quite right about your aunt's cleverness. Each time you catch her in an inconsistency, she patches her story. Of course,' Julian added, almost casually, 'she *could* be speaking the plain unvarnished truth.'

Tim nodded, although Julian's last remark was far from reassuring.

'About the book,' Julian continued. 'Yes, I certainly have heard of it. I've studied it. In fact, I happen to have a copy in my possession. It is, indeed, very old and very rare, just as your aunt says. I'm astonished to learn there's a copy here in Galen, even a mutilated, incomplete copy. No, Jennie's wrong about the binding. It isn't sheepskin. I've had tests made. It's human, all right, at least it is on my copy and I'll make an educated guess that it is on all existing copies. And it *may* have been peeled from living victims, but it just as easily may have been taken from cadavers, people who died natural deaths. No way of telling.'

Tim asked, 'What about the knife?'

'I'm inclined to believe it's exactly what your aunt says it is,' replied Julian. 'But I'm not admitting for a single minute, without evidence, that it possesses any superordinary properties. It probably *was* tempered in holy water. Hymeneal blood may very well have been added to the metal when it was in a liqueous state. Medieval people set great store by those substances, thought they had all kinds of magical powers. I know of a crusader's sword that's said to have had its owner's semen added to the molten metal, to give it virile strength, manly qualities, and so on.'

'The dreams?' asked Tim.

'You've had them, off and on, ever since you were a child?'

'That's right.'

'But they're never really distinct? I mean, you can barely remember them when you wake up?'

'I can hold on to them for just a few seconds,' said Tim, 'then they're gone.'

'But it's always the same dream? And it seems to be happening a long time ago, perhaps in a different century?'

'Just a vague feeling,' Tim replied. 'Something about the way the people are dressed, and the way they talk.'

Julian rose from the chair and paced the floor. 'Interesting,' he said. 'Any number of possible explanations, all perfectly natural, perfectly simple, and not the least bit sinister.'

He stopped pacing and turned to Tim. 'But there's also another possibility, *not* so simple.'

Tim waited silently for Julian to continue.

'You see, Tim,' said Julian, 'when I say I'm an agnostic in these matters, that's precisely what I mean: I have to be shown, I can't accept purely on faith. But I don't scoff. I keep an open mind. And I'm afraid my open mind tells me that all your aunt's fears *may* be valid. You *may* be descended from a pre-human race. And if you are, you may be the person who attacked all three of those women. You may have no memory of it, but when that part of you asserts itself and tries to mate with human females, it could take temporary control of your personality. And the control might not be only mental. Your body could undergo certain changes, too.'

'Hey . . . ' Tim held up a hand to stem the flow of Julian's speech. 'Slow down, Mr Trask, you're losing me.'

'Sorry,' said Julian with a smile. 'I get carried away when I start talking about my special field. Let's stick to one thing for the moment. Genetic memory.'

The two words seemed to contradict each other, Tim thought.

Julian continued. 'There's a considerable body of scientific opinion to support the belief that all of us may be able to remember things that happened before we were born . . . '

'Before we were *born?*'

'Before we were even conceived,' Julian went on. 'Before our parents and grandparents and great-grandparents were conceived. Our genes may carry memory-imprints from generation to generation, sealed into the DNA molecule, the building block of life. Those memories may be stronger in some people, weaker in others. They may be mistaken for hunches, idle reveries, foolish notions, groundless fears or depressions, bright ideas, the "inspirations" of poets and

81

other creative people. They may come as religious visions, to people we call saints – or madmen. And, of course, when we're asleep, relaxed, receptive, and the conscious mind is inactive, these genetic memories may take the form of dreams.'

Tim shifted in his chair, disquieted by Julian's words.

'There's a technique some of us have used in experimental situations,' Julian continued. 'It's not exactly legal, because it involves a drug that the law says must be administered by a doctor. I'm a doctor only in the academic sense; I'm not a physician. Still, I'll have to confess that I've broken the law on this point a few times. What do you say, Tim? Are you willing to be my partner in crime?'

Tim asked, 'What kind of drug?'

'It's new,' Julian replied. 'Chemically related to scopolamine, the so-called truth serum. It also has some of the properties of psilocybin – that's the drug that's been isolated from the sacred mushrooms of Mexico. We think it's more effective than either of them. It induces a hypnotic state in which the barriers of time dissolve, so to speak, allowing the mind to travel easily into the patient's past, and possibly into the past of his ancestors. We've had some remarkable results, and, so far, no bad side-effects. It's a harmless drug, used properly. Are you game?'

'Yes,' said Tim. 'I've got to know. One way or the other.'

'All right. Fine.'

'When can we do it?'

'No time like the present.'

'You have the drug here?'

'In my suitcase. Would you rather have some time to think about it? Sleep on it and come back tomorrow?'

Tim hesitated, but for only a moment. 'No,' he said, decisively. 'The sooner, the better.'

'You're sure.'

'Yes.'

'Roll up your sleeve and lie back on the bed,' said Julian. 'Make yourself comfortable.'

Tim kicked off his shoes and followed instructions, as Julian pulled his suitcase from under the bed. Opening it, he removed a small black leather case containing a vial of the drug, a.. ther of alcohol, cotton swabs, and disposable hypodermic syringes.

Adeptly, he swabbed a patch of Tim's arm with alcohol, then plunged in the needle. 'Count backward from one hundred, slowly,' he said.

Tim began counting. 'Hundred . . . ninety-nine . . . ninety-eight . . . ninety-seven . . .'

He felt as if he were floating, his body set free from the restrictions of space, his mind unchained from the tyranny of time. Although he continued to count, he soon lost track of the sequence of numbers. 'Ninety-six . . . ninety-five . . . ninety-four . . . ninety-five . . . ninety . . . five . . . nine . . .'

Scenes rushed backward past the windows of his memory; places, people, incidents, his childhood, school days, father, mother, aunt, faces both familiar and strange, voices warm with comfort and harsh with threat, a blurring spiral of flashing pictures, sucked up by the twisting black funnel of time's tornado, and falling now, for miles, for years, into a city, into a building, into a room, a cold and airless room where there are men in curious costumes and a girl, a little thing she is younger than twenty and more than usually pleasing to behold her face is pale in sharp contrast to the sunset blaze of her unbound hair . . .

## 19

. . . *at last two soul deep words come bleating from her mouth*

*succor me*

*the rackmaster treats her plea as a jest saying suckle thee dost think me a lewd fellow or an unweaned babe but thou hast suckled many a filthy pizzle ay and 'twere best for thee to tell of it leave off mockery says the interrogator waving him aside impatiently then bending over the fouled and near disjointed length of living meat he murmurs to succor thee child is my chiefest wish persist no more in willfulness for if thou dost then all of this day wilt thou be questioned thus and on the morrow we must needs again torment thee*

*through teeth gritted in agony with tongue and lips bitten till bloody the girl cries out again looking at none of the three men as she spews the words*

*succor me*

*dost call thy lover asks the interrogator he cannot save thee now*

*succor me*

*and then as if in answer things far outside of reason happen swiftly*

*the iron shackles of the rack sag and flake and crumble into powder loosing her bleeding hands and feet*

*a draft of chilling air makes the three men spin to look*

*the nearest wall is splitting stone from stone opening with a crunching scraping sound to permit the entry of an uninvited visitant*

*the three men howl in terror retreating stumbling backward falling scrambling to their feet crossing themselves covering their eyes clawing at the dungeon's iron door*

*and she rises from the rack to greet . . .*


'Her lover?' asked Julian.

Tim, his pupils still dilated by the drug, rubbed his eyes and shrugged. He was sitting up on the bed, slowly coming out of the trance-like state.

'I don't know,' he answered in a sleep-thick voice. 'It's a man, but somehow different. Taller, maybe. And those *eyes.* Like a lizard's or a snake's . . .'

'Anything else?'

Tim shook his head.

'Are you sure?'

Tim thought for a while, and said, 'He's always naked in the dream.'

'Yes?'

'And there's absolutely *no* mistaking him for a woman. Know what I mean?'

'Be specific,' Julian urged.

'Well, you know,' said Tim, hesitantly. 'I've never seen anything like it in my life.' After a moment, he added, 'Except maybe on a horse.'

Julian's heartbeat quickened. But he merely patted the boy's arm. 'Good, Tim,' he said. 'You've done very well. Lie back and rest now.'

What he did not tell Tim, what even Julian was struggling to accept, was that Tim had just given an accurate description of the legendary creature known to some as a dawn god but more usually referred to – in numerous accounts of the most loathsome sexual depths – as an incubus.

# TWO

# THE UNHUMAN

That superhuman beings, imperceptible to everyday sense, at times, for their own veiled purposes, seek union with men, and that this union is sometimes consummated, may appear to the majority very like moonstruck fustian. Meanwhile that which men vaguely describe as 'science' is slowly veering . . . to the quaint finding that many cast-by superstitions of the Rosicrucians lie just ahead, and bid fair once more to be 'discovered'.

James Branch Cabell
*Beyond Life*

# 20

THAT SAME NIGHT, Prue Keaton had gone to the Paradise with Charley Prescott.

Charley and his guests always got in free because his father owned the theater. This saved a lot of wear and tear on Charley's pocket, but it tended to limit the choice of entertainment he offered his dates. On that occasion, for example, Prue had said, 'Do we have to go to the movies *again*, Charley?'

They sat in the ice cream parlor around the corner from the theater. The sweet shop was as old as the Paradise itself, and had always been called the Sugar Bowl. Charley's father had told him that the original proprietor, long dead, had taken the name from a fictitious adolescent hangout in an old comic strip called *Harold Teen*. Both Prue and Charley drank iced tea, no sugar; she because she was dieting, he because of a diabetic condition.

'I thought you liked movies,' Charley said.

'Sure,' Prue replied, 'but why can't we do something different for a change?'

'Like what?'

'Like drive into Midvale, maybe.'

'What's so special in Midvale? Anyhow, I can't get the car.'

'Oh, all right. But I heard that the movie your dad is showing is a bummer.'

'That one closed last night. We're opening a revival today, *The Maltese Falcon*, Bogart, Greenstreet, Peter Lorre. A real classic. Of course, we could always just go to the park and –'

'With that maniac on the loose?'

'I'd protect you.'

'Who'd protect me from you? For all I know, *you* might be the nut.'

Charley mimed demented lechery, complete with bulging eyes, gaping mouth, and groping paws.

'Okay, let's see the movie,' said Prue. 'I do kind of like his pictures. He's sexy.'

'Bogie? I guess, if you like that type.'

'Not him. Peter Lorre. Weirdos turn me on. Why do you think I go out with *you*?'

Charley's response was another extravagant portrait of mad lust.

Prudence Keaton, who had recently celebrated her seventeenth birthday, had green eyes, chestnut hair, a slim and supple figure. She was the niece of the Reverend, whose stiff manner she sometimes mimicked. Her father, Ben, owned the big garage where Galen's cars were repaired and fueled. Her mother, the former Helen Barton, taught fourth grade at the elementary school. Prudence hated her given name, particularly when her more malicious coevals shortened it to Prude, and sometimes Prune. She was neither.

The Paradise Theater had been built in the heyday of silent cinema, when it had served the entertainment needs not only of Galen, but the surrounding communities as well. Families drove in to Galen in their flivvers to see the latest Valentino or Clare Bow picture. There was now a vacant niche where the Wurlitzer organ once had stood, its player pouring out the mighty sounds of chase and passion to match the action on the screen. Some of the old Twenties finery was still in evidence in the lobby: the art deco murals on the walls; the crystal chandeliers; even a few pieces of the pseudo-Grecian statuary, modestly fig-leafed. The original tapestries and carpets, however, had long since become the victims of dust and wear and time. The restrooms, discreetly relegated to the downstairs area, were as spacious as ever – far too spacious for today's spotty patronage – but the deep couches and oil paintings of chubby Biblical nudes that once had graced their antechambers were only memories shared by the older citizens of Galen. With the crash of '29, the theater had closed and stood dark for several years. With the television invasion of the early Fifties, it had closed again for a time, occasionally being rented out as a meeting hall or a place to hold charity theatricals. In 1959, Joe Prescott bought it cheap and reopened it again as a movie house. Somehow, he managed to make a living at it. Through all its permutations, the theater had never changed its name. It had always been the Paradise.

Charley and Prue arrived during the short subjects, waving at buxom Belinda Fellowes, the ticket seller, as they passed the box office. The pretty middle-aged woman waved back. After the cartoon (a good one, a Roadrunner) the house lights went up for a short intermission of popcorn selling. Charley and Prue, dieters both, stayed in their seats while Charley, a dedicated movie buff, regaled his date with lore about the feature they were soon to see.

'How old did you say this picture is?' she asked.

'1941.'

'God! What a relic! My mother was a little *kid* then!'

'It's an oldie, all right, but even so, it was the *third* film version of this same story.'

'They made it three times? It must be pretty good.'

'It's terrific. Based on a novel by Dashiell Hammett. The first movie version was ten years earlier, 1931. It had Ricardo Cortez in it and Bebe Daniels and Dudley Digges and Una Merkel. Directed by Roy Del Ruth.'

'Never heard of *any* of them.'

'They made it again five years later, in 1936, under the title *Satan Met a Lady*. William Dieterle directed it. Warren William, Alison Skipworth, Arthur Treacher, Bette Davis.'

'I've heard of *her*.'

'But this one we're going to see is the best, and the most famous. John Huston directed it. There was a radio version, too, 1943, Lux Radio Theater, with Edward G. Robinson. You've heard of *him*, haven't you?'

'Of *course*,' she said, haughtily.

'I have a tape of the radio show,' Charley continued. 'Want to hear it sometime? Laird Cregar played the Green-street part, and –'

'Shhhhh,' said Prue. 'It's starting.'

It was. The screen seemed like a postage stamp after the giantism of contemporary pictures; the images were black and white and pearly gray. To a soft cushion of ominous music in a minor key, and against a background of the black statuette of a bird, the main titles and credits came and went, dissolving and forming, finally to culminate in an introductory subtitle:

*In 1539, the Knight Templars of Malta paid tribute to Charles V of Spain by sending him a golden falcon, encrusted from beak to claw with the rarest jewels. But pirates seized the galley carrying this precious token, and the fate of the Maltese Falcon remains a mystery to this day.*

The foreboding music gave way to a sprightly urban theme, as a familiar American city appeared on the screen, accompanied by the subtitle, *San Francisco*.

*REHCRA dna EDAPS*, read the reversed lettering on the office window. Humphrey Bogart, sitting at his desk, looked up as his secretary entered the office. 'Yesh, shweetheart?' he said.

'There's a girl wants to see you. Her name's Wonderly.'

'Cushtomer?'

'I guess so. You'll want to see her anyway. She's a knockout.'

Bogie smiled like a piranha. 'Shoo her in, Effie darling, shoo her in.'

When the customer was ushered in by Effie, Prue turned to Charley and whispered. 'She's beautiful. Who is she?'

'Mary Astor,' he said. 'Played in silent pictures with John Barrymore. Real name Lucille Langehanke.'

'I inquired at the hotel for the name of a reliable private detective,' said Mary Astor. 'They mentioned yours.'

'Shupposhe you tell me about it,' Bogie suggested, 'from the very beginning . . . '

Before long, Charley had his arm around Prue's shoulder, and not long after that, it had strayed to the breast budding under her blouse. She kissed his hand casually, and placed her own hand on top of it, pressing his palm to her bosom.

Later, Bogart was having a drink with Sydney Greenstreet, a man huge in all directions, regally paunched, elegantly groomed, his bulk topped by a head with thinning white hair, pursed mouth, small glittering eyes, and the appropriate beak of a falcon. His voice was a modulated purr, and he spoke with the trace of an English accent: 'Now, sir, we'll talk if you like. I'll tell you right out that I'm a man who likes talking to a man that likes to talk.'

'Shwell,' said Bogie. 'Will we talk about the black bird?'

Greenstreet's laugh bubbled up in short spurts from the great globe of his body. 'You're the man for me, sir. No beating about the bush. Right to the point. Let's talk about the black bird, by all means. First, sir, answer me a question . . .'

Prue whispered to Charley, 'I'll be right back.'

'You'll miss the best part.'

She shrugged. 'When you've got to go . . .'

'Oh, all right.'

He got up to allow her to pass him. 'Don't be too long.'

Prue walked up the aisle and into the lobby. She bought a package of sugar-free spearmint gum from Mary Lou, the girl at the candy counter. She was about a year younger than Prue.

'How do you like the picture?' Mary Lou asked her.

'It's okay. Kind of old-fashioned. Charley *loves* it, of course.'

'Well, he's a nut for old movies.'

'He's just a nut.'

They chatted, for longer than Prue had intended, about boys, and the rapes, and other subjects. 'I'd better go,' she said, finally. 'See you, Mary Lou.' She put the gum in her purse and walked downstairs.

The ladies' room was unoccupied when Prue entered. She checked her face in the mirror, smoothed her hair, then locked herself into one of the booths.

Shortly after she had been seated, she heard the restroom door open and close as someone else entered. This person did not seem to walk farther into the room, but apparently remained standing, quietly, just inside the door. Prue heard no footsteps.

After a brief span of silence, she heard a *click*, and the restroom went totally dark.

'Hey!' she called out from the booth. 'What happened to the lights?'

The new arrival offered no reply, but Prue now heard footsteps drawing nearer and nearer to the booth in which she was sitting. When they sounded as if they were directly in front of her, they stopped.

Meanwhile, Sydney Greenstreet had chipped the black enamel coating from the falcon and discovered it to be a fake made of lead. Peter Lorre, slim, curly-haired, attired and mannered in the style of a preening homosexual, spluttered his rage at the fat man. '*Yiu,*' he said eyes bulging, a Central European color tinting his voice, 'eet's *yiu* who bahngled it . . . yiu ent your stupit attempd to buy it! . . . Kemidov fount oud how faluable it was . . . huh! . . . no wahnder we hat soch an easssy tam stealing it . . . yiu . . . yiu *eem*becile! . . . yiu bloated *eed*yot; . . . yiu stupit *fat*-head . . . yiu . . . ' He broke into tears of frustration, like a disappointed child.

Prue sat petrified in the ladies' room booth. 'Who's there?' she demanded. 'Who is it?' The darkness pressed upon her eyes like thick black jelly. She began to feel the nausea of fear.

Now the handle of the booth's door was seized and pulled. The locked door rattled. 'Stop that!' cried Prue. 'Who are you?'

The footsteps retreated, but only as far as the booth immediately to Prue's left. The person entered that booth. Soon, Prue heard sounds that told her someone had climbed up on the toilet seat there and now was standing on it.

She heard breathing above her head, and looked up. She sensed that someone was peering at her over the partition, but she knew that wasn't possible – she couldn't be seen in this blackness.

'What do you *want*?' she cried.

96

Then she screamed, as she realized that the intruder was attempting to climb over the partition and join her in the booth.

She stood quickly, yanking her panties up to her waist. With shaking hands, she unbolted the door. Panic squeezed her heart when she found out that the intruder had slipped something through the handle on the other side, locking her in. She shook the door frantically, but it remained closed. She screamed again.

The intruder's full weight dropped upon her from above, knocking the breath out of her, throwing her to the floor, her legs sprawled outside the booth, under the door. As she fell, she accidentally hit the flushing handle with her head, and the roar of the churning water filled her hearing. The left side of her face was pressed against the icy base of the porcelain bowl. She tried to scream again, but a hand covered her mouth.

It was hardly necessary: her screams, she realized, could not be heard. The restrooms were stoutly built, almost hermetically sealed from the remainder of the theater, buffered by antechambers and double sets of doors, and located in the lower level, far below the lobby and auditorium. But why oh why, Prue wailed in her mind, did no other women come into the rest room? In the same instant that she asked herself the question, she answered it: not only was the main feature still playing but the door probably had been barred by her attacker, like the door of the booth.

The molester's other hand reached under her skirt and tore off her panties with one strong tug. She struggled desperately, but it was no use; her captor was muscled like an athlete. Still, she continued to resist, twisting and wriggling under the crushing weight. She reached down to ward off the assault and prevent penetration. When her fingers touched the hard invading flesh, she was stunned by disbelief and terror. It was impossible, it couldn't be ...

She squirmed wildly to escape it, but could not.

Pain like a glowing sword pierced her, deeply gored her, pried her apart. The only mercy was that, even before her violator shuddered and keened in foaming, bursting waves of climax, she was dead.

As the movie ended upstairs, Ward Bond, as a police detective, was looking at the black bird with curiosity. 'What is it?' he asked.

'The, uh, shtuff that dreamsh are made of,' replied Bogie.

## 21

AFTER TIM HAD DOZED a bit longer on Julian's bed, sleeping off the residual effects of the drug, he awoke to find Julian at the desk, leafing through a large book he immediately recognized as a counterpart of the antique volume in his aunt's house.

Julian looked up when he heard Tim stirring. 'How do you feel?' he asked.

'All right,' Tim replied. 'A little spaced-out.' After a moment, he added, 'That dream. Genetic memory. It means I *am* descended from one of those witches, doesn't it?'

Julian looked steadily at the lad before he said, 'It might.'

He placed the book on the desk and sat on the edge of the bed, next to Tim. 'And it might not. First, you have to keep in mind that most, perhaps all, so-called witches were falsely accused, perfectly innocent. You might be descended from a woman who was accused of being a witch, yes. But that doesn't mean she was one. As for the dream, it may not be genetic memory at all, just a recurring nightmare, based on things you've read or heard about. For instance . . . '

Julian walked over to the desk and brought the *Artes Perditae* back to Tim. He turned the pages, then handed the book to him. 'Is this picture in your copy of the book?' he asked.

The entire page was devoted to a medieval woodcut of

a naked woman being broken on the rack, her arms and legs stretched out of their sockets, her mouth distended in an eternal silent scream. There were three men in the picture: one turned the crank, another stood patiently over her, the third sat in the background at a desk, writing.

Tim studied it. He shook his head, not in denial, but confusion. 'I . . . just can't remember,' he said. 'It may be one of the pages that's torn out. Or it may not.'

'Or,' said Julian, 'it may have been torn out *after* you saw it as a child.'

Tim nodded slowly. 'Could be.'

'If you ever saw this picture before, then the dream proves nothing, either way. It's a dream anyone might have after seeing a picture like this, particularly at such an early, impressionable age.'

'But the *detail* in the dream,' insisted Tim. 'The language . . . '

Julian shook his head. 'Those stories your aunt told you about witches being racked and skinned alive – she got them from your mother, didn't she?'

'That's what she says.'

'Isn't it possible that you heard or overheard those tales of your mother's when you were very young? Heard them again and again, perhaps? She may have told them vividly, dramatically. Or your mind may be combining your mother's stories with movies you've seen or books you've read. Your aunt said there was a seventh woman, who was rescued from the rack . . . '

'Just like the woman in my dream.'

'Yes,' said Julian, 'but your aunt got the story from your mother, and you may have heard the same story when you were a child.'

Tim nodded, somewhat reassured. 'Yes, I see . . . '

Julian put the book in the desk drawer, and turned again to Tim. 'Everything I've just said was in my role as devil's advocate, the hard-headed realist looking for holes in the story, finding natural explanations for allegedly supernatural events. *But*,' he emphatically added, 'there's another side to the coin.'

He stood over Tim, counting one by one on his fingers. 'One: the dream may be a genetic memory of a real event. Two: the woman in the dream may have had sexual intercourse with a survivor from pre-human times. Three: you may be descended from that union. Four: you may have parahuman qualities and powers. Five: you may be the one who attacked Gwen, Melanie, and Laura.'

Tim said, bitterly, 'Oh, I know I'm the favored candidate.'

'Not to Hank Walden you're not,' said Julian, 'or you'd be in the lock-up right now. That's because Doc Jenkins told Hank something that convinces both of them you can't be the culprit. I think I know what that something is, but it doesn't convince *me* because I know things Doc doesn't. Things about the peculiar abilities of parahuman beings. I have to be frank with you, Tim. If it were up to me, I'd keep you under lock and key until we could find out more about you. Not because I'm convinced you committed those crimes, but because I'm not convinced you *didn't*. And because I'd rather be safe than sorry. I don't want any more Galen women raped and killed.'

Wryly, Tim said, 'Guilty till proven innocent.'

Julian smiled. 'Something like that. Fortunately for you, I'm not the law.'

'But, Mr Trask,' said Tim, his face clouded, 'if I thought for one minute I was the one, I'd *want* to be locked up.'

'I know that, Tim. I know.' Julian patted Tim's shoulder and sighed. 'It's getting very late. I don't think there's any more we can do tonight. Go home. But – for your own sake – be very careful.'

Tim nodded, without knowing what he was agreeing to. 'What do you mean, exactly?'

'The pre-human race, according to legend, had power over the elemental forces, and could use this power against its enemies when it was hindered in any way, impeded, frustrated, in danger of capture.'

'Elemental forces?'

'Fire, water, earth, and air. You've already had one experience with fire.'

100

'That was an accident.'

'Probably. But I repeat: be careful. Even if you really are, as your aunt might say, "one of Them". They could turn against you if you opposed Them. In other words, you could turn against yourself. Your pre-human part could attack the humanity in you.' Julian escorted Tim to the door. 'But there's another reason to be careful,' he said. 'A very ordinary reason. The drug may not have completely worn off. Sometimes it takes a while. You may have a dizzy spell or two. You might even hallucinate. Don't be alarmed. Just try to get a good night's sleep, and you should be fit in the morning.'

They shook hands, and Tim left.

Shortly after, Julian's phone rang. It was Laura, with the news about Prue Keaton.

Julian met Laura at the Paradise. Doc, Hank, and Clem were already there. The body of Prue Keaton had been removed. They stood in the lobby of the empty theater, with the owner, Joe Prescott, his son, Charley, and the girl from the candy counter, Mary Lou. She was in tears. Charley, badly shaken, was repeating his story.

'Like I said, she just whispered that she was going to the ladies' room and she'd be right back. But she was gone a long time. I started to get worried, thought maybe she was sick. So after a while I came out here to the lobby and asked Mary Lou if she'd please go in there and see if Prue was all right.'

Hank Walden turned to Mary Lou. Haltingly, between sobs, she said, 'It was pitch black when I went in there. But I knew where the switch was, just inside the door, so I turned on the lights. Then I . . . saw her . . .'

Doc Jenkins said, 'Just take it easy, dear.'

After a moment, Mary Lou continued. 'Just her legs, that's all I could see. Sticking out from under the booth. Her stockings were all torn. One shoe was off. And there was . . . blood . . . all over the floor . . . ' She broke into uncontrollable tears.

'Clem, take her home in the patrol car,' Hank said, 'then

go on home yourself. I'll get a lift from one of these fellows.'

Clem guided the weeping Mary Lou out of the theater.

Joe Prescott spoke now. The big chubby current Mayor of Galen was obviously the original of which Charley was a younger edition. He had the same flaming-red hair, though now somewhat dimmed and thinned. 'As soon as Mary Lou came screaming out of there,' he said, 'Charley and I went in. It was just like she said. Blood everywhere. The booth was locked from the inside. I climbed up and looked over the partition. It was . . . like a slaughterhouse . . . I knew she must be dead . . . I didn't touch anything or try to move her. Called you right away, Hank. By that time, the last show was over, and folks started to file out of the auditorium. I kept everybody out of the ladies' room. Some of the ladies didn't like that, but I told them there'd been a plumbing accident. Christ, Hank, what the hell are you doing about these awful things? Folks are starting to climb all over *my* back because I'm the stupid asshole who got stuck with the mayor job this year, so I've got to jump on *your* back . . .'

While Joe and Hank tangled, Julian turned to Doc Jenkins. 'Is it . . . like the others?'

'Seems to be, superficially,' Doc replied. 'Won't know until I make a thorough examination. I'm going to the hospital now.'

'I'm going with you,' said Julian.

Doc asked Hank Walden, 'Has anybody told the girl's family?'

Hank said, 'That's my lovely job, as usual. Unless anybody wants to volunteer to relieve me of it this once?'

Laura said, 'I'll tell Ben and Helen.'

'Thanks, I appreciate it,' said Hank. 'You can break it to them easier. They see me coming this time of night, right away they know there's something bad happened. Doc, I'll come with you to the hospital.'

At about this time, Tim was arriving home. The old house was dark, not a single light left burning by his parsimonious aunt.

102

He felt abnormally tired as he walked wearily up the path to the front door; drained by the sharply-etched horror of the dream – if it was a dream – and troubled by the conflicting, comfortless theories expounded by Julian Trask.

He unlocked the door with his key and entered the house. He could have turned on some lights, but he did not bother. Years of living in the musty old rooms had imprinted every corner of them in his memory.

In the living room, as he passed the coffee table, he reached out his hand to feel for the old book. It was still there, the human parchment loathsome to his fingertips. He walked on, making his way in the dark to the staircase.

As he climbed the stairs, dragging his leaden limbs, he passed the portraits of Galens dead and gone. He could not see them in the dark, but he knew every line of their stony faces. Matthew, his father. Wallace, his grandfather, and his wife, Elizabeth. Great-grandfather Edmund and his wife, Naomi. All the way back to Calvin and Lydia Galen. The masters of the manor and their wives. Only Tim's mother was absent from the gallery. His aunt forbade her portrait to hang here. It hung in Tim's room, like a feminized mirror image of himself: the same high cheekbones, amber eyes, and pagan beauty.

With each step, Tim heard in his mind the voice of Julian, solemnly counting out the numbers of doom:

*One: the dream may be a genetic memory of a real event.*

*Two: the woman in the dream may have had sexual intercourse with a survivor of pre-human times.*

*Three: you may be descended from that union.*

*Four: you may have parahuman qualities and powers.*

*Five: you may be the one who attacked Gwen, Melanie, and Laura.*

As he continued to climb the stairs, the old boards creaked with each step. They seemed to be saying:

*Fire.*

*Water.*

*Earth.*

*Air.*

103

Over and over again, as he mounted the stairs: *Fire* . . .
*water* . . . *earth* . . . *air* . . .

At last, he reached the second floor of the house.

He passed his aunt's bedroom. The door was closed. He
tried it. Locked. Was she afraid he would rape her? He
smiled, sardonically. The only thing to be said in favor of
the rapist was that he had good taste. He preferred young,
pretty women. Tim walked on, to his own room.

Here, moonlight relieved the darkness, frosting the familiar
objects. He went directly to his dresser, his eyelids heavy
with fatigue. Like an automaton, he emptied his pockets
of keys, coins, wallet, placing them where he had placed
them by habit for years, next to his brush and comb.

Yawning, he stripped off his shirt, at the same time kicking
off his shoes. His jeans came off next. He aimed them at his
chair, and missed. They landed on the floor in a heap. 'Hell
with it,' he muttered sleepily, and turned gratefully in the
direction of his bed.

What he saw there made him scream and recoil with a
thud against the wall, displacing his mother's portrait. It fell
with a clangor of breaking glass.

## 22

HIS BED WAS GONE.

Occupying the space where it had been, where it had
always been ever since he could remember, was the medieval
machine of his dream: the rack. And, stretched upon it, red
hair matted, teeth clenched, naked body slick with the sweat
of agony, was the woman of that dream. Her pain-widened
eyes glowed in the moonlight, burning directly into Tim's.

'Succor me!' she pleaded.

Tim howled in phobic horror, his back to the wall, his
body shaking.

'Succor me!' she begged again.

He shut his eyes, slid with a whimper down the wall, and collapsed upon the floor, into the brittle shards of glass.

'Timothy!'

His aunt's voice. She had snapped on the lights in his room, and stood in his doorway in her nightgown. 'What's wrong?' she demanded. 'You're bleeding!'

He sat among the broken glass, clad only in his underwear. His knees and calves were cut by the sharp splinters. He had not opened his eyes.

'Timothy!' Agatha cried again. 'What is it?'

He groaned, and lifted an arm, pointing with still closed eyes in the direction of the rack.

Now he felt his aunt, helping him stand up. 'Careful!' she warned. 'You'll cut your feet.' She guided him away from the broken glass. 'Sit down here,' she said, and he felt her urge him to his chair. He sat down. He felt her hands on his legs, picking away pieces of glass. 'It's not as bad as I thought,' she said, 'not deep. Timothy, what was it? A nightmare?'

He was afraid to open his eyes. He whispered, 'Don't you see her?'

'See who?'

'That girl,' he moaned. 'Poor . . . girl . . . *there*.' Again he pointed with closed eyes in the direction of his bed.

'Open your eyes, Timothy,' his aunt said firmly. 'There's no one there.'

Reluctantly, slowly, he opened his eyes and looked at the spot where the rack had been. His bed stood there, in its customary place.

'You were having a bad dream,' said Agatha. 'About a "poor girl", you say, there on your bed. Don't you realize, Timothy, that your guilty conscience made you dream about her? A poor, violated girl, victim of rape . . . '

'No . . . ' He shook his head. 'Not like that . . . '

'Who was it? Gwen Morrissey? Melanie Saunders?'

'No, no, you don't understand. Forget it. Just a . . . hallucination. He told me I might have them . . . '

'Who told you? What do you mean?'

105

'Never mind, Aunt Agatha. I'm very tired. I just want to sleep.'

'All right,' she said. 'In a moment. Let me get something for those scratches first.'

She went into the bathroom. Tim sat, his body limp and fear-drenched, looking at the broken portrait of his mother on the floor.

Doc Jenkins had completed his examination of Prue Keaton's body, and pronounced its condition to be identical to that of the other two girls. He, Julian, and Sheriff Walden were standing in the first floor visitors' lounge of the hospital.

'Seventeen years old,' Hank said. 'God Almighty.'

Doc Jenkins turned suddenly and explosively on the sheriff. 'Damn it, Hank, you've got to *find* this maniac!'

'I'm doing everything I can,' Hank insisted.

'*Are* you? Do you really *want* to find him?'

'*Here,*' roared Hank, ripping the badge from his shirt. '*You* wear it!'

'Gentlemen, please,' said Julian, stepping between them. 'We're all on edge.'

'Sorry, Hank,' said Doc. 'I don't know what got into me.'

'I do,' said the sheriff, with gruff understanding. 'You're worried about your Jennie. You have a right to be. I'd be worried, too, if I had a pretty little daughter like her.'

'I know you're doing your best.'

'And I know my best is none too good. But what else can I do? Arrest Joe Prescott's boy? My hottest suspect is still Tim Galen, but you tell me he can't be the one, and anyway, he sure isn't the fellow Laura Kincaid shot. I'm stymied, Doc. Plain stymied. All I can do now is run a check on every male in town and find out where each one of them was at the time Prue was killed. And I may as well start with you two.'

'I was home in bed,' said Doc.

'Can you prove it?'

Doc shook his head. 'Afraid not. Martha and Jennie were both asleep when I got home. I don't think Martha even heard me get into bed. No, Hank, I don't have an airtight alibi. I *could* have attacked Prue and then had plenty of time to get home.'

The sheriff grunted and turned to Julian.

'I was in my room at the inn, reading,' Julian said.

'No witnesses, I don't suppose?'

'Tim Galen dropped by to talk to me, but if the time of death Doc told us is correct, he didn't arrive at my room until after it was all over. So, no – I have no alibi.'

'And if *you* don't,' said Hank, 'neither does Tim, most likely. Neither do I. Beautiful, just beautiful. Every man in Galen is a suspect.' He shook his head in frustration. 'Well, I better get started. Not getting anywhere standing around here. Guess I'll have that restroom dusted for latents, but I don't think we'll turn up anything but smudges. Didn't get any decent prints from Laura's office when he broke in there.' There was a hole in Hank's shirt where he had ripped off his badge. 'Ruined a brand-new shirt,' he muttered. Then he pinned the badge back on and lumbered out of the visitors' lounge.

'One more thing, Hank,' Doc called after him. Turning to Julian, Doc said, 'I'll be right back. Just a private matter I want to talk to him about.' Julian nodded. Doc joined the sheriff in the corridor outside the lounge, and spoke in a lowered voice:

'Now, I don't want you to make too much of this, Hank. But I'm duty-bound to report it to you. A minute ago, with Trask standing there, I said Prue's condition was the same as the other two girls. That's not quite true. There's one small difference.' He paused. 'There was a small amount of undigested protein and sugar in Prue's stomach . . . '

'Ice cream sodas at The Sugar Bowl before the movie.'

'No, Prue only had iced tea, Charley said. She was on a diet. Don't ask me why, slim little thing, but girls these days are crazy on keeping their weight down, my Jennie's the same way. This substance was, as I say, present in a very small amount, maybe about 90 cc's. It wasn't something she'd eaten hours before. It had been very recently ingested – probably only minutes before she was killed. Her stomach was relatively empty except for that – you know how these

107

kids are when they go on a diet, fanatics, she was probably starving herself. This stuff was a gelatinous protein containing an abnormally high proportion of fructose, a monosaccharide sugar that happens to be one of the sweetest of natural substances . . . '

'Get on with it, Sam. What the hell are you driving at?'

Doc's voice dropped even lower. 'The substance was human semen, Hank.'

The sheriff was indignant. 'You mean, before that son of a bitch raped her, he forced her to –'

'No, no. Fructose appears in this high proportion only in the semen of diabetics. And the only male diabetic in Galen is Joe's boy.'

'Charley? *He's* the one we want?'

Doc shook his head. 'He can't be. I know Charley's medical profile even better than I know Tim's, and take my word for it, neither of them is the rapist. All it means is that, when he and Prue were sitting there in the dark, watching the movie, well . . . '

'You *sure* that's all it means?'

'Yes. But I had to report it to you. The thing is, Hank, we can't let this get around. Best forget it. Not only would it embarrass Charley, but think of Prue's parents, Ben and Helen. And, Christ, she was the Reverend's niece. It's nothing horrendous, they were probably in love, but no father wants to think that his baby daughter's last act on earth was to . . . see what I mean?'

'I see what you mean, all right,' said Hank, 'but in my opinion any fellow who'd make a girl do a thing like that is capable of raping and killing her, too!'

'Keep your voice down. First of all, Hank, you're a damn Puritan. And naïve. Nobody *made* Prue do it. She did it because she wanted to. Second, no man who's just had *that* favor done for him is going to be able to rape anybody for a while. In fact, the very presence of Charley's discharge in her stomach is pretty close to proof positive that *he* couldn't possibly have raped her.'

'All right, all right, you're the doctor, but who *did*?'

Doc smiled. 'Like you just said, Hank, I'm the doctor.

*You're* the sheriff. *Your* job to find out.'

Hank snorted and left the hospital and Doc returned to the lounge where Julian was waiting for him. 'Hank's a good cop,' said Doc.

'I believe it,' Julian said, 'but this is something the best cop in the world isn't equipped to deal with. It's outside his field of competence. Outside yours, too. We're in my territory now, Doctor, and I think the time has come for you to tell me everything you can – about Melanie, Gwen, Prue, about Tim Galen. Medical ethics be damned. Three girls are dead. Another one had a narrow escape. I just might be able to help track down the culprit – but I need your cooperation.'

Doc Jenkins sighed. 'You've sold me. Get in your car and meet me at my office in ten minutes. I have a bottle of Scotch stashed in my desk.'

'Purely for emergencies, of course,' said Doc ten minutes later in his office, flourishing the whisky bottle. 'And if this isn't an emergency, I don't know what is.' He poured generously into two glasses, and handed one to Julian. 'Mud in your eye.'

They drank.

Doc perched himself on the edge of his desk. 'I remember reading in a book once,' he said, 'how Ivan the Terrible sometimes put people to death. Impaling, they called it, got the idea from the Turks. Condemned person was stripped naked and forcibly seated on top of a high narrow pole that had a sharpened point. With men, the point was inserted an inch or so into the anus. With women, of course, there was another possibility. Well, it wasn't *too* bad at first, but then gravity started to take effect and the poor soul began to slide down the pole, very slowly, inch by inch, pulled lower and lower by his or her own body weight, with that sharp pole pushing deeper and deeper into the body, rupturing everything in its path until the feet finally touched the ground. Took several hours, they say. Folks used to bring their lunches and spend the day, watching the fun. Must have been almost as entertaining as the Indianapolis 500. Well,

109

this being the humane modern age, I never had the dubious privilege of examining anyone who'd been impaled – until I saw those three girls.'

Julian said, 'I thought as much.' He sipped his drink. 'Would I be off base if I assumed that the rapist had to be physically abnormal? The polite word is overendowed.'

Doc nodded and took another long swallow from his glass. 'You've guessed it,' he said. 'Don't know how you did it, but you nailed it, all right. And that's why I know Tim Galen can't be the one. He's physically normal.'

'Proves nothing,' Julian said flatly.

'I know what you mean,' said Doc, 'but you're dead wrong. You're thinking the culprit might have used some kind of object on the girls. Wouldn't be the first time some sadistic maniac has done that. Used a beer bottle or a corn cob or something because he was impotent.'

'No,' said Julian. 'That's not what I mean. Because the rapist *wasn't* impotent, was he?'

Doc put his glass down on the desk. 'No, he wasn't. But how do *you* know that?'

'Just a guess. There was evidence of seminal discharge inside the girls' genitalia – correct?'

Doc nodded. 'Proving the rapist was potent.'

'Yes,' said Julian. 'And I'll make another guess. There was something unusual about the discharge. A normal ejaculation amounts to only a spoonful or so. But my guess is that, with all three girls, it was more.' Julian waited. 'Well?'

Doc nodded.

'Much more?' asked Julian.

'Yes'

Julian got up and paced restlessly. 'Doc,' he said, 'I think we're making progress. I feel we're on to something. Now, can we get very specific about a few details? You say the semen was much more than normal. *How* much more?'

Doc picked up his glass again and drained it. 'It was all over them,' he said. 'Gwen, Melanie, and Prue. They were dripping with the stuff.' He shuddered. 'God help, us, there must have been *pints* of it.'

He refilled his glass.

'In Prue's case,' Doc added – for he had decided not to withhold this from Julian – 'there was a very small amount in her stomach, too. But I happen to know – don't ask me how – that it wasn't the rapist's.'

'You're right,' said Julian, 'but not necessarily for whatever reason you may *think* you're right. Believe me, unlike so many other rapists of the common or garden variety, this one has absolutely no interest in fellatio.'

'You're awfully sure of yourself.'

'Doctor Jenkins,' said Julian, unconsciously reverting to a stiffly formal, British manner, 'you examined those girls. You alone. You saw with your own eyes exactly what the rapist did to them. You're the only one who can tell me what's involved here. The time for delicacy is long past. We're talking about a male genital of, what, double average size? Triple? Judging from the evidence of the girls' condition, what would you say?'

Doc took a large swig of whisky. 'You're not going to believe this,' he said.

'Try me.'

'From the condition of those girls,' said Doc, 'the extent of the ruptured tissues, the massive hemorrhaging, the lethal nature of the lacerations . . . ' He half-emptied his glass in a single gulp. ' . . . I'd say the damn thing had to be the size of my arm.'

Doc held his left arm straight out, dramatizing the statement.

'Not like anything I've ever seen on a man,' he added. 'More like something you'd expect to see in a zoo.'

Julian nodded, pensively. 'Strange,' he said, half to himself. 'Someone else made an animal analogy tonight.' He was thinking of Tim's reference to a horse.

Doc said, 'Now, wait a minute. I never said I thought it *was* an animal . . . '

'I know, I know,' said Julian.

'No animal tracks were discovered near Gwen or Melanie, and – '

'No,' Julian said in agreement. 'We're not looking for an animal, exactly. And we're not looking for a man, exactly,

111

either. What we're looking for is a rare creature who exists for only one reason. To mate with humans and perpetuate its race. It doesn't want to kill. It only wants to procreate. But its physique makes it deadly. It doesn't know that. It's blind to everything but that overwhelming sex drive. Rarely – maybe only once or twice in all of history – it succeeds in actually impregnating a woman. She gives birth. And that hybrid offspring lives, matures, and spawns children of its own. With each generation, the non-human strain becomes more diluted, weaker and weaker, but it's always there, invisible, undetectable, in a seemingly normal person, and every so often it surfaces, suddenly grows dominant, and . . . '

The doctor's phone rang. He did not answer it immediately. 'Does this "rare creature" have a name?' he asked, scorn souring his voice.

'Several,' Julian replied. 'One of them is incubus.'

Doc picked up the phone. 'Dr Jenkins,' he said. As he listened, Julian watched shock stamp his face.

'Oh, no,' said Doc. 'Oh God, no. . . . Yes, Hank, I'll be right there.'

His hand dropped the phone back into its cradle as if the instrument itself were a repulsive live thing.

'Not another one,' Julian said in disbelief.

The doctor looked at him. His voice was blanched of all color. 'No, not another one,' he replied. '*Two* more. Numbers Four and Five.'

# 23

ANITA GRANT, forty years old when she died, had been a robust and handsome woman. She remained handsome until her death, but her robustness, her unlimited energy, her hearty appetite for sports and civic activities, had come to an abrupt and cruel halt at the age of thirty-seven.

The most cunning fiend, using all his diabolic art to drive her mad, could not have devised a torment worse than that which her life had become. For a woman of such vigor to be condemned forever to bed and wheelchair, wheelchair and bed, was torture of hellish intensity.

And yet Anita Grant did not ever repine. Her spirit remained undimmed, her smile still cheering, her religious faith stronger even than before. Only once in a very great while, when she was alone, did she allow herself to weep. But the tears were never for herself. They were for her daughter, forced to work to support a crippled mother; and for her husband – jolly Josh, they used to call him – chopped down by blind fate at the crown of his maturity.

No, that was wrong thinking, she would tell herself. If fate was blind, then God was blind, and deaf as well to human prayers and hopes. If fate was blind, then life was nothing but a game of random chance, formless, pointless, where the good could be punished and the evil rewarded.

It had all been God's will, Reverend Keaton had assured her, and she believed that. She had to believe it, or go insane.

God's will. Or God's willfulness?

She could not help asking *Why?*

Why, in that dreadful accident, had her daughter been spared, herself made a helpless invalid for life, and Josh killed? What sense was there in that? What purpose? What plan, Divine or otherwise?

And the irony of the way it happened. The ridiculous irony. They had not been driving on a hazardous stretch of road – no serpentine twists or hairpin curves – just the smooth, straight highway between Midvale and Galen. It was about ten-thirty of a pleasant spring night. The air was sweet with laurel. Mary Lou, thirteen then, was in the back seat, singing along with the car radio, one of those rock numbers she was so fond of. Josh had issued a mock threat to switch to another station in the hope of finding Lawrence Welk, and Mary Lou's howl of protest made all three of them laugh.

Was ever a man loved as Josh had been loved? Mary Lou adored him, and Anita was passionately devoted to making

113

him happy. Josh reciprocated both lives, with expansiveness and warmth. 'I'm a lucky man,' he often said.

A car approaching from the opposite direction swerved suddenly for an absurd reason – to avoid hitting a skunk frozen in the headlights. Both cars were accordioned by the headlong collision. The other driver, alone in his car, was instantly smashed to pulp. So was Josh.

His wife and daughter lived. Mary Lou suffered only a few bruises and scratches, not even a broken arm. Anita was less fortunate. A part of her spine had been damaged beyond repair; certain nerves were totally destroyed; her legs forever after would be a pair of useless appendages. Two dead weights to drag from wheelchair to bed, bed to wheelchair, heavy lifeless lumps: those long, strong legs that had flashed so superbly on tennis courts, and had tightly held her husband in the grip of love.

Her legs could grip nothing now. She couldn't even move her toes. 'Prettiest toes in town,' Josh would say as he kissed them, sometimes varying the compliment with 'in the West' or 'in the whole wide world'.

Josh knew he was corny. He was proud of it. 'Best things in life are corny,' he said. 'Love, kids, friendship, fried chicken, dogs, even Mother Nature. Look at that sunset! Ever see anything cornier than that? I ask you.'

Anita had surprised everybody by marrying him – even Josh. 'You could have knocked me over with a feather,' he said. 'I wanted her like nothing else in my life before or since, but I didn't think I had a Chinaman's chance of actually landing her. Classy lady like that? But no harm in trying. And by golly if she didn't say yes. What on earth does she see in *him*? they all wondered. So did I. I still do!'

She saw goodness.

And now all that had been changed, in a moment, by a silly, meaningless quirk of chance on a road. All the goodness and love that had been Josh Grant: discarded. Her own usefulness: canceled. Mary Lou's life: blighted by grief and trauma and burden.

'It could have been worse,' the Reverend had said to her

114

soon after the accident, when she was still bitter, still out-raged.

'Oh, yes, Reverend,' she had replied, scathingly, 'I know that. No matter how bad things may be, they can always get worse. And probably will.'

She heard a key in the front door. Was it that late already? The last show at the Paradise over, and Mary Lou home? Time usually went slowly for her, not quickly, but tonight she must have dozed.

'Mom?'

'I'm awake, dear,' Anita called.

When Mary Lou appeared in the doorway of the bed-room, Anita knew immediately that she had been crying. 'Honey! What's wrong?'

'Oh, Mom!' wailed Mary Lou. 'It's Prue Keaton!' Her tears gushed afresh as she kneeled at the bedside to be comforted by her mother.

'What happened?'

Clem stood, shy, in the bedroom doorway. Anita was surprised to see the deputy. 'Clem, what is it?' she asked.

He told her, in bald official terms.

'Oh, God! How *horrible*!' Anita said, stroking the head of her weeping daughter. 'How terrible for Prue, and how awful for you, dear, to be the one to find her. Oh, Clem, what's happening in this town? Who's doing these terrible things? Why can't he be stopped?'

Clem shrugged and shook his head. 'Doing all we can, ma'am.'

'I know. Of course you are.'

'Well, Mrs Grant,' said Clem. 'I'll just look around the house and see all the windows are locked, then I'll be getting back. And, Mary Lou? You'd best lock and bolt the door after I leave.'

Mary Lou nodded, unable to speak. A few minutes later, when Clem announced all windows secured, she saw him to the door, then locked and bolted it, just as he had advised.

'Poor Helen,' Anita said when Mary Lou returned to her. 'And Ben. What they must be going through now. And the Reverend . . .'

Despite herself, an uncharitable thought crossed Anita's mind. Would Reverend Keaton still say it could have been worse? Would he talk about God's will? She hated herself for the thought.

'Dear,' she said soothingly, 'why don't you go take a nice hot bath? It will help you relax. You can sleep with me tonight if you want to.'

'Yes, I'd like that,' said Mary Lou.

'Run along, then.'

What kind of world had this become? the invalid widow asked herself when her daughter left the room. Where had joy gone? Could it truly 'be worse' than this? In a quiet little town like Galen, no vicious New York or Chicago, could such hideous events really be happening? The rape and murder of one young girl after another, the latest just seventeen . . .

Josh, darling, you're well out of it, she said in her mind. The world isn't corny sunsets and dogs and fried chicken anymore. It's pain and filth and death . . .

The soporific, steady sound of the tub filling with water in the bathroom down the hall acted like a lullaby to Anita. She drifted smoothly into sleep, into a merciful dream of happier days, of love with Josh, of picnics with Josh and Mary Lou, of swimming and tennis and kissing and laughing –

The *CRASH* exploded her sleep and brought her instantly awake. What was it? Glass? A window?

Immediately, Mary Lou's scream knifed through the house, followed by a frenzied splashing of water and another scream.

'*Mary Lou! What is it? Mary Lou!*'

Screams of fear and agony, screams of slaughter, a girl returned to childish cries not of 'Mom' or 'Mother' but 'Mama! *Mama! MAAA-MAAAAAAAA!*'

'*Mary Lou!!!*'

She knew. Anita knew. It was the rapist, here in her house, violating her daughter at this very moment. She reached for the phone on the bedside table. Her hand clawed at it, fingertips brushing it without effect. She rolled her helpless body toward the phone to get closer, lunged awkwardly at it, managed to separate the two sections of the instrument, heard the tone, dialed 'Operator' before the phone slipped from her fingers and fell with a jangling crash to the floor.

'*MAAAA-MAAAAAAAAAAAAAAAAAA!!!*'

Oh God: Spare her! Spare my daughter and take me, take *me*, this dead flesh, this useless half-woman, kill me, burn me in Hell forever but take *me*, not her, not her, not her, not –

The screams had stopped.

Anita could hear nothing but her own breathing. She knew what the silence meant. It meant Mary Lou was dead. Her baby was dead.

'My baby, my *baby* . . . '

New sounds. Footsteps. Wet, slogging, sloshing steps. Coming closer. Water dripping from a soaked walker. Plodding, sloshing, closer and closer to her bedroom . . .

Trapped by her lifeless legs, Anita had no choice but to await the beast – a man like that, to her mind, could only be a beast and did not deserve the name of man. She lay on her bed as on a heathen altar, a human sacrifice to a gruesome god, needing no tethers to tie her down, listening to the ever nearer, louder tread of the slosh . . . slosh . . . slosh . . .

Through the terror and grief that had reduced her to a quivering, moaning mass, she was appalled that there remained in her a remnant of curiosity about the frightful assailant whose every step brought him closer to her. So avid was her thirst to know his identity that she looked forward, with a mixture of fear and perverse eagerness, to the moment when she at last would see him and would know the name of the barbaric fiend who had ravished and killed her baby and so many other blameless girls.

Slosh . . . slosh . . . slosh . . . Anita fixed her tear-dimmed eyes on the bedroom doorway . . . in one more second she would know . . .

The trespasser stood in the doorway, trickling water and blood, Mary Lou's blood, upon the carpet, standing in a scarlet puddle.

117

Anita could not scream. The horror was too great for screaming, too much for mind to grasp. It was no man at all. It was a travesty of mankind, an obscene mockery, not human, that which now walked purposefully to her bed, its monstrously swollen erection jutting like a weapon. But it was not the unhuman aspect of the thing, not even the impossible size of its member, where the darkest horror lurked.

The despair that throttled Anita's voice in her throat was caused by the numbing knowledge, just before the dripping creature sprang upon her, that she *did*, indeed, recognize its face.

## 24

MARY LOU WAS LYING in a tub full of blood.

That was the first impression to blast eye and brain upon entering the bathroom. The tub was a period piece that stood well away from the wall, on four lion's paws. The girl's arms and legs hung out over both sides, red water still dripping from her fingers and toes. Her head rested on one shoulder, dead eyes open and staring. The rest of her was immersed in water so opaque, so densely incarnadined, that it appeared to be not water but pure blood.

Broken glass littered the tile floor. The window above the tub, though still locked, had been smashed in.

A ghastly trail of water and blood led out of the bathroom, directly to the bedroom of the girl's mother. She was sprawled on her back in a blood-sodden bed, legs pried grotesquely apart, her robe and nightgown pulled up to her waist.

Hank Walden's face was gray from the events of the night. 'Anita never had a chance,' he said to Julian as Doc Jenkins examined her body. 'She must have heard the crash of the bathroom window, heard Mary Lou scream, but she couldn't do a thing about it. Tried to use the phone – it fell to the floor. She couldn't move out of that bed without help. Her legs were completely useless. Paralyzed in the same smash-up that killed her husband, three years ago. So all she could do was lie there and listen to her daughter being slaughtered, then wait for that bastard to come into her bedroom and get her, too. She was a fine, brave woman. God *damn* it to hell! Three in one night!'

'It's accelerating,' was all Julian could think to say. The words sounded inadequate, even to himself.

'That's the second time he's smashed right through a locked window,' Hank said. 'He sure can't be afraid of broken glass. Don't understand it. Christ, I've known people to be killed by broken glass. But this son of a bitch takes it in his stride.'

Julian thought he knew why, but there was no point in voicing that hunch now.

Hank declared, 'I'm just going to have to issue firearms to every woman in Galen. Commandeer everything that shoots from Oscar Garrett's sporting goods store, including BB guns. The only thing that saved Laura Kincaid from ending up like the rest of them was that old revolver of her father's. And I may have to deputize every man in town, as well.'

'Speaking of deputies,' said Doc Jenkins, joining them in the living room, 'where's Clem?'

'I wish I knew,' said Hank. 'I wish to God I knew.'

'Who notified you about the Grants?' asked Julian.

'Switchboard operator. When Anita's phone got knocked over. She heard screaming, so she called me and I got over here quick as I could. But too late. Too God damn bitching *late.*'

'You can't locate Clem?' said Doc. 'Didn't he take Mary Lou home from the theater tonight?'

'That he did,' Hank replied grimly. 'Which makes him my number one suspect.'

At that moment, Clem walked into the Grant house.

'Where the hell you been?' roared Hank.

'Down at the beach, getting the air,' Clem responded, surprised at the ferocity of Hank's tone. 'Radio was squawking when I got back to the car. Girl said you been trying to get hold of me and I better get my tail over to the Grant place right away. What's wrong, Hank? It isn't . . . Mary Lou, is it?'

'You're damn right it's Mary Lou! *And* her mother!'

Clem slowly sank into a chair, his face in his hands. 'Jesus Christ Almighty,' he said.

Hank continued to roar at him. 'I want to know every step you took when you left the theater with that little girl – start talking!'

Clem looked up at him, baffled. 'I took her home, just like you said. Even came in the house with her. Said hello to her mother. Looked around, made sure everything was okay in here. Checked all the windows to see they were locked. Told Mary Lou to double-lock the door and bolt it after I left.'

Hank studied his deputy. 'Came in the house, you say. Said hello to her mother.'

'Seemed only right,' said Clem.

'What *else* did you do?'

'Nothing. Then I left. Had the car, so I drove around a little, and ended up at the beach.'

'That's the lousiest alibi I ever heard!' Hank shouted. 'You're going to have to do a whole lot better than that!'

'Alibi?' said Clem, dumbfounded.

'There are two dead women in this house, damn it! And unless you can come up with something better than "driving around a little", *you* are going to be on the wrong side of the bars, sonny boy!'

Clem was wilting fast under Hank's barrage. He was close to tears. 'Jesus, Hank, you don't really think *I'd* do a thing like that?'

'Why shouldn't I think it? What makes *you* above suspicion? Where were you when the Morrissey girl was killed? Where were you when Melanie was attacked on the beach? And when Laura Kincaid's office was broken into? And when Prue Keaton got it in the Paradise tonight? And when Anita Grant and her daughter were raped to death in this

120

very house less than half an hour ago? "Driving around a little", were you? Every time? "Down at the beach, getting the air?" '

'Gee, Hank –'

'Answer me!'

Clem gulped hard. Voice unsteady, he said, 'Where were *you* all those times, Hank?'

'Never you mind about me!'

Doc Jenkins interrupted. 'Cool off, Hank. He's right. You can't lock up every man in town. The only fellows who are pure as the driven snow are me and Trask. We can alibi each other. We were both in my office. And before that, we were at the hospital with you. But after you left the hospital, *you* had plenty of time to get out here to the Grant place. Going to lock yourself up, too?'

'Yeah, yeah, you're right,' growled Hank. He turned to Clem. 'But no more "driving around" in the patrol car! That's county property! And until this rotten business is settled, you and I are on duty twenty-four hours a day. I want to know where you are every minute. Do you understand?'

'Coming through loud and clear,' Clem assured him.

Doc Jenkins said, 'I'm beat to the socks, Hank. If you'll have the bodies moved to the hospital morgue, I'll complete my examination in the morning.' Doc then took Julian aside. 'Come home with me for a nightcap,' he said. 'We have a conversation to finish.'


When the two men had settled themselves in the doctor's living room, and Doc had gravitated toward the decanter, Julian said, 'Do you mind if we have the conversation without the nightcap?'

'Won't join me? Suit yourself. I never force drinks on anyone, at today's prices.'

'I think we should *both* keep our heads clear,' Julian said pointedly.

The Scotch decanter was already lifted over the glass when this suggestion was made. Doc put it down. 'Maybe

121

you're right,' he said. He sat down, opposite Julian. 'Yes, I'll need a clear head if I'm going to listen to more of your . . . shall we say *recondite* theories? Always liked that word. Hardly ever get a chance to use it.'

Julian was in no mood for wordplay. 'May I expect the courtesy of an open mind? And a minimum of ridicule?'

'Sorry,' said Doc. 'We tend to get into habits of manner. Mine is sardonic. Dry-country-doctor. Hard to kick habits like that. Harder than dope or booze. Okay, you'll get your open mind. That's what skeptic *means*. And I'll have to give you this – you've homed in on the two most distinctive elements all these cases have in common, and the best kept secrets in town. How you did it, I don't know, but you were right on target with that stuff about physical size and the amount of semen. So keep talking. Open mind, yes. Gullible, no. I'll try to poke holes in your theories every step of the way, I warn you. I'll play devil's advocate.'

Julian smiled. 'I used that term tonight myself, to Tim Galen.' Briefly, Julian sketched for Doc the gist of his conversation with Tim, and told him of the drug and of Tim's dream, or genetic memory, of the incubus.

'Incubus,' echoed Doc Jenkins. 'What is it, exactly?'

'Could we consult your Bible again?'

Doc nodded, and brought the volume from the bookcase. Julian said, 'I'd like you to read from the same place, if you don't mind.'

'Genesis, wasn't it?'

'Chapter Six.'

Doc found the place and began reading aloud: ' "And it came to pass, when men began to multiply on the face of the earth, and daughters were born unto them, that the sons of God saw the daughters of men that they were fair; and they took them wives of all which they chose." '

'Skip down to Verse Four,' said Julian.

Doc read again. ' "There were giants in the earth in those days; and also after that, when the sons of God came in unto the daughters of men, and they bare children to them . . . " '

Julian cut in: 'What do you think that means – the sons of God?'

The doctor shrugged and shook his head. 'It's all Mother Goose to me, I'm afraid. Very pretty mythology, but I don't believe a word of it. Sons of God . . . kind of an odd phrase, at that. I thought Jesus was supposed to be the only son of God, but obviously this doesn't refer to him. I imagine it means something like angels?'

Julian said, 'Theologians differ about the meaning, as you might expect. But there's one opinion I find even stranger than the passage itself. Wait, I'd better consult my notes . . .'

He reached into an inside pocket for his notebook. It contained the quotations he had received over the phone from Stefanski. 'Yes, here we are. Now, then. Regarding the Bible verses you just read, Pope Benedict the Fourteenth had this to say: "This passage has reference to creatures known as incubi and succubi," unquote. In medieval folklore, incubi were supposed to be male, and succubi were female, but a French Dominican named Charles René Billuart wrote: "The same evil spirit may serve as a succubus to a man and as an incubus serve a woman." He lived from 1685 to 1757, and –'

'Fascinating,' said Doc Jenkins, not without sarcasm. 'But, as I told you, it's all Mother Goose to me. Why should I care what some superstitious priests wrote centuries ago? Why should *you*? A scientist. A hard sell, you say.'

'As a scientist,' said Julian, 'I tend to be alerted by parallels, recurring patterns. And I try to ignore semantic traps, emotive terms, words like "evil spirits" – they're just outmoded labels for phenomena and life forms that haven't been catalogued by science. Not *yet*, that is.'

Doc Jenkins nodded and sat back in his chair, wearily. He yawned and closed his eyes. 'Just giving the headlights a rest,' he said. 'I'm listening.'

'According to another old book, the *Artes Perditae*,' said Julian, 'the incubi were reputed to have been metamorthropes. Shape-changers. They could control their shape, size, toughen their skin texture, take on new muscle tone and strength . . .'

'And you *believe* that?'

'Not exactly believe it,' said Julian. 'Let's just say I haven't ruled it out. I've seen chameleons change their color. So have you, I imagine. I've seen films of a little blowfish puffing itself up to a sphere many times its usual size. Happens instantly. A salamander can grow a new leg if you cut one off. My own skin, and yours too, can grow a thick tough shield over a wound, then discard it after it's served its purpose – a scab. Or what about an ordinary erection? When you stop to think about it, Doctor, isn't that a kind of minor miracle – the way that organ adapts itself to the task, changes its size and texture, then changes back again when the task is completed? We call those things natural. Well, why not an extranatural creature with powers similar to those, and yet different? That's why a "normal" physique doesn't make Tim Galen innocent – or anyone else, for that matter.'

Doc Jenkins grunted, eyes closed.

'I have a few other quotes I'd like to read to you,' said Julian. 'Try to regard them objectively, scientifically. Forget the archaic language. Remember, I'm impressed by certain patterns and parallels. Maybe you will be, too.'

He opened the pocket notebook again and turned the pages. 'This is from *Demonolatreiae Libri Tres*, by Nicholas Remy. Very old, 1595. Remy writes, "Alexia Drigie examined her lover's phallus when it was sticking up, and said it was always as long as some kitchen utensils . . . " '

Doc Jenkins chuckled grimly, his eyes still closed. '*Very* scientific, Mr Trask. Very exact and precise. Hell, some kitchen utensils are only three or four inches long. What about an ordinary corkscrew?'

'Just a couple more, if I may,' said Julian. 'This is from Henri Boguet's *Discours des sorciers*, 1602: "His member was *like that of a horse*." And this is the last one I'll inflict on you tonight, Doc. It was published in 1612, ten years after the Boguet treatise. Written by Pierre de Lancre. The title is a jawbreaker: *Tableau de l'inconstance des mauvais anges et démons*. But the quotation is very short: "He always had a member like a mule's . . . it was as long and as thick *as an arm* . . ." '

Doc Jenkins suddenly opened his eyes and looked at his guest penetratingly.

Julian closed the notebook. 'Ring a bell?' he asked.


## 25


AFTER A LONG MOMENT in which Doc digested the quotations from the old books, he said, 'Impressive. I have to admit it. Even if it's only coincidence, it's an impressive coincidence.'

'I don't believe it's coincidence,' said Julian.

Doc rose from his chair and wandered aimlessly around the room, rubbing his stubbled chin with his hand. Turning to Julian, he said, 'Correct me if I'm wrong. You're suggesting that there's someone here in Galen, someone we've all known for years, who's physically normal most of the time, but is capable of changing, because he has this hereditary strain in his blood from a remote ancestor. Right so far?'

'Right. The old Greek legends of Pan, and the Roman Faunus, and Priapus, all the satyrs of mythology, the fertility gods, may have been started by ancient people who'd had fleeting glimpses of the incubus. Distortions, horns, hooves, and so on, probably crept into the legends later.'

Doc continued. 'This person, according to you, this otherwise quite ordinary townsman, impelled by a para-normal sex drive, actually changes into an . . . incubus, and becomes – what was that delicate word you used in my office tonight? – overendowed.'

Julian nodded.

'All right,' said Doc. 'A question or two Why has it happened so abruptly? If this incubus of yours is someone who's been living right here in Galen all along – someone like

Tim or Hank or Clem – why hasn't he gone on a rampage before this?'

Julian replied, 'Look at it from a medical point of view. A genetic defect, physical or mental, can lie dormant fo. years – even for generations – and then manifest itself almost overnight, for no apparent reason. Isn't that true?'

'Yes, it is,' said Doc. 'Fair enough. But why Galen?'

'Why *not* Galen?'

'Why only here?'

'I never implied it was only here. I'm convinced it's happened before, in other places, but it wasn't recognized for what it was. It may be happening somewhere else right now. And it may happen again. How many unsolved case of rape and mutilation do you think there are in the police files of every town, city, country in the world, collected over the years, over the centuries? How many of them might have been committed by an incubus? No town is immune, no place or time.'

'This change,' said Doc, 'this metamorphosis – does the incubus control it? Or does it just *happen*, like an epilepsy attack?'

'I don't know,' answered Julian.

'Well, that's honest,' said Doc. 'You made some very cryptic remarks about those six bullets Laura fired. What was that all about?'

Julian briefly paraphrased the *Artes Perditae* passage about bronze and iron weapons.

Doc's eyes surreptitiously stole a sidelong glance at the Scotch decanter, then snapped back to Julian. 'Another question,' he said. 'When the incubus is in the normal, human state, is he aware of the hideous things he's done? Is he standing there laughing at us making fools of ourselves. knowing all the time that he's the one we're looking for? Or is it like a schizophrenic condition – the left hand doesn't know what the right hand is doing?'

'I'm not sure,' Julian replied, 'but I tend to think it's the latter. A clean split between the human and the non-human personalities. One thing that leads me to believe this is that the crimes are so *pointless*. All the incubus wants to do is

126

procreate, preserve its race. Pure, naked instinct. But it doesn't succeed because the women are killed by the procreative act itself. If there were a rational human mind operating during the periods of change, the incubus would realize the futility of its acts.'

'Makes sense,' said Doc, 'of a sort. But, on the other hand, it makes it all the more difficult to credit.'

'Why?'

'You *do* realize what you're saying, don't you? You're saying that *any* man, not only in Galen, but in the whole world, could be an incubus and not even know it. A Philadelphia lawyer, a student at UCLA, a New York cab driver, a member of the House of Lords, an Italian tenor, a Chinese rice farmer, a Hindu mystic, a Soviet commissar, you name it.' Doc shook his head, as if to clear his brain of cobwebs. 'Any man, anywhere. A potential menace. A possible hybrid with the powers of the incubus locked inside his genes, dormant, ready to surface at any time, causing him to rape and kill without ever being aware of it . . .'

Doc rested one long arm on the mantelpiece and rubbed his bristly jaw again with his hand. 'You build a very tall tale, Trask. But the damn thing does hold water. In its own cockeyed way. As crazy and wild as it is, I can't seem to spring a leak in it. That's the trouble with being a skeptic. If a man hands you a theory that's consistent within its own system of logic, you can't disbelieve him. You don't have to believe him, but you don't dare *dis*believe him.'

'Coming from you,' said Julian, 'that's almost a compliment. But don't you have another question?'

'Don't think so,' said Doc. 'Not at the moment.'

'I'm surprised,' said Julian. 'You haven't asked the biggest question of all.'

'What question is that?'

'If every woman who ever had intercourse with an incubus died – if there were *never* any survivors – how could there be a part-human descendant among us now?'

'No,' said Doc. 'I wasn't going to ask that. Because I know the answer. And so do you, I expect. We're on my turf now, the human body. Some women – they're extremely rare

127

– have enormous physical capacity in that way. Pathologically so. They're usually nymphomaniacs or prostitutes or both, but not always. One of the most degraded forms of sex peep-show is a prostitute performing with an animal. Krafft-Ebing said, "The intercourse of females with beasts is limited to dogs," but the old boy was wrong. A great scientist, but curiously naïve in some ways, and his book was published almost a century ago; it's full of misinformation and wrong guesses. Catherine the Great was rumored to . . . well, never mind, it was only gossip. As I say, it's extremely rare, and it's certainly repulsive, but it isn't impossible.' After a moment, he added, 'Few things are.'

Doc became reflective, his eyes focusing on unseen vistas. 'The human body and the human mind,' he said. 'They're capable of things beyond our most fantastic dreams. Sublime heights and shocking depths.' He snorted and turned back to Julian. 'Sorry about that,' he growled. 'Didn't mean to turn philosophical.' He consulted his watch. 'Especially at this late hour,' he said. 'Look at the time. Sun will be up before we know it. I'm dead on my feet. Both of us better get some sleep. Big day ahead. Three funerals.'

He accompanied Julian to the door. As his guest was leaving, Doc said, 'I'm not converted, you understand. But I'll play it your way unless somebody comes up with a better idea. Till then, you're running the only game in town.'

'I also have a plan,' said Julian. 'I'll tell you and the sheriff about it after the funerals.'

The fog, as if it knew that golden sun and crystal skies were inappropriate to the occasion, moved somberly in from the sea to be a soft gray shroud over the churchyard.

The dead of Galen, for generations, had been buried in the cemetery of the church. Many of the gravestones were smoothed by time. On this sad Saturday, three fresh graves had been dug, three gaping cavities in the earth. A bizarre but fitting triple funeral would be held, the mourners moving from one grave to another, to the last homes of Prue Keaton, Anita Grant, and her daughter, Mary Lou.

The body of Gwen Morrissey, an out-of-town girl, had

128

long since been claimed by her parents and buried elsewhere in the state. Melanie Saunders no longer had any family in Galen at the time of her death, but a cousin in Nevada had requested that the remains be shipped there for final services.

Most of the people of Galen attended the triple funeral, shivering in the unseasonable early morning chill and damp. Everyone had either known or been related to the dead. The two Grant women had no living family to mourn them, but all of Galen had been fond of them. They were buried next to Josh, their husband and father. Prue Keaton was mourned by her parents, Ben and Helen; by her older brother Paul, a medical student who had flown from New York to be at his parents' side; and by her uncle and aunt, the Reverend and Mrs Keaton.

Julian also was present, although he remained discreetly at the rim of things, since he had not known the dead or their families. Laura stood with him.

Prior to the individual encomiums for the three departed, Reverend Keaton delivered some general words.

'We are gathered today in sorrow and in shock,' he said, his lean, skull-like face softened by the fog, 'to mourn the loss of three of our beloved sisters. In sorrow and shock, but not in anger, which our faith forbids. And yet we would be less than human if we did not feel a sense of deep outrage at the untimeliness and violent manner of their passing. Who among us is so perfect a Christian that he feels no wrath, no rage at the man who took their lives with such ferocity and lust? Still, we are taught that we must pray for him, as well. It is difficult, my friends, to do so. No one knows better than I how difficult. We want to curse him, damn his soul to the vast caverns of Hell. But vengeance is not ours. We must forgive, as our Saviour would have forgiven.'

Reverend Keaton's eyes raked the faces of the assembled mourners, as he repeated, 'We must forgive.'

He opened his Bible and continued. 'In the Book of Job are written words that, if they are no comfort for us in this hour, reflect the dark, conflicting feeling in our hearts.'

He read: ' "Man that is born of a woman is of few days,

and full of trouble. He cometh forth like a flower, and is cut down ... yea, man giveth up the ghost ... " '

His voice rose, crackling whiplash resonance, and Julian was struck by the strange significance of the Biblical words: ' "I have said to corruption, Thou art my father: to the worm, Thou art my mother, and sister." '

His eyes sparkling with new tears, he closed the book and hoarsely muttered, 'Let us pray.'

All heads bowed with his, as he said, his voice breaking at several points, 'O Lord, remove the bitterness and hatred from our hearts, and help us, that we may accept and resign ourselves to Your will. Make us to understand the working of Your ways, for Jesus' sake. Amen.'

A ragged 'Amen' was echoed by the fog-draped mourners.

Laura moved away from Julian to speak to Tim.

'I've closed the *Signal* office today,' she whispered. 'There's no need to come in.'

Tim nodded.

Laura asked, 'Your aunt's not here?'

'Not feeling well,' replied Tim. 'So she says.'

Laura returned to Julian.

Reverend Keaton had begun the eulogy of Anita Grant, but Tim was not listening. In his mind, the words of the Book of Job had become distorted to *Corruption, Thou art my mother.*

*We want to curse him, damn his soul to the vast caverns of Hell*, the Reverend had said, and Tim felt he had been looking at him when he said it, as well as when he had spoken of *the man who took their lives with such ferocity and lust.*

As far back as he could remember, his aunt had filled his mind with venom about his tainted blood, his evil mother, and yet he had never believed her. His memories of his mother, though he had been little more than an infant at the time of her death, were of a tender woman with gentle hands, a smoothing voice, a soft kiss, a smile that comforted small childish hurts.

But what if his aunt's poisonous tales were true? What if his mother had been evil, descended from a woman who had mated with a creature that was not a man?

The woman on the rack: was she only a nightmare, or a genetic memory of his own ancestor? Her rescuer, the awful-eyed monstrosity with the obscene genitalia: was that thing, too, his ancestor?

The fog soaked into him, chilling his marrow. He drew his coat closer around his body. The Reverend's voice droned on.

No, Tim told himself. His aunt's conception of evil was a naïve mixture of superstition, jealousy, and ignorance. The 'disgusting rites' and 'bestial acts' she had always hintingly attributed to his mother were actually something quite different.

He had come to know this only in recent months. Angered by Agatha's vilification of his mother, he had, not long before, demanded some specific example of the dead woman's so-called degradation. Agatha had demurred, had evaded and avoided him, but Tim had been insistent, and finally she had said:

'Very well. It turns my stomach to think about it. No decent person would speak of it. Certainly it is nothing a woman should describe to her nephew. But you force me to it. One night, long ago, before you were born, when my brother and his wife were living here, I wished to speak to him alone, and I chose a time when I thought your mother was out of the house, visiting friends. Oh, yes, she had plenty of friends; pretty women always do. I went to Matthew's room and opened the door . . .'

Agatha had broken off, and turned away from Tim. 'How can I say it? She was not visiting friends. She was with him. They were so preoccupied, they didn't know I'd opened the door. I closed it at once. A glance told me everything, even though the room was almost dark, one small lamp burning. They never knew I'd seen them at their filthy ritual.'

Tim's aunt had blurted out the final words of her disclosure: 'She was naked. So was he. He was sitting in his armchair, and that woman was . . . *kneeling* before him . . . doing a thing so vile . . . depraved . . . I can't say more. And, God forgive him, he was enjoying it. She had corrupted him, dragged him down into her own slime . . .'

131

The story had amused Tim when she had told it. He had laughed with relief, and Agatha had been horrified at his laughter. A fond caress, a gift from wife to husband, a loving tribute of a sort Jennie would not think twice about bestowing upon Tim, had been twisted and magnified into the nameless 'rites' so often darkly whispered of by Agatha. Now it was out in the open. And, if anything, it made his mother dearer and more human in his heart.

Reverend Keaton's eulogy continued, but still Tim's thoughts were of other matters:

And yet, he told himself uneasily, those other things might still be true. The transforming of a shameless secret into a blameless love scene did not, alone, prove his mother innocent of different sins.

Tim waited until all three ceremonies were over and the churchyard had been deserted by the mourners. When he was alone, he walked among the gravestones in the fog until he found the one he sought.

It read:

KATE DOVER GALEN
*Beloved Wife and Mother*

He knelt beside the grave. He touched the stone, stroked it, pressed his cheek against its cold, rough surface. He kissed it, reverently. His eyes brimmed with tears.

'Mother,' he said, 'tell me what to do.'

Instantly, like a coin sliding into a slot, a thought entered his mind, and he knew exactly what had to be done.

## 26

JULIAN'S PLAN was put into effect later on the Saturday of the three funerals.

'Don't tell Hank Walden any more than he actually needs to know,' Doc had advised him. 'Just tell him you have a scheme to smoke out the molester, and spell it out in detail. But don't start airing your incubus theory or you'll lose him. He'll just think you're a crackpot and he won't listen. Hank's no dumbie, but he's not ready for *that*. I'm not sure I am, either.'

Julian followed the doctor's advice, and when the two men met with Hank and Clem in the sheriff's office, Julian outlined his plan in the most practical terms.

'It's very simple,' he said. 'We never know where he's going to strike next, and we're always caught off guard. All I want to do is fix it so that we *know* where he's going to strike.'

'How you aim to do that?' asked Hank.

'By rounding up every woman in Galen. Every woman, every girl, literally every human female, and locking up all of them in the same place.'

Clem said, 'Our two-bit jail won't hold them. Where you going to find a place big enough?'

'I've already found it,' Julian replied. 'The dormitories of Galen College. It's summer vacation, and they're both empty. This is a small town – the female population isn't that big. Plenty of room in the dorms for all of them, if they double up or triple up.'

'Keep talking,' said Hank.

'We give them a week's supplies. It won't exactly be fun, but it will be livable. We make sure all windows are boarded up and all doors are barred and barricaded from the *inside*. Only the women can unlock them, no possible way of unlocking them from the outside. And they're told they mustn't open up for *anybody*. Not for you, or me, or their own husbands or fathers or brothers. *Nobody*. Rigidly enforced. They'll be in touch with the outside world by telphone, and that's *all*. We post armed deputies around the dorms twenty-four hours a day.'

Clem grinned sheepishly. 'Going to be a whole lot of frustrated men and women in this town for a week,' he said with a giggle.

'Hush, Clem,' growled the sheriff.

'Clem's right,' said Julian. 'That's exactly what I'm counting on. And the molester will be the most frustrated of all. His sexual appetite is abnormal, insatiable, and he'll have no way of gratifying it. There won't be a woman left in town, except in those dormitories. He'll be in torment, ready to explode. He'll try to get into the dormitories. He won't succeed, but he'll try. And when he does, we'll have him.'

Hank nodded slowly. 'I like it,' he said. 'We'll have to check it out with Joe, just for courtesy's sake 'cause he's the Mayor, but he'll go along. There'll be some opposition from the ladies – and their men-folk – but I don't think they'll put up too much fuss.'

'We have to move quickly,' said Julian. 'The molester strikes only under cover of dark, so those women have to be locked in before nightfall. We have a lot to do.'

'Have to contact every home in Galen,' said Hank.

Doc said, 'And get the market to deliver a week's supplies of canned goods to the dorms.'

'Cook-stoves,' said Clem. 'Electric hot plates.'

'And carpenters to board up the windows,' added Julian.

Hank rose to his feet. 'What are we sitting around here for?' he said. 'Let's get going.'

It took the rest of the morning and all of the afternoon to 'corral the quiff', as some of the men coarsely but aptly had put it. But before sundown, it had been accomplished.

There were, as Hank had predicted, a few objections, but only Agatha Galen had flatly refused to go into a dormitory. 'I was born in this house,' she said, 'and I have never spent one night under another roof.' She was the only exception. The dilemma was solved by Tim moving to the inn for the week, and by boarding up and barring the windows and doors of the Galen mansion. A newly deputized armed guard, Charley Prescott, was stationed outside, to be relieved by three other men, all working six-hour shifts.

Julian said privately to Doc, 'Miss Galen probably would be safe enough even without all these precautions. The incubus appears to have an instinct for women of child-bearing age.'

Doc said, 'Other rapists have been known to attack any-

134

thing in skirts, old women, little girls.'

'But I think the creature we're looking for can actually *scent* nubility. The victims have been no older than forty and no younger than sixteen.'

The women of Galen had been evenly divided into two groups, and split up between the men's and women's dormitories of the college. Each group elected a leader, or 'den mother'. The Reverend's wife, a notable organizer, thus became the natural leader of the group inhabiting the women's dorm. Laura Kincaid, as a prominent local business woman, was the den mother of the men's dorm group.

Shortly before the women were sealed inside their manless worlds, Julian, standing outside the men's dorm with Laura, asked her. 'How are the ladies taking it?'

'Pretty well,' she replied. 'Some of them consider it a kind of camping trip or pajama party, I think. Of course, they'll get restless when they start missing their husbands and boy friends.' She pouted. 'And you and I were getting along *so* well,' she said.

'Abstinence makes the heart grow fonder,' he reminded her.

'By the time I get out of here,' she said, 'I'll be so fond I'll be a candidate for a strait-jacket.'

'And I'll be right on hand, with Dr Trask's Handy Cure-All For Feminine Ills.' He kissed her. 'Any other complaints?'

She shook her head. 'Some of my girls are a bit unhappy about being put in the men's dorm, but they'll survive.'

'What's wrong with the men's dorm?'

'Not enough booths in the john,' she said. 'Those wall things are *very* impractical.'

At the same time, the other women of the town were taking leave of their men.

Martha Jenkins and Jennie had been assigned to Laura's group in the men's dorm. They stood outside it, giving instructions to Doc. 'Your good socks,' said Martha, 'are in the top right-hand drawer. Don't take the socks from the bottom drawer – they have to be darned. Are you sure you know how to use the new coffee-maker?'

'I refuse to mess with it,' said Doc. 'I'll drink instant.'

'You hate instant.'

'Then I'll break my fast at the inn until you're sprung.'

'Dad,' said Jennie, '*please* don't forget to feed Queenie.'

'Don't worry. That damn turtle will outlive us all.'

While Martha gave Doc further directions about how to run the Jenkins household in her absence, Jennie turned her attention to Tim, who was hovering nearby. He was carrying a small canvas bag and a large package wrapped in paper. 'Is that a ten-pound box of chocolates for me?' asked Jennie.

'No way,' he said. 'I don't want you coming out of that dorm next week with pimples all over you.'

'Will you miss me?' she asked, smoothing her hair.

'Hell, no.'

'Liar.'

'If I start to miss you too much,' he said, 'I'll just break in and pay you a little visit.'

Jennie frowned. 'Don't even *joke* about that,' she said.

They kissed.

Jennie said, 'I've got to go now.'

'I'll phone you,' said Tim. He walked away, in the direction of the inn.


Also assigned to the men's dormitory was the bereaved Helen Keaton, Prue's mother, her eyes still swollen from incessant weeping. Her husband, Ben, and her son, Paul, stood with her outside the dorm before lock-up time.

She said to Ben, 'I don't want to leave you alone at a time like this. I should be with you.'

'I won't be alone,' Ben reminded her. 'Paul will be with me.'

'We'll be all right, Mom,' Paul said. 'Don't worry about us.'

'You should go back,' she said. 'Back to New York. You're neglecting your studies.'

'That's what I told him,' said Ben.

Paul shook his head. 'I'll be waiting here with Dad when

you come home,' he said. 'And I'm not leaving Galen until they catch or kill that maniac.'

Ben said to her, 'Now, you promised not to cry anymore, remember? You'll hurt your beautiful eyes. Why, they're so puffed up and slitty already you look like a Chinese lady.'

The remark was meant to amuse her, and it achieved its purpose. She smiled. 'When I was young,' she said, 'I could cry all day and still look fine in the evening. But now that I'm an old ruin . . .'

'Best-looking ruin I've ever seen and forty-two is not old,' Ben said mock-sternly. 'You're just fishing for compliments, as usual. Now, I want you to call me at *least* once a day. Call me at the garage during business hours and at home at night.'

She nodded, adding, 'There's only one phone in the dorm. I can't monopolize it.'

'You can monopolize it whenever nobody else is monopolizing it,' said Ben.

Helen Keaton kissed her husband and her son and entered the dormitory.


'I just hope this fool scheme works,' Sarah Walden was saying to her husband, Hank, as they stood outside the other dorm. 'Cooping us up like a bunch of hens.'

'Hens is right,' said the sheriff. 'Just listen to you clucking away.'

'I'm not used to living with a lot of women,' she said. 'Brought up by three brothers, then I married you and had myself a couple of sons. I like plenty of men-folk around me.'

'Yes, you're man-crazy, always have been,' he said, with gruff affection. 'But now that our two galoots have grown up and flown the coop, there's only *one* man-folk in your life, and it'll be good for you to get shut of me for a while. Make you appreciate my fine points all the more when you get back out.'

She hugged him roughly. 'Well, one thing,' she said, 'you won't be able to chase any other women while I'm away. They'll all be in here.'

'Don't be so sure,' said Hank. 'Might just take a notion to drive into Midvale and pick me a young one.'

'She'd wear you out,' said his wife. 'I'm over half a century old and I even wear you out.'

'Quit your bragging. Get on in there before I slap that big fanny of yours.'

The Reverend Keaton and his wife also stood near the women's dormitory, of which she was the elected leader. They enjoyed the peculiarity of sharing not only a last name, but also their Christian names. The spellings were different, Francis and Frances, but the phonetic sameness had threatened to cause confusion until, early in their marriage, they just naturally became known as Frank and Francie. Doc Jenkins had once offered his own home-grown rule for knowing which name was masculine and which was feminine. 'All I have to remember, Reverend, is that the male form of the name has a big stiff erect "i" sticking straight up from it. When I think of that, I never make a mistake.' The Reverend had received this bit of lore frostily, but his wife had smiled.

Now, he was saying to her, 'God will be with you in there.'

'I know, dear.'

'I'll pray for you constantly.'

'You take care of yourself, Frank. Don't forget to take the pills Doc Jenkins gave you for your hypertension. It's twice a day now, you know. He increased the dosage.'

'You must pray, too.'

'Why, of course I will, Frank. I always do.'

'And for him. You must pray for him.'

'I know I should,' she said with a sigh, 'but I can't promise. I don't know if I'm a good enough Christian to forgive him for what he's done.'

'You'll try?'

'Yes. I'll try.'

'And perhaps, if you could lead the other ladies in a daily prayer meeting . . .'

'Daily? Well, tomorrow, anyway. It's Sunday.'

In these ways and in others, the women of Galen bade farewell to their men, submitting voluntarily to segregation and imprisonment.

Just before the doors were locked, Reverend Keaton asked everyone to pray with him for a moment. All of Galen, gilded by the setting sun, stood outside the dormitories, silent, with bowed heads.

'Let us pray,' he said, 'that this small sacrifice, this temporary discomfort and loneliness, will bring to an end the fearful reign of death and terror that is despotizing our peaceful town. For Jesus' sake, amen.'

And so began the first night's vigil.

## 27

Gresham's Law ('Bad drives out good') originally applied to money, but can be seen at work on many levels of our lives, not excluding everyday language. Accurate, vivid words and phrases are constantly being driven out by the juggernaut of illiteracy, and replaced by fuzzy-minded nonsense.

Try to think, for example, how long it's been since you heard the phrase, 'I couldn't care less.' It is now in the process of being dethroned – in daily speech, in print, in TV dialog – by 'I could care less'. This is *not* intended to mean the reverse of the other phrase. It's used in exactly the same way, for the same purpose, in the same tone of casual contempt, and with the same intended meaning as the older form, which may be paraphrased as: 'The subject in question is so unimportant to me, I care so little about it, that it's impossible for me to care *less* about it than I do now.' In other words, 'I couldn't care less.'

Doc Jenkins stopped writing for a moment. He was at home, in a house empty except for himself and Queenie, the turtle. It was an oppressively quiet Saturday night without Martha and Jennie. A perfect time, he had thought, to work on another Will Clemens piece for the *Signal*. But this one didn't seem to be turning out right. He couldn't put his finger on what was wrong, however, so he just kept on writing, his pencil flying over the paper:

Illiterates (including a great many journalists and television writers) have imperfectly heard the original, true, logical phrase, and have misrendered it as 'I could care less'. Worse than meaningless, this garbled version *has* a meaning, all right – but it's a meaning exactly opposite of that intended by the unthinking user. And yet this phrase is taking over; the original phrase is being pushed out.

There are, in current use, two terms to describe the type of tape recorder that doesn't use cassettes – 'open-reel' and 'reel-to-reel'. The latter is lame-brained because cassette recorders are reel-to-reel, too. The reels are small, and are tucked inside the cassette, but they are very much *there*, and they operate on the same principle as the other reels – the tape winds from one reel onto the other, during recording or playback, like a typewriter ribbon or a strip of movie film. Reel to reel, right?

So 'open-reel' is the more intelligent term. It accurately and succinctly describes and distinguishes the unhidden, out-in-the-open reels of the non-cassette machine. The term has the additional advantage of coming more easily to the tongue and being shorter to write and type.

Despite its superiority, however, 'open-reel' seems to be losing ground. In a few years, 'reel-to-reel' will probably be firmly seated in the common language, snug, smug, secure, and unbudgeable. 'Open-reel', on the other hand, will be greeted by blank stares of incomprehension, and people who should know better will bow to the tyrant Usage and say 'reel-to-reel' just to be understood.

Or what about 'jury-rigged'? It's fairly obvious how this abomination was formed. Inattention and a rich lode of wax-in-the-ears conspired to confuse and merge the terms 'jerry-built' and 'rigged jury' – two very different concepts – in the minds of a few individuals with sluggish brains and hyper-active mouths. Soon it spread, even to people of some intelligence. Intimidated, afraid to be out of step with the mob, many began to say 'jury-rigged' when they meant 'hastily, sloppily constructed' – in other words, jerry-built.

I could care less. By which I mean that I *do* care. Unlike Gresham (that's Sir Thomas Gresham, English financier and advisor to Henry VIII and Elizabeth I), I refuse to resign myself. I'll fight the trend, singlehandedly if need be, obeying Clemens' Law ('If you can't join 'em, lick 'em').

Doc put down his pencil and read over the pages he had written. What was wrong with the piece? It was logical, pointed, literate, and it made a good case. It was also curmudgeonly and caustic – valuable qualities in a homespun satirist of the sort Will Clemens aspired to be.

He dropped the pages on his desk and sighed. Yes, it was all that. There was just one little thing wrong with it. It wasn't funny. And if Will Clemens couldn't make his points without bringing a little smile to the faces of his readers, he wasn't worthy of his two great idols, Twain and Rogers.

Was he getting too old and sour and crotchety to see the humor of things? Or was it the ghastly shroud of tragedy smothering the town that had killed the comic spirit?

Maybe a little of both, he told himself.

It was too lonely in the house with the women gone. Doc had half a mind to drop by the inn and chat with Jed.


'But why Galen?'

Doc had asked that question of Julian during their recent conversation, and Julian had replied, 'Why *not* Galen?'

It had seemed an adequate answer at the time, expressing Julian's thought that the incubus had not singled out Galen for a special reason.

Later, he was to have other feelings on the subject.

There was, for instance, a copy of the rare, near-legendary *Artes Perditae* in this town. That in itself was so remarkable that it challenged the easy explanation of coincidence.

There was the curiously unCalifornian look and feel of the place, an atmosphere presumably inherited from the original home of Galen's founders: new England, a region steeped in dark associations of witchcraft, torture, dire punishment of death.

Did this uniqueness of Galen have a connection with the current horrors? Was there a possibility, however remote, that an element of retribution figured in the violent events? Had a witch of old Salem or of some earlier, European culture, smashed the barricades of time, working vengeance on her persecutors' posterity through the medium of her own descendant?

Was the Biblical word in this way being fulfilled? *For I the Lord thy God am a jealous God, visiting the iniquity of the fathers upon the children unto the third and fourth generation...*

And what of Julian's own involvement with Galen, years before? What force had guided him when, out of several offers, some more lucrative, he had chosen Galen College in which to teach for a term? His interest in paranormality had bloomed only later; at that time, he had been purely an anthropologist. What chance or destiny had pulled him to Galen then, and subsequently kept alive his affection for the town, even to the extent of subscribing to the *Signal* long after he had left? Was he a pawn on some vast cosmic chessboard?

Questions. A buzzing, stinging hive of questions; but no answers.


In the men's dormitory, the unknown molester's most distinctive physical feature had quickly become common knowledge.

Doc Jenkins had made private mention of the fact to Martha, and now that she and Jennie were in the exclusive company of women, with little to occupy them, she had confided it to her daughter, and it had spread throughout the dorm.

Many of the women, such as Belinda Fellowes, flatly refused to believe it. A few giggled. Some were struck silent with horror. Most of them were gripped by morbid fascination.

Jed Purdy's wife, Ruth, said, 'Years ago, when Jed and I took over the management of the inn – my, I was still a spring chicken back then! – we couldn't afford to hire extra help, so I had to make up the beds and change the towels myself. Worked like slaves, both of us, day and night. Well.

142

we had this regular, Mr McIntire, a traveling salesman. Always used to stop at the inn on his way through town. Real nice fellow, very soft-spoken, bald, wore glasses. And one morning, I didn't know he was still in the room, and I waltzed right in with my arms full of sheets and towels and pillowcases, and lo and behold he came walking out of the bathroom naked as a jaybird, and I swear he had one about like a salami. I never saw anything like it before or since. I dropped the whole pile of sheets and things on the floor. He just said, "Oh, excuse me," and turned around and went back into the bathroom. Such a *mild*-mannered little man, too, you'd never have thought it. But, you know? He never came back to the inn after that. Drove right through town without stopping. I think maybe he was ashamed of it. My goodness, you'd think he'd be proud as a peacock. I told Jed about it at the time and he said he heard that fellows like that can't get it hard. Seems a pity, doesn't it?' Then Ruth laughed. 'But maybe Jed was just envious!'

'The coloreds are supposed to be built like that,' observed Mona Garrett, wife of the sporting goods proprietor.

'Oh, that's not so at all,' said Jennie.

'How do *you* know?' asked her mother.

Jennie blushed and replied, 'There was this black boy, Clayton Bradshaw, went to Galen State. He graduated last year.'

'I remember him,' said Ruth Purdy. 'Used to eat his dinner at the inn once in a while. Black as coal, but a real good looker.'

'Well,' said Jennie, 'he modeled for us in art class sometimes . . .'

'I thought they always wore a jock strap when they did that,' said Mona.

'They do,' Jennie assured her, 'and he always changed behind a screen, but one day after class I forgot my purse and went back to the art room for it, and he thought everybody had gone, and I caught a glimpse of him. It was just the same as – well, anybody's. Except darker.'

She blushed again, and her mother asked, 'Are you *sure* that's how you happened to see it?'

'Oh, *Mom*,' said Jennie, and the women laughed.

Laura stayed out of most of these discussions, preferring to remain close to Helen Keaton, with whom she shared a dormitory room. She felt that, of all the women in the dorm, Helen was the one who needed her most. The recent dreadful death of her daughter, the ordeal of the funerals that same morning, and now this imposed isolation, the enforced separation from her husband, and the chatter of nervous women, all could be too much for her to bear.

Helen was lying on her bed, staring with blank eyes at the ceiling. Laura sat on the bed and took her hand. 'You should close your eyes and try to rest,' she said.

'I can't.'

'Do you want a sleeping pill or a tranquilizer? Doc Jenkins gave me a supply, for anyone who might need them, with strict instructions about doling them out.'

Helen shook her head.

'Are you sure? Just something mild to help you relax? You've been through so much.'

'No. Thanks anyway.'

'Maybe a nice hot shower?'

'I'd just like to stay here,' said Helen.

'All right, dear, whatever you want,' Laura said. 'I think I'll hit the showers, though, while the others are busy gossiping.'

As Laura was leaving the room, in her robe, Helen said, 'You won't be long?'

Laura smiled down at her. 'Two shakes.'

'I don't want to be alone.'

'I understand.'

A few minutes later, while Laura was soaping herself in one of the shower stalls, Helen appeared, in a robe, carrying towel and soap.

'Change your mind?' asked Laura.

'I got lonely,' Helen replied.

'Welcome aboard,' said Laura.

Helen removed her robe and stepped out of her sandals. Her body was mature and full, but still firm. The bearing of two children, years before, had left no sign unless it may have been a certain ripeness and roundness that declared her flesh to be a deep reservoir of life. She did not step into a shower stall, but moved in front of the stall in which Laura stood, and looked silently at the newswoman's body, shiny with water and suds. The superficial scratches on Laura's shoulders and upper arms were already beginning to heal.

'You're very beautiful,' said Helen.

Laura, somewhat surprised, responded nonetheless heartily. 'Why, thank you, ma'am,' she said, with a broad mock-Western drawl. "You're a fine figger of a woman yourself.'

Helen stepped forward, into the same stall with Laura. The warm water sprayed down on both of them. She encircled Laura with her arms. Their breasts touched. 'I just don't want to be alone,' she murmured.

'I know,' said Laura.

'I want someone to hold me.' She embraced Laura more tightly. Their toes mingled.

Laura maternally patted the other woman's wet back. 'Yes, yes, of course,' she said. 'It's terrible for you. To be away from Ben, now of all times.'

Helen Keaton's hands slipped slowly down Laura's soapy back and rested on the soft lyre of her hips.

Then she said, 'My God,' and stepped back quickly out of the stall. 'What am I doing?'

'It's nothing,' said Laura.

'I've never done anything like that before.'

'It's all *right*.'

'You probably think I'm a –'

'I think you're exhausted and lonely and afraid, that's all,' said Laura. 'So am I. So are all of us. But you even more than the rest, and with good reason.'

Helen started to say, 'If you want to change your room . . . '

'Don't be silly,' said Laura. She handed Helen a washcloth and turned to face the wall, saying, 'Here, do my back, will you? And then I'll do yours.'

'No ... I couldn't ...'

'Nonsense.'

But Helen, dropping the cloth and donning her robe in a flash of panic, ran out of the lavatory in tears.

## 28

IN THE WOMEN'S DORM, the wives of the Sheriff and the Reverend were testing the stoutness of the boarding that had been hammered over the windows.

'Pretty good job,' said Sarah Walden, tugging at some of the boards. 'They sunk those nails in good and deep.'

'Thick, strong wood,' said Francie Keaton.

Sarah nodded. 'Nobody's going to be coming through that.'

'How about some coffee, Sarah?'

'Just half a cup, dear. Otherwise it might keep me awake.'

Mrs Keaton lifted the pot off the hot plate and poured a small portion for Sarah and a full cup for herself. 'I didn't care much for that canned hash we had for dinner,' she said.

'I can eat most anything,' Sarah said. 'Cast iron stomach. Now, *Hank*: there's a finicky man.'

Francie smiled. 'I guess there has to be one in every family. I'm the fussy eater in ours. Frank never gives a thought to food. Just eats whatever I put in front of him. Never complains. "I eat to live," he says. "I don't live to eat."'

'That's a neat way of putting it,' said Sarah.

Francie sipped her coffee, then said, 'I never thought about this before, but you're married to a lawman and I'm married to a minister of the Gospel. Have you ever wished you were married to a man with a more mundane job, Sarah? Storekeeper or insurance salesman or something?'

'Oh,' Sarah replied, 'I suppose once in a while I get fed

146

up with the awful hours. Hank being hauled out of bed in the dead of night, and all. But it's just as bad for Martha Jenkins.'

'Yes.' Francie Keaton sipped again from her cup. 'I wasn't really thinkng of the hours. Frank's hours aren't bad. Maybe what I mean is he's so dedicated. I know Hank and the Doc are dedicated to their work, too, but they're not clergy. Frank is such a pious man. He really believes. It's hard to keep up with him. Sometimes I think I'm the wrong wife for a man like that. I'm nowhere near devout enough.'

'Exactly why you're good for him,' said Sarah. 'You help keep his feet on the ground. A man like that has to be reminded, once in a while, that he's a *man*. Not some kind of saint or angel up in the clouds. Why, dear, they're all pretty much the same, you know. A mouth to feed, two arms, two legs, and the thing in the middle. And they're all babies, just big babies. Frank's no different. The President of the United States is no different.'

Francie Keaton said, 'It would have been better if we'd had children.'

'Don't be too sure about that,' said Sarah. 'I love those two big apes of mine, I'd die for them, almost *did* die birthing the first one, but if I had it all to do over again? I don't know. You work your tail off for them for so many years, wear yourself out, and when they grow up and leave you – and God knows they *must* – you're right back where you started except a lot older. What's it all for? That's what you ask yourself. But there's that old biological urge, as Doc calls it, hammering away at you and your man, so he keeps on plowing you like you were a field and planting that seed, and before you know it you're all swelled up as big as a house again. "Increase and multiply," that's Scripture, isn't it?'

Francie nodded.

Sarah asked, 'Whose fault was it, dear, yours or his? Or don't you want to talk about it?'

Francie said, 'If you can keep a secret?'

'Tightest lips in town,' said Sarah.

'Even Frank doesn't know this. Only me and Doc Jenkins. We tried and tried to have children when we were first married – just kept on "plowing", as you put it – but nothing happened so we went to Doc for some tests. Well, the long and the short of it was that there was nothing wrong with me. It was Frank. Doc told me that privately, and I made him swear he wouldn't tell Frank. Then, when *I* told Frank, I just reversed it and told him I was to blame. It's the only time I ever lied to him. Maybe I was wrong.'

Sarah said nothing for a moment. She walked over to the coffee pot and filled her cup. 'Guess I will have a little more,' she said, and took a long sip. 'No, Francie,' she said, 'I don't think you were wrong. You've got to ask yourself, what good would you have done by telling him? Just hurt him, that's all. Hurt him real bad, right in his manhood. You did a loving thing when you told him that lie.'

'Thanks, Sarah,' Francie said quietly.

Sarah chuckled and shook her head. 'Men,' she said. 'You know that thing they always say about us? Can't live with 'em, can't live without 'em? Well, that's *twice* as true of *them*!'

When Julian returned to the inn after nightfall, Jed Purdy told him, 'The Galen boy checked in a little while ago. And he wanted to see you. His room wasn't made up yet, so I thought it was all right to let him wait in yours. Since you know him and all. He's up there now, I expect.'

'Thanks, Jed,' said Julian.

When Julian opened the door of his room, he called, 'Tim?'

Tim wasn't there. Julian picked up the phone and spoke to Jed, who was tending the switchboard. 'Will you ring Tim Galen's room, please? He's not here in my room now.'

Jed rang the other room. There was no answer. Julian asked, 'Are you sure he didn't leave the inn? He would have had to pass the desk, wouldn't he?'

'Well, I did take time out to answer a call of Nature, Mr Trask. He might have left then.'

'What room did you give him?'

'Six.'

'All right, Jed, thanks.'

148

Julian left his room and walked down the hall to Six. He knocked. Nobody answered. He tried the door. It was unlocked, and he walked in. 'Tim?' The room was empty. He shrugged, and returned to his own room, where he pulled off his shoes and stretched out on the bed with a weary sigh.

A moment later, a flicker of anxiety ran up his spine. He sat suddenly upright on the bed.

The book. The *Artes Perditae*. The last time he had used it was when Tim had visited him, and he had not locked it into his suitcase afterward. He had merely put it in the desk drawer. Tim had seen him put it there. And the drawer had no lock.

In a second, Julian was off the bed and had yanked out the drawer of the desk. He exhaled a long breath of relief. The *Artes Perditae* was still there, next to the Gideon Bible. Julian closed the drawer.

It was not a book to fall into the wrong hands. The edition in Tim's house was probably harmless, because the most dangerous pages had been torn out. Julian's copy was complete.

On his first afternoon in town, when Laura had come up to his room after lunch, she had uttered two words, in the primordial language, from the book. He had stopped her before she had repeated them, and the outcome had been only a rumble she had assumed was a small earth tremor.

Now, something nagged at his mind. The book in the drawer . . . was there something different about it?

He turned back to the desk and opened the drawer again. Was the parchment binding just a shade darker than he remembered it? Or was it merely a trick of light or memory?

He lifted the heavy volume out of the drawer, and began to turn the pages.

Sections of the book were missing, ripped out. This was Tim Galen's copy. Tim had switched them.

Julian's heart pounded with fear. He seized the phone and yelled into Jed Purdy's ear, 'Get me the Galen house! Right away!'

'Yes, *sir!*'

After an agonizing interval, the phone was answered by Agatha.

'Miss Galen? My name is Julian Trask. Is Tim there with you?'

'I'm alone, Mr Trask. Buried alive. A prisoner in my own house. But surely you know that. I understand the whole thing was your idea.'

'Do you know where I might reach him?' asked Julian.

'He told me he would be staying at the inn.'

'He's not here.'

'Then I can't help you. Good night, Mr –'

'It's vitally important. If you hear from him, will you ask him to get in touch with me right away?'

'Why? So you can encourage the worst side of his nature?'

'Miss Galen, I only –'

'Whatever bond may exist between you and Timothy,' Agatha said sharply, 'I want nothing to do with it.'

She hung up.

The phone hummed in Julian's ear. He put it down. An icy drop of sweat crawled down his back.

He had to find Tim. Julian was far from certain that the eerie rumble he and Laura had felt that afternoon had been just an ordinary tremor. He knew what Laura did not: that the words she had spoken were an ancient incantation to revoke the irrevocable and reverse the strictest canon of natural law. With it, a man could shatter the foundations of life.

That book, in Tim's hands, was like a hydrogen bomb in the hands of a baby.

## 29

'MOTHER, TELL ME WHAT TO DO.'

When Tim had torn that groan from his heart, kneeling in the fog-soaked cemetery, his face crushed to the damp stone marker of Kate Galen's grave, he suddenly saw in his mind Julian Trask's copy of the *Artes Perditae*. In particular, he saw a certain page of that copy. It was one of the pages that had been ripped out of the edition in his aunt's house. A single phrase appeared in the center of the page, surrounded by an ornamental border of entwined skeletons, under a heading and introductory material. The language of the phrase was bizarre – pothooks and squiggles, a little like Arabic, with the faintest hint of ancient Egyptian cuneiform. Printed directly under the phrase, within the same border of entangled bones, was not a translation, but what Tim correctly took to be a transliteration, a phonetic rendering in the Roman alphabet of the arcane phrase above it. The general heading at the top of the page was in Latin, and even an imperfect scholar like Tim knew what it meant.

It was this heading that had fluttered like a banner in his mind when he had asked his long-dead mother what to do.

He had arisen from the side of her grave and walked home through the morning fog. All the way, he was thinking. Should he simply ask Julian Trask to borrow his copy of the old book? Trask would ask him why he wanted it, and he would have to make up some lie. Very well: what lie? A feeble remark about his natural curiosity and interest? That would be thin and ineffectual. What other lie, then? It would have to be good. Tim could think of nothing.

Besides: even if he could concoct a credible and effective story, Trask would not entrust to a comparative stranger a treasure of such priceless antiquity.

When he returned to his aunt's house, she was in her room, still in bed, but not asleep.

'Feeling any better?' he asked.

'Much the same.'

'Shall I call Doc Jenkins?'

'There's nothing wrong with me but old age, Timothy. Only one Doctor can cure that.'

'Whatever you say.' As he began to leave her room, he said, 'I'm tired. Got up too early. Why do they have to hold funerals at such an ungodly hour? I'm going to lie down for a while. Do you want me to get you anything first?'

'No, thank you, Timothy.'

'A cup of tea? A magazine?'

'No. You're being very considerate today.'

Tim shrugged. 'My *good* half, no doubt.'

He left her room, but did not go to his own. He returned downstairs, to the old escritoire, in which the *Artes Perditae* and the skinning knife were locked. His aunt kept the key in her purse, but the purse was in her room. He wanted no further discussions with her on the subject of the heirlooms. Using a letter opener, he jimmied the lock and removed the book and the antique blade. Then he carried them up to his room.

The book would have to be wrapped in something – paper, anything. He couldn't carry it through town like this. He left his room again and foraged in the kitchen until he found some wrinkled brown paper from an old package, and returned with it to his room.

Before wrapping the book, he flipped casually through its pages, noting again the rough discrepancies where leaves had been savagely torn out. On one of the pages that remained was an engraving. The picture was crudely executed, depicting a nude and fleshy woman in sexual union with a hideous demon. The leering creature was scaled like a lizard. His hands and feet were clawed. Horns sprouted from his head and a pointed tail from the base of his spine. His organ was sinuous, snake-like, unhumanly long, and trifurcated, divided into three distinct prongs. One of these performed normal coitus upon the woman; another curled behind and was

152

buried between her buttocks; the third reached up to her face where it was encircled by her lips.

He remembered his dream, or whatever the gruesome vision was: *did he do sodomy upon thee as well or didst receive him into thy mouth*

Tim turned the page, and another, and was about to turn another when he saw a small rose-colored envelope wedged tightly into the gutter of the book. At that moment, the telephone rang, and he went out into the hallway to answer it.

It was Sheriff Walden, explaining Julian's dormitory idea. In the next few minutes, Tim had relayed the gist of it to Agatha, who had refused to leave her home, and Tim had worked out with the sheriff the alternative measure to guard and board up the house. 'I'll move into the inn this evening,' he concluded, thinking how well it fit into his plans to obtain Julian's book.

That completed, he returned to his room. He had forgotten the envelope he had discovered in the book, and now he examined it closely. It was addressed simply to 'Matthew', in lavender ink, in a neat feminine hand. The envelope was still sealed.

Tim quickly ripped it open.

It contained a letter. Tim's eyes skipped down to the signature – 'Kate'. It was a letter from his mother to his father. A letter his father had never read.

With a sense of excitement, Tim read his mother's words:

Dear Matthew,
   Please forget me. The world is full of women, fine women. Choose one who will be a good mother to little Timmy. Take her and him away from here.
   My dear, I cannot go on living in this atmosphere of hatred and suspicion. You say your sister does not hate me, but she does, I know she does. I used to think it was because of this obsession she has about the old rumors, the ancient gossip. I do not think so anymore. I think she would hate any woman who became your wife. That is why I say, take Tim away from this house, away from Agatha, and marry again, and be happy.
   I begged you to do it many times but you always said you

had a duty to your sister and could not leave her alone. Oh Matthew darling, your duty was to me and to our son. Perhaps what I am now about to do will finally convince you. You must not bring your new wife into this house. If you do, it will start all over again. Agatha will hate her. She will hate her because she loves you, and not in the way a sister should love a brother. I know I am making an offensive accusation, and I know how loyal you are to her, how closely the Galens band together against any outside threat, but you must believe me. Your sister wants you in the way a woman wants a man. I have seen it in her face when she looks at you. She dies inside herself every night when you take me to bed. She hates me because she wants to lie beside you in my place. I know. A woman can sense these things. Leave her, dearest Matthew, before her terrible passion destroys you and our son.

Never tell Timmy how I died. He might think I did not love him enough to live. Just tell him I got very sick and the angels took me away like they took away the puppy we gave him last Christmas. Tell him I love him and will always love him and will wait for him, and for you, in Heaven.

And please forgive your
Kate

Tears were running down Tim's cheeks when he finished reading the letter. He kissed it, and put it carefully into the envelope again, and slipped it inside his shirt.

In his mind, he said: Damn you, Father, for letting it happen. And damn you for not having the decency to read her last words. Or – the thought flashed quickly through him – had it been Agatha who had found the envelope and quickly hidden it, meaning to destroy it later, but forgotten?

He sighed. It didn't matter anymore.

In preparation for his move to the inn, he threw a few things into a small canvas bag, and then began to wrap the *Artes Perditae*.

As night fell dense and black upon Galen, Tim crept into the churchyard. The early morning fog, which had burned off during the heat of the day, had now returned. It hung in thick slabs, like smoke in an airless room. Had anyone else been there to see him, he would have seemed to appear and disappear as he walked in and out of the chalky layers, on the way to his mother's grave. He carried Julian's copy of the *Artes Perditae* under his arm.

Visibility was poor: the moon was choked by fog. But Tim had no need to see the page. The incantatory phrase was short, only two words, and he had already committed it to memory. He had also haltingly read the Latin introduction above the phrase, recognizing references to Jesus, and Lazarus, and King Arthur, and other names, unknown to him. The implication, as near as he could make out, seemed to be that Christ had used this very incantation on Lazarus and that it would be used on that apocalyptic day when Arthur would be awakened from his long slumber to lead his people out of chaos.

Tim stopped at the grave marked KATE DOVER GALEN. He opened the book to the page. *Mortuos Resuscitare*, read the Latin heading: *To Raise the Dead.*

Gathering courage for the awesome act he was about to perform, he licked his dry lips and took a long, deep, shuddering breath. If he had rightly understood the Latin instructions, it was needful to do no more than to utter the words clearly and slowly, and to repeat them again and again until the deed had been completed.

He raised his head and spoke the words:

'Oreela boganna.'

The fog, whipped by a sudden gust of sea breeze, refracted the moon into a grotesque form.

'Oreela boganna,' he said again.

Dead leaves skittered across his mother's grave, and the pages of the book were riffled.

Tim swallowed a lump in his throat and repeated the incantation: 'Oreela boganna.'

He heard a rumble, faint and far away, like distant thunder or muffled drums.

'Oreela boganna.'

The wind grew stronger, bending the tall cypresses in the cemetery, and a baleful flash, like heat lightning, briefly and starkly illuminated the gravestone.

'Oreela boganna.'

The muffled rumble grew louder, deeper, nearer. Tim felt chilled, and it was only by a supreme effort of will that he kept his teeth from chattering.

'Oreela boganna,' he said once more.

*succor me*

What was that? Had he actually heard a voice? He looked around, in dread. He was alone. He told himself it must have been the wind.

He breathed deeply and repeated the incantation: 'Oreela boganna.'

*tell me child*

This time, the voice was accompanied by a flashing instant from his recurrent dream: for the slimmest fraction of a second, he saw the dungeon, the girl, the rack, the three men, as vividly as if they were with him in the graveyard. He rubbed his eyes. Julian had warned him of hallucinations, but Tim had hoped that the bloody vision in his bedroom had been the first and last of them. Filling his lungs with the damp air, he spoke the words yet again:

'Oreela boganna!'

*thou wilt be dismembered*

The rumble seemed closer now. Tim disregarded it.

'Oreela boganna!'

*why shouldst thou suffer*

He also disregarded the brief lurid images of torture that vexed him like insects.

'Oreela boganna!'

*that wretch thy lover hath betrayed thee*

Tim gritted his teeth and went on:

'Oreela boganna!'

*confess the sinful congress thou hast enjoyed*

'Oreela boganna!'

*speak now whilst yet thou art unbroken*

The graveyard blurred; Tim's eyes went out of focus; his senses swam and he was plagued by nausea. Still, he continued:

'Oreela boganna!'

*a quarter turn to start my lord*

A disquieting high whistling sound, almost beyond the

human range of hearing, whined and twisted in Tim's ears.

'Oreela boganna!'

*did he do sodomy upon thee as well*

'Oreela boganna!'

*or didst receive him into thy mouth*

'Oreela boganna!'

Wild hyena laughter, the cackling of madmen, cries of ultimate despair.

'Oreela boganna!'

*another and another until this bitch of hell doth speak*

Partial faces, pieces of grasping hands, disembodied leers, rushed upon Tim like swooping bats. In a frenzy, he repeated the incantation over and over:

'Oreela boganna, oreela boganna! . . .'

*rack and be damned*

*rack and be damned*

*rack and be damned damned damned damned*

'Oreela boganna, oreela boganna, oreela boganna!'

The whistling sound corkscrewed painfully into his ears, his brain. The rumble darkened to a deafening roar. The ground beneath him heaved, like a sea-swell. Tim struggled to hold his footing, as – with a noise of cracking and rending – the soil of his mother's grave trembled and split open like the fissure of an earthquake.

'*Mother!*' he cried.

All sounds abruptly ceased, chopped off by a thud like a guillotine blade, and he was transfixed in silence, a fly in amber, unable to move, unable to breathe, unable to hear even the beating of his own heart; able only to feel, from behind him, the horrid weight of a hand upon his shoulder.

# 30

At that touch, Tim screamed and fell to the ground, dropping the book.

'Let her rest.'

Sprawled and trembling on the cold graveyard soil, Tim turned fearfully and looked upward at the source of the voice.

'Let your mother rest,' said Julian.

Tim was shaking. He got to his feet, clods of damp turf clinging to his clothes. The wind, the whistling, the rumble had stopped. His mother's grave was smooth and undisturbed, the sod not split. He passed a hand, incredulously, over the unruptured earth. He whispered, 'I thought I saw . . .'

'Forget what you saw,' said Julian, 'or thought you saw. Put it from your mind.'

Julian picked up the fallen book from the ground. He took Tim's arm and began to lead him away from the grave, out of the churchyard.

As they walked back to the inn, Tim said, 'I'm sorry about taking your book. I was going to give it back.'

'It's a powerful book,' said Julian. 'It contains secrets men once knew, but chose to forget. Millionaires have offered fortunes just to look at a single page. People have killed for it. Others have died under torture rather than reveal where they'd hidden it. It's driven some people mad. The title means *Lost Arts*, and it can be taken in two ways – lost in the ordinary sense, but also lost in the sense of damned. As when we speak of a lost soul.'

After a moment, Julian echoed himself: 'A lost soul. We say it so easily. It's become a cliché. But have you ever stopped to think what it means? There's a warning somewhere in the book, about people who trifle with the lost arts

158

being doomed – "immutably, eternally". I'm not a religious man, but those two words have always given me a chill. To be doomed *immutably* – never to change. *Eternally* – without end. Without hope. Think of it. All life is change. Change is healthy, natural, good. Even death brings change – decomposition at the very least; and to religious people a change of a different kind. *"We shall not all sleep, but we shall all be changed,"* the Bible says. A thing that never changes is a monstrosity, against all the laws of Nature. And for a person to be sealed into a doom that's unchanging and lasts forever – *immutably, eternally* – frozen into Hell for the rest of time . . . I shiver whenever I think about it.'

They walked on, unspeaking, for a while, before Tim asked, 'Did it really happen?'

'Did what happen?'

'I saw the dungeon, and those men, and the woman. I heard them talk. And there were sounds, and wind, and my mother's grave *opened*. Did you see it?'

'I felt the wind,' said Julian. 'As for the other things, I arrived only at the last minute. I told you, it's a powerful book. And all of its power is evil. Nothing good has ever come out of its pages. What if you had succeeded? What if you actually had raised the corpse of your mother out of the grave? You would have committed a horror.'

Tim muttered, 'I only wanted . . . to talk to her.'

'How do you know she would have been able to talk? How do you know she wouldn't have been a mass of rot, without a tongue, without a brain, unable to talk or think? And consider this, Tim – although there's an incantation to raise the dead, nowhere in that book is there one to lay them to rest again. Not in all of its pages. Be thankful I came along when I did. Thankful not only for yourself, but for your mother. For all of us.'

They were approaching the inn. 'I suggest you go straight to bed,' said Julian. 'We can talk in the morning.'

Tim nodded. 'I'd like to phone Jennie, but I guess it's too late.'

'I think so. The ladies are probably having a hard enough time getting to sleep in strange beds.'

159

Doc Jenkins was sitting all alone in the dining room as they passed. He hailed them. Tim merely waved and went up to his room. Julian walked over to Doc's table. Jenkins obviously had several drinks under his belt.

'Now this,' he said, pointing to the glass in front of him, 'is twenty-five-year-old Scotch. Jed breaks it out only for very special customers or very special occasions. I'm a very special customer, and this is a very special occasion. The first night in history when the whole town has gone stag. Any town, probably. I'd take it very kindly if you'd join me.'

'With pleasure,' said Julian. 'Just let me drop off something in my room first.' On his way past the desk, Julian had a second thought. 'Jed,' he said, 'do you have a safe where your guests can keep valuables?'

'Sure do,' replied Purdy. 'Good one, too.'

Julian placed the *Artes Perditae* upon the desk. It had been wrapped again in Tim's brown paper. 'I'd like to put this package in it.'

'No problem. Just step this way.'

When the book had been locked inside the safe, and Jed had given him a receipt, Julian rejoined Doc in the dining room. The doctor had rounded up another glass and had already poured out a drink for him.

'Heard a toast when I was a college boy,' said Doc. 'Never forgot it. Seems kind of appropriate, considering how the whole town, the atmosphere itself, seems permeated with sex, charged with it, like electricity.' He raised his glass. 'Here's to it. The birds do it. The bees do it and die. The dogs do it and get hung to it. Why don't you and I?'

They drank. 'You and I?' said Julian. 'Are you making a pass?'

Doc smiled. 'No, but you raise an interesting point. We've cut off the supply, right? The poor sex-starved incubus, or whatever he is, is presumably going bananas because he can't get at the women. Well, what if he gets so frustrated he starts going after the *men*? Happens in prisons. Anything in your book of regulations to rule that out?'

'In a way,' said Julian. 'Sexual perversion is pretty much a human trait. And, no matter how horrible these attacks

160

have been, they were, in one sense of the word, normal. If we discount the elements of rape and genital size, they were ordinary coitus.'

'Or what is sometimes known as The Missionary Position.'

'Precisely. None of those girls were attacked orally or anally. And yet it happens all the time with human rapists. The Galen molester is obsessed with only one thing – impregnating women.'

'So you figure we men are safe from his attentions?'

Julian nodded.

'I'll buy that,' said Doc. After taking another sip of Scotch, he added, 'What about what my grandfather used to call the sin of Onan?'

'Onan, you'll remember, cast his seed upon the ground precisely because he *didn't* want to impregnate a woman. It's not mere sexual gratification this creature wants, not just *any* kind of orgasm. It feels it has a mission, a purpose. Homosexuality or masturbation don't serve that purpose.'

Doc said, 'I've been re-reading the classics. Remember your Plutarch? That thing about Thamus, the ship's pilot? During a voyage to Italy, he heard a voice out of the wind call his name three times. Then it gave him a message to pass on to the world. *Great Pan is dead.* But if your hunches are right, that was an unconfirmed news flash, hm? Reports of his death have been greatly exaggerated. Our word *panic* comes from Pan, you know that? He had the power to make people go berserk, run amok, stampede like cattle, scatter pell-mell in "panic" frenzy. Interesting study, the origins of words.'

Doc gazed into his glass, as if it were a magic crystal brimming with secret doctrine. 'Sex,' he said. 'You'd think the Almighty could have made it simpler. Just a function, like eating or going to the bathroom. But it's all mixed up with romance and love and poetry on one side, and on the other side it's all dark and ugly – jealousy, frustration, rape, sadism, masochism, every conceivable kind of perversion and unhappiness. Motive for murder, cause of war, lies, deceit, pain. Yes, Lord,' he said in summation, raising his glass in

161

the general direction of the ceiling. 'You really fucked up that one.'

In Room Six, Tim was lying on the bed in his clothes. He reached under his shirt and took out his mother's letter. It was wrinkled now, and damp with his sweat. He read it again, and when he finished he read it yet again. Tears scalded his eyes each time he read the final sentence: 'Tell him that I love him and will always love him and will wait for him, and for you, in Heaven.'

His father, even though he had never read the letter, had told Tim only that his mother had passed away in her sleep. Now Tim realized it was probably the literal truth – she presumably had taken an overdose of sleeping pills. Was it possible his father never knew it was intentional? He could not believe his father would have left her last letter unopened. All the more, he believed Agatha must have discovered the envelope, correctly assumed it to be a suicide note, and whisked it away.

Less than a year later, his father had died in an airplane crash.

'Your sister wants you in the way a woman wants a man.' Of course. That explained a lot: her hatred of Kate, her horror at the love scene she had walked in on. The act itself was not what repulsed her, although she may not have realized it. She wanted to be the woman kneeling naked before Matthew Galen, and it was her own desire that appalled her.

Tim wanted to thrust the letter in his aunt's face, taunt her with it, accuse her of perverted fantasies, mental incest, hear her croak out denials. He wanted the awful knowledge to kill her.

But what would be the point? She would die soon enough. She was old and sick. There was a surfeit of bitterness between them already.

His thoughts turned to Jennie. A drowsy warmth began to steal over him, and erotic feelings suffused and stiffened his flesh. He jarred himself into full wakefulness. Now, his love for Jennie disturbed him. What if this surge of good warmth was the prelude of a paranatural change? He had never before been ashamed of his desires. Now he was more than ashamed. He was afraid.

His throat was parched with thirst. He rose from the bed and walked into the bathroom for a drink of water. As he turned on the tap, he looked up at the mirror above the basin.

A face not his own looked back at him.

After the first shock, Tim willed himself to look directly at it. It was the face of the rackmaster. *Drink deep*, it said, *drink all thou wilt* ...

Tim shut his eyes and gulped the water. When he opened his eyes, the face in the mirror was his own.

Downstairs, in the dining room, Doc Jenkins laughed and said, 'You know, Trask, I think I know the mystery of life. Ah, sweet mystery of life – remember that song? Nelson Eddy, Jeanette MacDonald? No, you're a little too young. Well, the mystery of life isn't so sweet. You know what it is? Simply this. God isn't dead, like they say. Hell, no. God is *drunk*.'

Doc refilled their glasses. 'God is blasted out of His mind. Plastered, fried, stiff as a goat. Staggering around the streets of Heaven like the old lush that He is, falling flat on His face, sleeping it off in some cosmic doorway, then waking up with the biggest, rottenest hangover in the whole universe. And taking it all out on us. That's my exclusive for tonight, my friend. Remember you heard it here first.'

Julian said, 'Well, it's an original theory, at least.'

Doc Jenkins drank deeply from his glass. 'Look at the world,' he said. 'War, starvation, torture, slave labor camps, smog, rape, cancer. Not to mention politicians and athlete's foot. How can anyone in his right mind believe in a benevolent God? Either there's *no* God, or He's a sadistic fiend, or the poor Son of a Bitch is suffering from the d.t.'s. I favor the latter explanation. And, by God, I'll drink to that.' He did.

'I think I'll be getting up to bed,' said Julian.

Doc put down his empty glass. 'All right. I told Jed to

163

put this on your bill. You've drunk plenty of *my* Scotch in the past few days.'

'That I have.'

'Everybody thinks doctors are rolling in money. Surgeons, yes. *Plastic* surgeons. That's what I should have been. A plastic surgeon. Creating beauty out of ugliness. Look at those hands. Like the hands of a great sculptor. Instead, I stick my finger up people's asses.'

He rose from the table, imperially. 'Guess I'll be wending my way home. Nothing to go home *to*, though. Martha and Jennie both in the slammer. I'll have to talk to the turtle. You know that damn turtle likes to be sung to? Favorite song is *Mighty Lak a Rose*.'

'Sure you're okay to drive?' asked Julian.

'Me? That implies that I'm drunk. Well, maybe I am. But no drunker than God. If He can do it, so can I.'

'But He's making a lousy job of it, remember?'

'True. Say, I just thought of something. You know that expression, "drunk as a lord"? Well, what it should be is "drunk as *The* Lord," see what I mean?'

'I think you've hit on something,' said Julian. 'I'll walk you out to your car.'

When they had stepped outside the inn, Doc Jenkins said, 'Fresh air feels good.'

The sheriff's car hurtled out of the darkness and screeched to a stop inches from them.

'Christ, Hank!' Doc roared. 'You damn near killed us!'

Hank Walden shouted from the car: 'Get in! Both of you!'

'What's wrong?' asked Julian.

'What the hell you *think* is wrong?' cried Hank. 'It's happened again! He got into one of the dorms and slaughtered another woman!'

# THREE

# THE FACE

. . . but there's no bottome, none
In my Voluptuousnesse: Your Wives, your Daughters,
Your Matrons, and your Maides, could not fill up
The Cesterne of my Lust, and my Desire
All continent Impediments would ore-beare
That did oppose my will.

*Macbeth:* IV, iii

## 31

'Who was it?' Doc and Julian asked simultaneously as they clambered quickly into the sheriff's car.

Hank hit the gas and the car lunged forward, away from the inn.

'Don't know,' he replied. 'I was on my way to relieve Clem outside the dorms and take over as captain of the midnight shift. Got a whole posse of men out there with guns, you know. The pussy posse, Clem calls 'em. Idiot. While I was on my way, I got this call from him on the car radio. He said the girls in one of the dorms started screaming. He couldn't get in, of course, and they were too scared to unlock the doors and *let* him in. He couldn't make out much of what they were saying. Just screaming and yelling, hysterical, something like "He's here!" and "She's dead!" '

'Which dorm?' asked Doc, suddenly cold sober.

'Don't know that, either. We'll find out soon enough.'

The car rolled onto the campus and turned into the dormitory area. A detachment of Galen's male citizens blinked in the glare of the headlights. Excited dogs barked and wagged their tails, ambivalently. Each man was holding some kind of firearm.

'Which dorm is it?' Hank shouted as he drove.

'Men's dorm,' Oscar Garret shouted back, running alongside the car. 'Clem's there now.'

Doc's lips were pressed tightly together. With both of his women in the men's dorm, he had more to fear than Hank or Julian.

The car jolted to a stop in front of the dormitory. Clem came running over. Seeing Doc, he said, 'Thank God you're here. Maybe they'll open up for you.'

The three men piled out of the car and followed Clem to

the locked door of the men's dorm. Clem called out: 'You ladies? . . . Listen, here's Doc Jenkins.'

Doc heard a voice from within say, 'Sam?'

It was his wife. A flood of relief washed over him. 'I'm here, Martha. How's Jennie?'

'We're both all right.'

'Will you open the door for us, dear?'

'Yes . . . ' A sliding of bolts, the clicking of a key, and Martha Jenkins swung open the dormitory door. Jennie and some of the other women stood behind her, huddled, fearful, tear-stained. 'Oh, Sam,' said Martha, 'it's so horrible!'

He embraced her. 'There, there.'

Behind Doc, many of the other men were impatiently asking, 'Who was it?'

Doc gently put the question to his wife. She was sobbing so uncontrollably that she could not reply.

Jennie stepped forward. Her voice shook as she said, 'It was Helen, Dad. Helen Keaton.'

A single cry erupted from among the assembled men: 'Oh, God! *No!*' It was Ben Keaton. He pushed through the crowd to the door. 'Not Helen!' he said, in disbelief.

Jennie lowered her eyes. She could not look at him. She felt guilty of being alive.

'No!' Ben cried. 'Not Prue, then Helen! *No!*' He rushed into the building. 'Where is she?' He called: 'Helen? Helen? . . . '

'Ben, don't!' said Doc. 'Don't go in there!'

But Ben already had pushed his way past the women and was running into the interior of the dorm.

Hank was asking Clem, 'How did the bastard get in?'

'I don't *know*, Hank! I checked every window – they're all tight as a drum. Still boarded up. There's nothing broken in. And that door was locked and bolted until just a minute ago when Doc's wife opened it up. I can't see *how* he got in!'

From deep within the dormitory, a long hoarse wail of anguish went up. Ben had found his wife.

Doc turned to the Sheriff. 'Come on, Hank. We'd better get in there.'

Hank said to Clem, 'Just me and Doc. Keep all the other fellows out.' He entered the dorm with the doctor.

Now, Laura squeezed past the jam of women at the door and called to Julian.

'Laura!' he said, and took her in his arms. 'I was afraid it was you.'

Her voice was unsteady. She said a curious thing. 'It *was* me.'

'What?'

'It was my fault.'

'What are you talking about?'

'If I hadn't left her alone . . . ' She began to weep, adding fresh tears to those which had begun to dry on her face.

'Now, now,' said Julian, 'what nonsense is this?'

'Oh, Julian, she was alone, all alone. She was the only woman who had a room to herself. I shared it with her at first, but she begged me to leave . . . '

'Why?'

'It doesn't matter why. She's dead. I didn't want to leave her, but she insisted, so I moved in with Martha and Jennie.'

Martha came forward and put her arm around Laura's shoulders. 'It wasn't your fault, dear. What could you have done to help her if you'd been there? You would have been killed, too.'

Laura shook her head, still weeping. 'No. He chose her because she was the only one who was alone. The only one.'

Martha Jenkins told Julian, 'We didn't even hear any screams. He must have covered her mouth while he did it.'

Laura said, 'I woke up and walked down the hall to the bathroom. As I passed Helen's room, I thought I'd just look in and see if she'd been able to get to sleep. And when I opened the door, I . . . saw her.'

Julian held her more tightly. 'You didn't see the molester?'

She shook her head. 'He was gone by then.'

Hank and Doc came out of the dormitory, supporting Ben, who had all but collapsed. The man's face was white, his eyes glazed. As they passed, Doc said to Julian, 'I'm going to take him to the hospital and shoot him full of dope.'

Julian jerked his head in the direction of the dorm. 'Is it . . . ?'

Doc nodded. 'Same as the others.' He and Hank walked on, with Ben Keaton. When the sheriff had helped Doc put Ben into the doctor's car, he returned to Julian.

'Well, Mr Trask,' he said, 'it was a good idea except for one thing. It didn't work. And I'm damned if I know *why* it didn't work. No evidence of break-in. There is just no way anyone could have gotten into that building. Unless he turned himself into a puff of smoke and floated in under the door. Or – unless somebody *let* him in.'

Martha Jenkins said, 'Hank, talk sense. Why would any of us let in a homicidal sex fiend?'

'I'm grasping at straws, Martha,' said Hank.

'Well, go grasp somewhere else.'

Julian asked the sheriff, 'Are you sure you checked all the windows thoroughly?'.

'And double-checked.'

'No sign of boards carefully pried away, perhaps, and put back?'

'No. Everything nailed down just as it was this morning. Good and tight.' He took off his hat and scratched his head. 'Well, I better get on over to the women's dorm and see if everything's all right in there. If Sarah will let me in.' He walked off.

'I better get back to Jennie,' said Martha, and returned to her daughter.

Julian led Laura to a nearby bench under a tree. 'Sit down here,' he said, and sat beside her.

'If only I'd insisted on staying with her,' she said.

'Don't keep on blaming yourself. But I can't quite understand why she was so adamant about being alone. Do you know?'

Laura nodded. 'But I can't tell you.'

'Why not?'

'If it ever got back to Ben . . .'

'It won't.'

172

'All right,' said Laura, 'but it has to be just between the two of us.'

'It will be,' he assured her.

'Helen was afraid of herself,' said Laura. 'Afraid of her own feelings. Something happened in the showers. She was frightened and lonely. God knows she had a right to be. She put her arms around me, started to fondle my body. We were naked. It lasted only for a second, but it horrified her. She began to apologize, and then she ran out of the shower room, crying. Later, she said she didn't trust herself to sleep in the same room with me. She was afraid she might . . . try to make love to me. I told her that was silly. What happened in the shower was perfectly innocent, I said. She asked me to move in with some of the other girls. I refused. She dropped to her knees and kissed my feet. "Please, I *beg* you," she said. What could I do? I moved out. You see why Ben must never know? If there was anything unnatural about Helen – and I don't think there was, not really – we mustn't let it poison his memory of her.'

'No, of course not,' said Julian. 'Poor Ben. First his daughter, now . . . ' After a moment, he asked, 'Do you have any idea how the intruder got in?'

She shook her head. 'It's just as Hank said. No breakage. And the men were outside with guns. How is it possible? Unless he were hiding in there all the time, *before* it was boarded up?'

'No,' said Julian. 'We searched both dorms thoroughly.'

'Do you suppose there's any point in keeping us here any longer?' she asked.

'No. As the sheriff said, it was a good idea that didn't work. You'll all be just as safe – or as unsafe – in your homes.'

Hank walked by soon after, and he confirmed Julian's assumption. 'Yes, we'll be sending them all back. And we'll be giving each of them a firearm. Laura, you have the revolver at home?'

'I certainly have.'

'Then I don't see any need for you to hang around here. Will you see she gets back, Mr Trask?'

173

'Right away.'

For a moment, Hank stood staring blankly at empty air. 'Getting too old,' he said. 'Things are beginning to be too much for me. Can't figure out anything anymore. When this whole mess is finally over – if it's *ever* over – damned if I don't think I'll throw in the towel and take my pension.'

It would not have been surprising if the series of bloody fatal rapes had put a damper on all sexual feeling in Galen. But, in fact, the opposite was true. As if to defy death and reaffirm the force of life, every man who had a woman cleaved to her on Saturday night. Doc Jenkins, fatigue and whisky notwithstanding, took pride in bringing multiple gasps of joy from Martha. Tim, in response to a phone summons from Jennie, climbed the pepper tree to her bedroom window. Sarah Walden was manfully 'plowed' (as she would have put it) by Hank. In the inn, Jed Purdy and his Ruth comforted each other in the same way. So did Oscar and Mona Garrett. After Julian had seen Laura to her house, the act of flesh had followed naturally, as a matter of course, but there was nothing matter-of-course in its fire. The Reverend and Francie Keaton, although devastated by his brother's double loss, brought the solace of their bodies to one another with a depth of satisfaction they had not known for quite some time. Joe Prescott, many years a widower, had an arrangement of long standing with Belinda Fellowes, the pleasantly upholstered woman of dyed blonde hair and indeterminate age who sold tickets in the Paradise box office, and on this night they surprised each other with their ardor. Many other people surprised their partners with the intensity of their lovemaking, and all of Galen, by these acts, laughed at the grave and imbued carnality with its rightful, restorative glow of goodness.

One man in Galen had been cruelly deprived of the only female companions of whom he had ever felt truly fond. Prue Keaton had been more or less his steady girl of late; he had dated Mary Lou Grant occasionally; and once he had tested his mettle on the generosity of Melanie Saunders. But, one by one, they had been brutally erased from the lists of the living, and now the ache of loneliness settled like a damp, cold pall on Charley Prescott.

Huddled on his bed in the fetal position, he lay alone, awake, eyes open, weeping.

## 32

WHEN CHARLEY finally got to sleep, he saw Prue and Melanie and Mary Lou. Sometimes they merged into one girl; conversely, one of them would divide into a pair, both the same; but these transformations did not seem strange – Charley took them for granted. His dream was at times blankly mundane: images of the most commonplace strolls through town with one or other of the girls, dull conversations, flat photographs of placid experience. But these lusterless scenes were suddenly spangled by fantasy, the air itself sang shimmering music, human eyes glowed like hot coals, a nebula of nipples and navels pinwheeled into a starburst of unparalleled sweetness and Charley awoke, with a groan, in a clammy little puddle of his spent desire.

It was dawn, as gray and chilly as his mood. For a brief span of sleep, the wizard of dreams had brought the three girls back to life, but now cold reality bludgeoned him with the truth. He would never see them again, except in dreams, only in dreams.

The odor of his spillage repelled him. He was ashamed of it. These nocturnal spurtings had never been a source of shame to him before, but now, with the girls dead, he felt dirtied by the involuntary act. He arose, peeled off his soiled pajamas, and walked straight to the shower where he cleansed himself with punishing needles of icy water.

Then he dressed and left the house.

Few people were astir in Galen at this early Sunday hour. Charley walked alone past his father's theater, quiet and empty now. Through the glass doors he could see the candy counter where Mary Lou had worked. Outside, the garish posters for *The Maltese Falcon* seemed to taunt him. He regretted the enjoyment he had felt while watching the film, because at the same time, in the restroom, Prue had been dying horribly.

He walked on, and turned the corner. The Sugar Bowl was closed and empty, too, at this time of day. Peering through the window, he saw the booth where he and Prue had sat, sipping their iced tea.

'Why don't we do something else for a change?' he heard Prue say again. 'Like drive into Midvale, maybe.'

She hadn't wanted to go to the movies. Had she had a premonition? But he had talked her into it. He winced at the memory.

He walked on, and passed the inn. All was quiet here, too. Through the dining room windows, he saw the tables where Melanie had worked as a waitress, where she had often served him coffee and swapped provocative remarks with him.

Charley's wanderings led him eventually to the beach, not far from the spot where Melanie had been attacked. There was no wind this morning, and the sea was like an expanse of thick gray gruel.

What would it be like to step into it? To strip off everything and walk naked into the waiting water? To Charley, it seemed to beckon. After all, life originally came from the sea, didn't it? He seemed to remember something like that from school. What could be more natural than returning to it? To be disinfected by salt water so cold it would numb the flesh like Novocain – numb the mind, too, and the memory. To walk into that purifying water, and feel it rise to waist and chest and chin; and to keep walking till it rose above the eyes, until the feet could find no hold; and still to delve farther into the water, leaving loneliness behind on the shore, pushing farther and farther into the freezing final darkness.

Charley began to take off his clothes. One by one, the

176

articles dropped to the sand. Now, nude, he walked toward the sea.

When the chilling ocean touched his toes, he was startled out of his reverie. He looked down, saw his bare feet in the water, saw his nakedness, and stepped back, suddenly afraid. What was he doing? He looked around quickly, hoping nobody had seen him. He was quite alone. Shivering now with the cold, he put on his clothes again, and walked rapidly away from the beach, his feet crunching gritty sand inside his shoes.

He passed the church. He went there every Sunday with his father, sang the hymns, daydreamed through Reverend Keaton's sermons. But from one Sunday to the next, he never gave another thought to the church, unless it was to laugh at Prue's irreverent remarks about her uncle.

Charley saw her uncle, now, entering the church. Something made him stop and follow the clergyman inside.

Frank Keaton turned, surprised to find someone here at this hour.

'Good morning, Charley.'

'Hi, Reverend.'

'Can I do something for you?'

Charley shrugged. 'Oh, no, no. I just thought it might be all right if I sat down for a while in one of the pews. I won't be in the way.'

'You're welcome at any time, of course.'

Charley sat down and watched the Reverend walk among the pews, beginning with the back row, working his way forward, placing a small printed leaflet in each hymnal. They contained Gospel messages and church-oriented announcements. Charley was restless and shuffled his feet.

'Feel like helping me, Charley?' asked Keaton.

'What? Oh, sure, Reverend.'

Frank Keaton handed him a batch of leaflets. 'I've already done these pews,' he said. 'Why don't you start over there?'

The two men worked silently for a time, then Charley said, 'I sure am sorry about your niece and sister-in-law.'

'Thank you, Charley. Yes, it's been terrible, particularly for my brother.'

177

'I know,' said Charley. After a moment, he said, 'I liked Prue. A lot.'

'I figured you did,' said the Reverend.

'I think maybe . . . ' The lad hesitated.

'Yes, Charley?'

'Would it be wrong, now, for me to say that I loved her?'

Keaton looked up at him. 'No, Charley. It wouldn't be wrong. Not if it's true.'

'It's true. I *think* it's true. What I mean – I never thought about it before, while she was alive. I didn't know I loved her until now. When it's too late. I should have told her, shouldn't I?'

'Don't worry about it, Charley. If you loved her, she probably knew it without your telling her. Women are like that. Oh, they want us to say it, once in a while, in so many words, same as they appreciate a bouquet of flowers, but it isn't really necessary.'

Charley said, 'I'd like to think that she knew.'

They went silently from pew to pew, slipping the leaflets into the books. Charley said, 'Do you think she *does* know? I mean right now?'

'Perhaps,' replied Keaton.

They had completed their chore. All the hymnals had received the leaflets, and the two men stood at the front of the church, near the Cross. 'Well, thank you, Charley,' said Keaton. 'Nice to have a little help. It would have taken me twice as long without you.'

'Reverend?'

'Yes?'

'Will I ever see her again?'

Keaton turned away from him. 'What do you mean?'

'Like after I die? Will I see Prue then?'

'How can I answer that, Charley? I've never been there.'

'But if anybody knows these things, it would be someone like you, right? A minister? You know about God and all. You've studied up on it. Is Prue still alive, somewhere, in some way?'

Reverend Keaton looked up at the sorrowful, near-naked figure on the Cross. He saw the mutilated feet and hands.

178

He met the anguished eyes under the tormenting thorns. But he received no answer.

'Is she?' Charley repeated. 'What happens to us when we die?'

'Nobody knows,' replied the Reverend.

At the same dawn hour when Charley was roaming the streets, Tim was climbing down the pepper tree, hoping that no early rising neighbor of the doctor's had seen him leave Jennie's window.

It was probably the last time he would be able to use the tree. 'It's convenient,' he had said to Jennie as he was dressing to leave. 'Too convenient. If I can climb it, so can that molester. Talk to your dad today. Ask him to have that limb cut off. The sooner the better.'

'But I love that old tree. It's been there outside my window all my life. It's older than I am.'

'If you want to get any older, do as I say. I'm not asking you to kill the tree. Just lop off that limb. It's an open invitation to any nut.'

With a giggle, she said, 'Takes one to know one.'

'Very funny.' He kissed her and left.

Now, walking rapidly away from the Jenkins house, he was undecided whether to return to the inn or to his aunt's home. Conscience urged him to look in on his aunt. After all, she had been ill.

Agatha, wrapped in her robe, was sitting up in the living room, in an old bent-wood rocking chair.

'How are you feeling?' he asked her.

'A little better.'

A shotgun leaned against the fireplace. 'Did the sheriff loan you that?'

'Yes, last night, when they removed the boards from the windows. He insisted I take it, but I have nothing to fear.'

'I happen to agree,' said Tim. 'The rapist is interested in younger game.'

'That is not why I have nothing to fear,' said Agatha. 'This rapist is a judgment on the town, on its sins of the flesh.'

'Have it your way,' said Tim, not wishing to start an argument.'

'Just look at them,' Agatha went on, 'the women he's killed. Melanie Saunders. Everybody knew what she was. And the Reverend's niece – she openly mocked him, and God alone knows what she and that Prescott boy did together.'

Tim refused to listen to such drivel without at least registering an objection. 'What about the first one, Gwen Morrissey? An out-of-towner, you don't even know anything about her.'

'A college girl. We all know what *they* are, these days.'

'Mary Lou and her mother?'

'Anita Grant was always flaunting herself, half-naked, on tennis courts, in swimming pools. Spawning impure thoughts among the men. She received a terrible punishment: her husband killed, herself paralyzed, and then she and her daughter raped and murdered. The Lord is a God of vengeance. His ways are hard, but just.'

Tim was fascinated. He was curious what she would say about Helen Keaton. He mentioned her name, adding, 'A schoolteacher, respected by everyone. Devoted wife and mother. And no flaunting herself in bikinis or tennis shorts. A very sedate lady. What about *her*?'

Agatha sniffed. 'Oh, no doubt she's been a pillar of the community in recent years. But when she was a high school girl, before you were born, there was ... talk.'

'And Laura Kincaid?'

'For all I know,' answered Agatha, 'she's a virtuous woman. That may be why she only received a warning.'

'She would have received a lot more than that, if she hadn't had a gun handy.'

'It's no use discussing such matters with you, Timothy. Have you come home to stay?'

He hadn't made up his mind one way or the other before this moment, but now his aunt's uncharitable remarks about the dead women decided him. 'No,' he said curtly. 'Just came to pick up a few more of my things. I'll be out of here in ten minutes.' He started to walk away.

'Timothy . . . '

He stopped and turned. 'What?'

'My escritoire has been broken into. Do you know anything about it?'

He sighed. 'I did it. It was locked, and you were sick, and I didn't want to bother you for the key. I'm sorry about the lock. I'll have it fixed at my expense.'

'But why, Timothy? What have you done with the book?'

'It's mine, isn't it? Part of my legacy, you told me. What I did with it is my business.'

"Don't take that tone with me!'

'Aunt Agatha, in a few minutes I'll be out of your life. Let's not quarrel anymore.'

'The skinning knife? You took that, too?'

'You told me it was mine.'

'Evil things from your evil mother!'

Tim's amber eyes blazed dangerously. He wanted to hit her. His hand slid inside his shirt and touched the skinning knife and his mother's letter. He was sorely tempted to show the letter to her, to rub her nose in her own evil, she who accused everyone else of evil. But he resisted. She was a crazy old woman, and he would soon be out of the house, away from her nagging voice. And yet such hatred filled him that he wished her dead. He considered her his mother's murderer.

'Just don't say another word,' he warned her quietly.

In the next county, a man named Raymond Hunt was receiving some bad news on the telephone. His father-in-law was very ill.

The days ahead would bring him news far worse than that.

# 33

*(1.) Gwen Morrissey, 18. Raped in park. Dead on discovery.*

*(2.) Melanie Saunders, 20. Raped on beach. Survived, but committed suicide in hospital.*

*(3.) Laura Kincaid, 28. Attacked in office, repelled attacker with gun, suffered minor scratches.*

*(4.) Prue Keaton, 17. Raped in theater restroom. Dead on discovery.*

*(5.) Mary Lou Grant, 16. Raped in bathtub of home. Dead on discovery.*

*(6.) Anita Grant (her mother), 40, paralytic. Raped in bed. Dead on discovery.*

*(7.) Helen Keaton (mother of Prue), 42. Raped in dormitory. Dead on discovery.*

*None younger than 16 or older than 42. Average age, a shade under 26.*

And what did it all add up to, Hank Walden asked himself after he had carefully drawn up the list of facts and figures on a sheet of yellow legal paper. Nothing. Not a hint of a clue. He pushed the pad and pencil away from him and leaned back in his swivel chair. The springs shrieked their thirst for oil. Clem kept forgetting to lubricate them. Sometimes Hank wondered why he didn't fire Clem. He wasn't good for much. Maybe, Hank told himself, I keep him on because he always lets me beat him at checkers.

Three days had passed since Helen Keaton's death. She had been buried next to her daughter, Prue. Her son, Paul, attended the funeral, as did most of Galen, but Ben Keaton was still in a state of shock in the hospital, heavily drugged most of the time.

Whole families were being wiped out.

Hank felt helpless, useless, a man without purpose, a

man who could not justify his badge, his salary, his existence.

Julian felt much the same as Hank. After Helen Keaton had been attacked, he had run out of ideas.

Doc Jenkins had sarcastically asked him, 'This metamorphic business you spoke of – would that include shrinking down to the size of an ant and crawling into the dorm through one of the cracks? And then swelling to full size? And then shrinking down again to escape?'

Julian chose to treat the question seriously. 'Hank made pretty much the same remark,' he said. 'A puff of smoke was the way he put it. No. There's nothing in any of the lore to indicate that extent of metamorphosis.'

'Then how did he get in? What's your latest guess?'

'I don't have any,' Julian admitted. 'I'm up against a stone wall.'

'Join the club.'

So sharp was Julian's frustration that, on this morning, he decided to call Henryk Stefanski again. He would have to go into detail, be specific, and he did not want to risk being accidentally overheard on Jed Purdy's switchboard. After first stopping off at The Galen Bank for a supply of quarters, he drove out of town.

On the highway, halfway between Galen and Midvale, he spotted a public telephone at the side of the road. He approved of the fact that it was not the newer, open style of public phone, but a real old-fashioned *booth*, with a door, totally private and enclosed, like an upright and transparent coffin. Pulling over, he parked the Porsche, and, as he walked to the booth, he performed a superstitious ritual, uncharacteristic of him. To insure the phone being in working order, he crossed his fingers. So many public telephones, these days, were inoperable due to vandalism or neglect, one of the many signs of civilization's galloping race toward collapse.

His fears were ungrounded. The booth's light was burned out, but the phone was in perfect order, and he needed no artificial light at this bright hour. Within seconds, he had direct-dialed the Boston number and soon heard the phone ringing at the other end. But – to his surprise, because

Stefanski lived alone – it was answered by a female voice.

'I think I have the wrong number,' said Julian. 'I wanted Henryk Stefanski.'

'I'm the professor's nurse, Miss Rudden,' the woman replied. 'May I ask who's calling?'

'Is he ill?'

'His heart. He had an attack a few days ago. May I please ask – '

'Julian Trask is my name. But I'd rather not bother him now.'

'Yes, he's not taking any calls.'

'I understand. You might just tell him I phoned.'

'Julian Trask?'

'That's right.'

Julian could hear the unmistakable sound of Stefanski's voice in the background. He could also hear the nurse, even though she had covered the mouthpiece with her hand, say, 'No, sir, you're not to tire yourself.' Then another string of words from Stefanski, vehement this time. Now Miss Rudden spoke to Julian: 'He *insists* on talking to you, Mr Trask. But please don't keep him long.'

'I won't. Thank you.'

In a moment, he heard Stefanski's voice, weak but clear. 'Julian?'

'I'm sorry to trouble you while you're ill, sir.'

'Nyeets!' Julian recognized the syllable of the Polish word, *Nic*, meaning Nothing. 'A twinge,' said Stefanski. 'They make much fuss, the doctors. I am sitting up in bed with my books and papers, working, so why not speak upon the phone? Tell me, what is happening with you?'

Julian's pile of quarters shrank as he gave Stefanski an account of recent events in Galen, culminating in the inexplicable death of Helen Keaton. Stefanski uttered expressions of shock and dismay, in both Polish and English, but the scientist in him also compelled him to interrupt, at several points, with a number of cogent questions.

When Julian had finished, Stefanski said, 'A sealed dormitory. Doors locked from inside. Windows boarded. No, Julian, in all my researches, never have I seen anything to suggest that the incubus has the power to become a smoke-puff or so small like an insect. The answer is something else, but what, what? . . . '

Julian said, 'If you could just think about it, sir. Maybe something will occur to you. If it does, and if you're able to, I'd like you to call me.' He gave him the number of the inn.

'I am writing,' said Stefanski. 'Yes, Julian, I will call, if I have any – how do you say? – brainflash?'

'Brainstorm. But only if you're feeling well enough.'

'I am perfectly pink, do you say it? In pink? But my pretty nurse, she frowns on me and wants me to hang up.'

'Good-bye, sir.'

'Good-bye, Julian. And – this is *very* important that I say, even to a so modern atheist like you – God bless you.'

Julian left the phone booth, unaware that it would soon figure in the Galen mysteries in a very different way.


She was a woman in her mid-thirties, with a plain, strong face, at the moment haggard with long weariness and worry. She had spent many nights at the bedside of her ailing father, getting no sleep or only scattered moments sitting up in a chair, her head lolling. Now that her father's condition had been stabilized, his doctor had assured her there was no further need for her presence. Her, father, too, had insisted she return to her husband and children. Finally, she had agreed. Having done so, she had been seized by a desire to see them immediately, and so, instead of waiting until morning, she decided to return at once, even though it was already past midnight and the drive was long.

Now, as she drove along a stretch of lonely road, she was beginning to regret she had not stayed over one more night and left in the morning. She was very tired, and was having difficulty staying awake. She turned on the radio, just in time to hear:

'More Music-of-the-Night in just a moment. The time is now twelve minutes past one a.m., and I'm your host, Ken Baxley. If you're interested in saving money – and, these days, who isn't? – then you'll want to drop in and meet the friendly folks at –'

185

She clicked it off again, with a sigh. Why couldn't she ever turn on a radio when the commercial was just ending, rather than just beginning? But that was the least of her problems, for now she heard the car engine begin to cough and splutter. She looked down at the gas gauge, and groaned when she saw it indicated an empty tank. The car slowed down and drifted to a dead stop.

She cursed her own stupidity at not having checked the gas before leaving. Here she was, in the middle of nowhere, stuck someplace between Midvale and Galen, not another car on the road, in the dead of night, and miles away from a phone.

Or was she?

Far ahead of her, at the side of the road, barely reached by the beams of her headlights, was that a reflection upon glass? The glass of a telephone booth? She turned off the useless engine and switched to battery, so the headlights would stay on. It was a dark night, and she needed them. Clutching her purse, she climbed out of the car and began walking up the road, toward what she hoped was a phone.

Her trim form was silhouetted in the car lights as she walked. In the quiet of this hour, the only sound was the click of her heels on the asphalt and the song of a single distant mockingbird, earnestly proffering its entire repertoire of varied calls: trills, tremolos, roulades, cadenzas, swooping portamentos, cooing, warbling, chirping, pseudo-laughter, ghoulish cackling...

It took forever, so it seemed to her, to reach the phone booth. It was farther from the stalled car than she had originally thought. She hoped the headlights would not drain the battery. An empty gas tank was bad enough.

Finally, she reached the booth and opened the door. The light did not go on automatically when she did so; it was obviously burned out. She would have to dial in near-darkness, aided only by the feeble light of the far-from-full moon.

As she entered the booth, she was watched.

She opened her purse and took out some coins. Lifting the phone off the hook, she slipped two dimes and a nickel

into the proper slots, the coins making th
metallic clunk in the quiet of the night as they
dialed, slowly and carefully, ten digits, area co
number, the clicking and whirring of the di
loud in her ear. She listened with eroding patience as the
phone at the other end rang once, twice, three times . . .

The mockingbird was now mimicking the coo of a dove.

The phone rang a fourth and fifth time, and then a Shape
stepped silently between her and the moonlight, filling the
open doorway of the booth. She had heard nothing, but was
aware of the sudden plunge into darkness, and turned away
from the phone to see the cause.

She screamed.

The phone dropped from her hand. She could not see
what stood there, blocking her exit. It was too dark, and the
Shape itself cut off what dim light there was. She was aware
of mass, of strength, of deep and steady breathing, and the
pungent marine odor of sex. That scent, moreover, was
amplified a thousandfold, as if it were a distillation of the
male and female nectars, the elemental essence, sex personi-
fied, flensed of all irrelevance and concentrated to an infinite degree of potency; narcotic, overwhelming.

She screamed again as the Shape stepped forward and
joined her in the narrow booth, pinning her to the wall.
Efficient hands, incredibly strong, tore away her lower gar-
ments; and now her mind did battle with an impossibility,
fought against reason to believe the size of the organ that
pressed against her. She tried with all her will to pull away,
but her back was crushed to the wall of the booth, a wall of
thick hard glass, and there was no escape from the unearthly,
flesh-ripping length of the thing that now slid into her body,
deeper and deeper, as she screamed and screamed . . .

Her screams mingled with the attacker's high, loon-like
wail of orgasm, and a sea of seed was convulsively pumped
into the ravaged depths of her flesh.

Its mission achieved, the violator left the telephone booth
and vanished into the roadside green.

The woman was slumped on the floor of the booth, in a
pool of her own blood, quite still. The phone dangled by its

187

..There was no one, now, to hear the miniature parody a masculine voice that squawked from its earpiece:

'Hello? Hello? Who *is* this? Do you realize what the hell *time* it is? God damn it, is there anybody *there*? . . . '

As if echoing him, the mockingbird urgently repeated a query of its own: three notes with a rising interrogatory inflection: wit-wit-*wee*? . . . wit-wit-*wee*? . . . wit-wit-*wee*? . . .

It was the only ornament on the naked silence.

## 34

'HER NAME WAS CARRIE HUNT,' said Hank.

He was standing in the hospital morgue with Doc Jenkins and Julian. The body of the violated woman was supine on a slab, the traditional tag tied to a toe; the head and shoulders visible above the sheet. Now Hank covered her face.

'Thirty-six, married, two children,' he continued. 'Lived in the next county. She'd been visiting her sick father, over in Midvale. Driving home, she must have run out of gas and tried to phone her husband from that booth. It was the last thing she ever did.'

Hank rolled the sheet-draped slab back into its refrigerated niche and closed the door. 'Husband will be claiming the body if you're through with it, Doc?'

'I'm finished,' Doc said. 'It's no different from the others.'

'The only difference,' said Julian, 'is that the molester broadened his field of operation. This is the first attack that's taken place outside of Galen.'

'Easy to see why,' said Hank. 'Our women are all armed now. Bullets may not kill him, but they sure.as hell scare him off. Laura Kincaid's the proof of that. He must be afraid of the noise attracting attention, or maybe of getting hit in the head or the groin. I figure he's wearing a bulletproof vest.'

Neither Julian nor Doc mentioned the paranatural alternative as given in the *Artes Perditae*.

Hank added, 'Wish he'd get clear out of my county. This one didn't happen in town, but it was still in my jurisdiction.' He smiled apologetically at the other two men. 'Sorry. Guess I'm getting callous.'

'Numb,' said Doc, giving Hank a comradely slap on the shoulder. 'All of us are numb. Shock victims. Unable to feel anymore. It's as if we've come to *expect* these outrages. It's not just you, Hank. When you phoned to tell me there'd been another one, I almost said, "What else is new?".'

The three men left the hospital morgue and split up, going their separate ways.

The doctor went directly upstairs to Ben Keaton's room. Ben's son, Paul, was sitting next to the bed when Doc arrived. He looked up at Jenkins and shook his head slowly.

Doc glanced briefly at the patient's chart, then spoke to him. 'How are you, Ben?'

'Just fine, Sam,' Ben replied, 'How's yourself?'

Doc exchanged a quick look with Paul, as he answered, 'Can't complain.'

'Jennie and Martha all right?'

'Quite fit, thanks.'

'That's good,' said Ben. 'You should spend more time with them.'

'Well, I try, but I've been awfully busy, what with one thing and another.'

'You have to *make* time,' Ben said earnestly. 'There's nothing like a family, Sam. I'm busy, too, but I'm going on a picnic with my family today. Right, Paul?'

'That's right, Dad.' His son's voice was choked.

'Just the four of us,' Ben continued. 'Me and Helen and the kids. My wife makes the best fried chicken in town. Oh, Martha's no mean cook herself, I know that, but when it comes to fried chicken, my Helen's got 'em all beat, hands down. And Prue says she's going to make the potato salad.

189

Paul and I are going to do our part, too. We're going to eat it all up!' He laughed gleefully.

'That's fine,' said Doc.

Ben turned to his son. 'Thought we might make a side trip to Happytown, what do you say? Ride the rolly coaster?'

'Sure, Dad,' said Paul. Happytown was an amusement park that had glittered on the other side of Midvale. It had been torn down years before. A vast shopping center now stood in its place.

'I'm really looking forward to it,' said Ben.

'You get some rest now,' said Doc, and motioned to Paul to follow him out into the corridor.

Outside the room, Paul asked Doc, 'How long will he be like this?'

'I wish I could tell you. He's suffered two powerful shocks, one right after the other. This is his defense. It might pass quickly, and then he'll sink into deep depression. That's when we'll *really* have to watch him. On the other hand . . . '

Paul finished it for him: 'He might stay like this forever.'

'Chances are, no,' said Doc. 'It's not likely. These things usually pass. Gradually, he'll come to accept the truth. Of course, no one comes out of something like this exactly the same as he went in. There are always scars. But there's also scar tissue. Good tough mental scar tissue to seal the wound.'

Paul was persistent. 'But he *might* be like this the rest of his life.'

'You're a budding med man,' said Doc, 'so there's no use trying to kid you. Yes, he might never pull out of this. I repeat: the chances are, he will. With luck.'

'Luck! That's exactly what he doesn't have.'

'Luck can change. Look, Paul, I'm ordering a stiff sedative for him. He'll be out cold in a few minutes. You'll be no use to him then. I want you to go home and get some sleep. Doctor's orders. And then, later on today or tomorrow, I want to talk to you like a Dutch uncle about returning to school.'

'What for?' said Paul, bitterly. 'So I can learn how to stand around in hospital corridors and say, "These things usually pass"?'

Doc smiled. 'Granted, well over fifty percent of being a doctor is mastering the fine art of bullshit. But that's true of *any* profession. If your father were himself, he'd be urging you to go back to New York. If your mother were alive, so would she. They can't do it, so I'm doing it for them. All I'm asking, for now, is: don't burn any bridges while you're in this state of mind. Promise?'

Paul nodded, saying, 'Okay.' He looked at the door of his father's room. ' "Rolly coaster",' he said. 'He hasn't called it that since I was a little kid.'


When Hank Walden left the morgue, he returned to his office. Clem was seated in the sheriff's swivel chair, feet on the desk, reading. As Hank entered, he sat up quickly, and the chair screeched.

'Haven't you oiled that spring yet?' said Hank.

'Sorry. I keep forgetting. But –'

'Do it now.'

'Okay, Hank, but first I want to show you –'

'*Now.*'

Clem got up quickly and dropped his reading matter on the desk. 'Anything you say, Hank.'

As Clem was getting the oil out of the supply cabinet, Hank picked up what the deputy had been reading and began to look through it.

'What the sam hill kind of trash is this?' he muttered.

It was printed on cheap paper, and the plain cover bore several lines of type: HERE'S OUR LATEST CATALOG! IT'S NEW FROM COVER TO COVER! Under BULK RATE/U.S. POSTAGE PAID, was the discreet legend, SEX-UALLY ORIENTED AD.

'That's what I wanted to show you,' said Clem, on his knees under the swivel chair, oiling the spring.

Hank leafed through the murkily-printed pages. ALL COLOR SIZZLING UNRETOUCHED PHOTO MAGA-ZINES FROM DENMARK, proclaimed one advertisement. SEXUAL INTERCOURSE PLAYING CARDS, offered another. On the following page, THE MOST FAMOUS STAG MOVIES EVER MADE! were proffered. They included such 'long-sought-after classics' as *The Nun,* which was guaranteed to be 'Complete with masturbation scene, rape scene, and assorted sexual activities. This is the original uncut and uncensored version!'

'Jesus, Clem,' said Hank in disgust, 'is this what the county pays your salary for? So you can sit around the office reading this stuff and playing with yourself?'

*Oral Sorority House* ('with over two dozen crystal-clear photos') was among the ADULT BOOKS advertised on the next page; as was *Pamela's Punishment,* in which 'pretty Pam suffers the tortures of the damned in Marquesa de Sade's bizarre finishing school. FULLY ILLUSTRATED!'

'Aw, Hank, you know me better than that,' said Clem, uncurling himself from under the chair. 'There – not a squeak left in her,' he added, testing the spring.

'About time,' Hank mumbled. His jaw had slackened in disbelief as he turned the page and saw an ad offering for sale INGRID! THE SCANDINAVIAN SEX DOLL!

'She's five feet tall,' the ad went on, 'with soft, smooth vinyl skin that feels almost real. And she comes complete! Yes, all of Ingrid's exciting female components are built right into this living doll. Her open mouth works on the principle of air suction. Just gently squeeze the back of her head and feel her pulsating mouth come to life. And, for *low-*down pleasure, she has a 6-inch-deep canal that's also available in a battery-operated version! Ingrid will really turn you on when you turn *her* on! And she makes a great gift item ...'

Hank contemptuously threw the catalog into the wastebasket. 'What the hell is the world coming to?' he said.

'Hey, don't do that,' Clem protested, rescuing the catalog. 'Look here, Hank. On this page, right here. This is what I wanted to show you.'

It was a page offering a number of artificial phalli in a variety of sizes and shapes. MR WONDERFUL was the name of one. KING PLEASURE was another. But the item to which Clem pointed had a less seductive name:

*JOCK THE RIPPER*

'Christ,' said Hank, 'look at that thing.' The photo showed an unnaturally lengthy piece of merchandise that was advertised as being '14 inches long – 1¾ inches thick.' The accompanying text declared: 'This will *knock 'em dead!* Designed for those who demand bigger and better things. Now you can extend your influence where it counts! Make your presence *felt* – as it's never been felt before! Have a rip-roarin' time and *really* tear one off with JOCK THE RIPPER!'

'See what I'm getting at?' asked Clem.

'I sure do,' said Hank, 'and it's a good thought, but Doc Jenkins says it couldn't have been anything like this. First thing I asked him was if any kind of object had been used. He said absolutely not.' Clem looked crestfallen. 'But it shows you've been thinking,' Hank added, to make him feel better. He shook his head at the catalog and asked, 'Where did you get this thing?'

'Found it,' said Clem. 'In the alley, back of the Paradise. See here?' Clem pointed to a blank space on the catalog's cover. A printed word read simply TO:

'There must have been one of those little address labels pasted here,' said Clem, 'like magazines use? You can see how it's been torn off. Wonder who it belonged to.'

'I wonder.' said Hank.

He wondered, also, if Doc had been right about no object being involved. But he allowed that thought to remain unvoiced.


After Julian had left the morgue with Hank and the doctor, he stopped by the *Signal* office to see Laura. Tim Galen and Bill Carter were hard at work, but their employer was not on the premises. 'She's home,' said Bill.

'Packing,' added Tim. 'Says she's leaving town.'

Julian headed immediately for Laura's house. When she opened the door for him, he saw her bags standing behind her, already packed.

'Tim mentioned something about you leaving,' he said.

'Come in, Julian.'

He entered the house. Laura said, 'I tried to phone you

at the inn, but you weren't there. Yes, I'm getting out of town.'

'I can certainly understand,' said Julian, 'but – '

'We've all been fools,' she cut in, almost in anger. 'Fools to sit around just *waiting* to be raped and killed. It's insane. This town is ... I don't know ... cursed. I had a very close call, and I'm not going to tempt fate by staying here one hour longer. I'm getting out. Any woman with an ounce of sense will do the same, and that's what I'm advising them to do in this afternoon's edition. Bill is setting the type right now.'

Julian took her face in his hands and lightly kissed her lip, 'Don't print that in the paper,' he said.

'Why *not*?'

'Because you'll only make things worse.'

'How much worse can they get? Julian, whose side are you on?'

Julian turned away from her. He was worried. He felt the mystery growing, deepening, all hope of apprehending the incubus slipping through his fingers. And he continued to be convinced it was an incubus.

Turning back to Laura, he said, 'Look, dear. When the molester runs up against difficulty in Galen, he seeks his prey elsewhere. Seeks it and finds it, as he did last night. What will happen if you and all the other women leave? You won't be safe just because you're not in Galen. He's already struck outside town. If Galen becomes even more difficult for him, he'll range farther and farther afield. No woman will be safe, anywhere. And he'll become impossible to contain. As long as he stays here in Galen, or nearby, we have a *chance*, at least, of putting a stop to him. But if the women leave, so will he. And the attacks will spread, like a deadly disease. We'll *never* be able to stop him then.'

Laura sat down, slowly, on the couch. 'You may be right,' she said, 'damn it.'

'I hope to God I am,' he said. 'If anything happens to you because I persuaded you to stay ... '

'Then I'll never speak to you again,' she jauntily responded. 'Hand me the phone, will you?'

He did, and she dialed the newspaper office.

'Tim? Let me speak to Bill.' While she waited, she looked up at Julian. 'You and your scientific logic,' she said. Then, speaking into the phone again, she gave brisk instructions: 'Bill, kill that special editorial. . . . Yes, *that* one. . . . Put one of my rainy-day columns in its place. The one about the State Legislature. . . . I'll see you later.' She hung up. 'All right,' she said, turning to Julian. 'The exodus is called off. I certainly hope you know what you're doing.'

'That makes two of us,' said Julian.

He said nothing of the other danger. The incubus did not like impediments. When foiled or hindered, it struck back in arcane ways. As he'd told Tim, it had power over the elemental forces, those primordial essences of which the world was made. When its race was young, and when those forces were new, it learned the secret of taming them to its purpose. Fire, water, earth, and air: it could command them, at need, when humans put obstacles between it and its desire.

Galen, by arming all its women, had done exactly that.


# 35


When Julian returned to the inn, Jed handed him a letter that had just arrived. The return address was Stefanski's, but the envelope was typed, instead of being written in Stefanski's near-illegible scrawl. Julian opened it at once and read it on the way up to his room:

My dear Julian –

The so neat and clear electrical typing you see comes to you by the hands of Miss Rudden, who out of great goodness of heart is putting into order some of my notes. My Old World charm and handsome profile she cannot resist. Why did I not ever use this wonderful dictating before? I sit in great comfort in my bed, propped up by pillows, my books open all around me, and talk one mile a minute into a little microphone clipped to the lapel of my pajamas. My words go onto a tape and later Miss Rudden listens with an ear bug that looks like a hearing aid and she types. In this way, I finish some of my more important work, while still I am hearty and hale. I do not wish to alarm you, for I feel fine, but I am after all a very old antique, and would hate to leave things up in the sky (air?) when I am paid a visit by my old friend, Azrael, the Angel of Death.

I have given much thinking to what you told me on the telephone. This way and that, that way and this, from all sides And I must tell you that I share your conviction that the 'author' of the tragedies is what in this dictated letter I must refer to only by the initial 'i'. All evidences point to it. All our studies support it. Incredible it may be to such as your medical friend, but you and I have seen things in this world we never thought possible, is it not so?

And therefore I tell you again, dear friend who is like my own son, and kindly Miss Rudden please to type this in biggest letters possible, BE VERY CAREFUL. You are dealing with something not you, not I, perhaps not anyone now alive has had experience of. Things I could tell you, heard in my youth, in villages deep in valleys where life was lived as in centuries past, of powers, of evils, of death by fearful and ungodly forces, so again I say in big letters, PLEASE BE CAREFUL.

I have had as yet no 'brainstorm' as to how the 'i' got into the dormitory. It puzzles. But I will phone you if the lightning and thunder hit me on the head.

God protect you
Henryk

The signature was scrawled in a familiar yet markedly unsteady hand. The old man, obviously, was very ill.

That evening, Joe Prescott was looking at an unlit light fixture on a bedroom ceiling. It began to blur as his eyes went out of focus. A sound, not unlike that of deep despair, escaped him; and a whimper, as if of anxiety; then a string of sharp, barked, angry-seeming words: 'Oh! God! Oh! God-oh-Jesus!'

He sighed contentedly, and stroked Belinda Fellowes' chemically blonded head, and whispered, 'You're too good to me, Linda.'

196

She kissed the red bristles of his midriff, but said nothing.

'You know,' he said, after lighting a cigarette, 'I've never understood what a woman gets out of that. All the pleasure seems to be on the man's side, nothing in it for the woman. I don't know why you do it.'

'You like it, don't you, Joe?'

'I love it.'

'I love what you love, that's all. My pleasure is giving you pleasure. What's to understand?'

'But, afterward, I'm not even any good for you Not at my age.'

'There's always tomorrow,' she said. 'You'll build up another head of steam by then.'

He looked with admiration at the ampleness of her body. She was like those corny old paintings that used to hang in the Paradise: Bible scenes of Susannah and the Elders, Eve and the Serpent, Samson and Delilah. Those women were all built like Belinda. Wide hips, round bellies, deep navels, breasts like Persian melons. Statuesque, that was the word. But Belinda was no statue. She was warm and soft and fragrant. No chicken, but then neither was he. Sure, she dyed her hair, but he kind of liked it that way, even if it didn't match the rest of her when they were in bed like this. She was a damn fine woman.

'When are you going to let me marry you?' he asked.

'Are you going to start that again?'

'Well, what have you got against marriage?'

'Two ex-husbands.'

'I'm not like them. You told me so yourself. Nolan was a chaser and Fellowes was a drunk. And neither one of them could hold a job. I'm the Mayor this year, and I've got a good business and money in the bank and I don't hit the bottle. As for women, sure I used to go into Los Angeles or Frisco every once in a while after my wife died, and even before, I admit it, because she didn't satisfy me the way you do. She was a wonderful woman, but she just wasn't the same as you. But, I swear, in all the years that you and I have been going together I never once had another woman. You believe me, don't you?'

She patted his abdomen affectionately. 'Yes, I do. If you had, I'd have known it.'

'Then why don't you marry me?'

'I don't know,' she said. 'I guess I just don't see the point of it. It's not as if Charley needed a mother. He's practically grown up. And you and I get along pretty well the way we are. You sure can't tell me you want more kids? We're both of us too old to start raising a family.'

Joe crushed out his cigarette in the ashtray next to her bed. Belinda didn't smoke; she kept the ashtray there for him. 'But the whole town knows about us,' he said.

'I'd be surprised if they didn't, by this time.'

'Don't you care?'

'Do you?'

'I guess not.'

'Does Charley?'

'I doubt it.'

'Well, then.'

Joe was persistent. 'I want to do the right thing.'

'You do the right thing every time you come to my bed,' she assured him.

'Hell, that's not what I mean.'

'I know what you mean, Joe. Make an honest woman of me. Well, in my own mind, I *am* an honest woman. I don't need a preacher or justice of the peace to tell me I am. I'm not a whore. I take your money, but I work for it in that box office, same as anybody else.'

'But damn it, Linda, I love you.'

'Oh, that's *different*,' she said, sarcastically. 'Why didn't you say so?'

'Now you're making fun of me,' he grumbled.

'No harm in a little fun,' she said. 'I appreciate you asking me, Joe. I really do. And I love *you*, too, you know that. As for the wedding bells . . . ' She broke off, giggling. 'Oh, for goodness' sake,' she said.

'What is it?'

'You old goat. Look at that. You've built up another head of steam already.'

As she embraced him, and he responded with vigor that

belied his years, neither was aware of the perfervid eyes that watched their union.

Charley Prescott was selling tickets in the Paradise box office, as he often did on Belinda's night off. Years before, he used to wonder why his father always just happened to be absent from the theater whenever Belinda was, but as he grew older, the probable reason dawned on him, and it pleased him that his father had found a companion, even though he seriously doubted that people of such ancient vintage were capable of really *doing* much of anything together.

Tim and Jennie walked up to the box office.

'How's business?' asked Tim.

'So-so,' said Charley.

'People staying away because of what happened to Prue?' Jennie asked.

'They're sure staying away from the ladies' room,' he replied.

'Charley,' said Tim, 'how does your dad have the nerve to charge admission for an oldie like *Maltese Falcon?*'

'Oldie-but-*goodie*,' said Charley.

'Yeah, but it's on TV all the time.'

'Between deodorant commercials, sure. This is uncut and uninterrupted, the way it was *meant* to be seen.'

'Okay, okay, I'm sold,' said Tim, laying out the money.

Tim and Jennie entered the Paradise, arm in arm.

Belinda Fellowes lived in a small single-storey house surrounded by high shrubbery, of which she was extremely proud. She trimmed it herself, happily snapping the hedge clippers and humming. 'Why don't you let me do that for you?' Joe had asked her more than once; and she had replied that it was good exercise for the pectoral muscles. 'Wouldn't want me to sag, would you, Joe?'

The disadvantage of the shrubbery, now, was that it provided a hiding place for the Shape that crouched low behind it in the dark, its eyes fixed upon the narrow aperture where Belinda's bedroom window shade did not quite reach the bottom of the glass. Only half an inch of window was left uncovered, but it was enough to allow this intruder to watch the lovemaking within. Joe always liked a small, soft lamp illuminating the bedroom, the better to admire Belinda's Rubensian proportions, and this furnished sufficient light for the voyeur's eyes.

As the two lovers coupled, the watcher's member swelled, rising to meet the hand that reached between crouching legs to hold the thickening, lengthening presence and caress it, encourage its growth, exulting in its rapid change from supple snake to bludgeon.

Joe, the tension of his desire relaxed by Belinda's earlier affections, was now able to give prolonged attention to her needs.

Outside the window, the watcher gazed as if mesmerically transfixed. Both hands gripped the jutting member, slick with anticipatory ooze.

It pleased Joe to return in full measure the pleasure Belinda had given him. He was proud of his strength and glad of the gratification she was so obviously receiving.

'Oh, Joe. Oh gee, Joe.'

The inflamed mace in the watcher's hands throbbed with fevered pulse. A strand of diamond-clear seepage hung like spiderwork from the bulbous crown.

'*Joe!*'

Belinda's climactic cry was better than any song to Joe's ears. Upon hearing it, he permitted his love to fountain itself into her.

Outside, a string of thick saliva slowly descended from the watcher's gaping mouth.

'Want a cigarette?' Belinda asked Joe as he lay panting beside her.

'Be the death of me,' he said hoarsely.

'Smoking?'

'No,' he replied with a chuckle. 'Not smoking.'

Soon, he dressed and left to relieve Charley at the theater. Belinda, profoundly satisfied, did not get up. She stretched and yawned luxuriously on the bed, sumptuously nude, a billowing marshmallow Juno.

Tortured by her maddening musk, pungent even through the locked window, the watcher flung itself against the glass and shattered it.

Belinda turned quickly in the direction of the sudden noise, and saw someone, something, starting to climb in the window. She acted with a speed surprising in a woman so generously fleshed, rolling immediately off the bed, on the far side, putting the bed between herself and the window, and at almost the same time reaching behind the headboard for the hunting rifle that had been supplied her from Oscar Garrett's store.

'Stop or I'll shoot!' she yelled.

The lower part of the intruder's torso had become visible to her behind the flapping window shade, and, although its face was still unseen, there could be no doubting its sex. Undeterred by Belinda's shouted warning, it persisted in trying to scramble through the window. Belinda was horror-struck by the sight of its grotesque dimensions, but her horror did not prevent her from putting the rifle stock to her naked shoulder and taking aim.

'Stop, I said!'

When it did not stop, she squeezed the trigger. The explosion was like a ton of dynamite in the small room, and the recoil cruelly jolted her shoulder. What was left of the window was shattered by the bullet, and the intruder fled with a howl of bestial fury. There was a neat hole near the top of the shade.

Now that the danger had passed, Belinda began to shake, all her great curves bobbing and quivering like overripe fruit. Throwing down the rifle, she lunged at the telephone, dialed the operator, and sobbed out a frantic call for the sheriff.

## 36

THWARTED AND SEETHING, the molester turned his attention toward the other women of Galen.

While it was stalking its new prey, the sheriff was hurrying to Belinda's house. When he arrived, she was dressed in a robe, tossing down a stiff drink of Bourbon, and still trembling. She showed him the broken bedroom window and told him what had happened.

'The shot went high,' Hank said, examining the bullet hole in the shade. 'You probably missed him.'

'I got rid of him, though.'

'Good thing our women all have guns.'

'You want a drink, Hank?'

'No, but you go ahead and have another. You look as if you need it.'

'I sure do,' she admitted, filling her glass again.

'Belinda,' said Hank, 'are you certain you didn't see his face? Just for a second, maybe?'

She swallowed a large gulp of the drink and shook her head. 'Like I told you, the window shade was in the way. But I sure did get a good look at the lower part of him. I'd recognize *that* if I ever saw it again, and I hope to God I never do.'

'Feel like telling me about it?'

'Well,' she said, 'it's not the sort of thing a lady likes to talk about to a man.'

'I understand. But this is real important. Even though you didn't see his face, you're the only gal who got even a halfway good look at him and lived to tell about it. It was too dark for Laura Kincaid to see him – he smashed the only light that was on in her office. Melanie Saunders was in shock, couldn't do anything but scream, and then she killed herself. All the others . . . '

Belinda nodded and sipped her drink. 'I know, Hank. Listen, I got an idea. You go talk to Martha Jenkins, the doctor's wife. When we were shut up in that dorm, she started a rumor about this maniac. Something Doc told her. It just seemed silly to me at the time. I didn't believe a word of it. But you tell Martha that I believe it now. Tell her everything she said is absolutely true. Then get her to tell you what she told us that night.'

At the precise moment that Belinda was mentioning her name, Martha Jenkins was in danger. The watcher that had crouched outside Belinda's window was now climbing the pepper tree outside the Jenkins house, under cover of night. Boiling desire had drowned all cautious instincts. Making use of the limb that had not yet been cut down, it flung itself through Jennie's locked window with a heedless crash. Finding the room unoccupied – Jennie was at the movies with Tim – the Shape sprang into the hallway. It yanked open the door of the master bedroom.

Empty. The hour was not late, and Doc was still out making house calls.

The intruder's head lifted. Its nostrils flared, detecting an intoxicating scent. Like a compass needle magnetically sucked to a lodestone, the Shape slowly turned, stopped again, then padded down the carpeted stairs to the source of the irresistible aroma.

At the foot of the stairs, it hesitated for a moment, then turned unerringly toward the recreation room. Its nostrils flared again and its organ became suddenly tumid. On the other side of the door was a woman.

Martha was alone in the rec room, watching television. A cooking show. This week, soufflés. She had taken the precaution of locking the door, and an air rifle stood beside her chair. She wasn't sure she would be able to use it. She hated guns.

The door rattled. Martha turned away from the TV screen and saw the door knob being twisted impatiently back and forth. She got to her feet and snapped off the TV set.

'Sam?' she said.

The only answer was an angry rattling of the door.

'Jennie?'

With a loud thud, the intruder threw itself against the door. Martha was appalled by its strength – she heard the wood begin to crack.

She picked up the air rifle. 'Get out of this house!' she shouted, but again the thing on the other side hurled its body against the door, splitting the central panel.

Martha couldn't stand the thought of shooting anyone or anything. She pointed the air rifle into a metal waste-bucket and fired.

The noise was gratifying – and effective, for the assaults on the door stopped instantly, and she heard the intruder scamper quickly away.

Martha reached for the phone.

Frustration was churning inside the creature, rising like hot lava in a volcanic crater, as it skittered from shadow to shadow, criss-crossing Galen, a will-o'-the-wisp, hiding behind trees, dropping behind bushes, parked cars, trash cans, dashing in and out of alleys, keeping low, running at a crouch, alert for the smell of Woman.

One thing it had been created to do, and no other thing was of importance. Food, drink, rest, none of them mattered. Bodily harm to itself did not matter, except as that would affect its purpose. It was the custodian of precious seed that must not be allowed to die and pass away from the world. This it knew, and this was all it knew. The knowledge had been born deep within its flesh, its bones, its blood, a knowledge without words, without thought, an urgent compulsion that prodded and whipped and drove it to the deed.

Impressions flashed luridly in its dark mind, spasmodic lightning in a blackened sky: sights and smells and sounds and flavors and feelings: the taste of female skin . . . the glistening sight of labia, splitting to receive . . . the feeling, as that moist sheath contracted around its own hard flesh

. . . the liquid sounds of frenzied coupling . . . the dizzying, maddening bouquet of female musk . . .

The scent was evident again outside the home of Oscar and Mona Garrett.

Crawling on its belly along the foundation of the house, it found a cellar window, which it immediately smashed with one hand. With great effort, it squeezed its muscular body through the narrow opening, unmindful of broken glass, and dropped to the concrete floor of the cellar. Rising to its feet, it began to walk quietly to the door which led to the upper part of the house.

Pain struck its ankle with a metallic *snap!* The merciless jaws of a bear trap, biting with steel teeth, dug deep into its flesh to the bone. Oscar had brought home several of the traps from his sporting goods store. The creature's breath hissed and rasped with the effort to keep silent. It shook its foot in a frenzy, but could not dislodge the trap. Dropping to one knee, it applied both hands to the metal jaws and began to pry them apart. The spring of the trap was strong, but the hands that battled it were stronger. In a few more moments, its ankle was free, and the trap was flung furiously away, with a clatter.

'Who's down there?' Oscar Garrett called through the locked cellar door.

At his voice, the intruder retreated to the broken window, squeezed through it again, and ran away from the house, limping.

The scent was tormentingly powerful near the inn. Pain of two kinds goaded the creature. Its ankle stung and throbbed from the savage bite of the bear trap, but far more savage was the pressure of unfulfilled lust. This was like a knife in its guts. As a cloud drifted over the moon, the Shape took advantage of the diminished light to lope in dual agony to the inn's nearest window.

Here, yes, here – waitress, diners – the watcher was pummeled by the force of their combined musks.

The waitress screamed and dropped her tray with a crash.

She had seen a face at the dining room window. Only a glance she had before it turned away, but in that moment, even in the dark, the unhuman hunger of the eyes had horrified her.

An upper window of the inn opened. Ruth Purdy pointed a shotgun into the darkness below and fired wildly. Buckshot sprayed, sending the creature hobbling away into the shadows.

'After him, Jed!' shouted Ruth, but by the time the innkeeper had reached the outer door, a gleaming automatic in his hand, the Shape was nowhere to be seen.

As it limped away from the inn, a mighty rage was towering in its heart.

Julian, who had been in his room, ran downstairs to find out what had happened. Jed told him, briefly. He talked to the waitress who had seen the face, but all she could say was, 'His eyes!' And she shuddered.

*His eyes like furnace doors ajar.* The line from Logue's translation of the *Iliad* blazed in Julian's mind. 'Was the face in any way familiar?' he asked. 'Anyone you may have seen before?'

'I've never seen *eyes* like that before,' she replied. 'The face was gone before I could notice anything else about it.'

Back in his room, Julian stretched out on the bed and read Stefanski's letter again. 'Things I could tell you, heard in my youth, in villages deep in valleys where life was lived as in centuries past, of powers, of evils, of death by fearful and ungodly forces . . . '

He was so engrossed in the letter that he took no notice of a low-starting rumble until it had grown to a tremor that shook his bed. The phone rang, startling him. He leaped from the bed to answer it.

'Hello?'

'Mr Trask, this is Miss –'

The rumble was a roar now, boards creaked, a powdering of plaster sifted down from the ceiling, the floor rolled suddenly and threw him off his feet. Looking upward, he saw a crack appear in the ceiling over the bed. The split widened, flakes of plaster fell like snow. With thunderclap blast, a large section of ceiling dropped upon the bed. A small hill of sundered wood and brick and plaster flattened the mattress, smashing it down through the springs and bedframe to the floor.

In another moment, the tremor was over and it was quiet again, except for a steady hum. It was a dial tone from the telephone Julian still held in his hand. He had been disconnected. He got to his feet and left the room, to learn the extent of damage to the inn.

'You okay, Mr Trask?' asked Jed Purdy, whom he met on the stairs.

'I think so,' Julian said, as he dusted plaster from his hair and clothes. 'Anybody hurt?'

'No,' Jed replied, 'just a bit shook up. We get these little quakes every so often. Broke a couple of dishes in the kitchen.'

'It broke a good deal more than that in my room,' said Julian. 'Come take a look.'

When Jed saw the massive slab of ceiling that completely covered and crushed Julian's bed, he whistled in awe. 'That's one bed that'll never be fit to sleep in again,' he said. 'If you'd a-been lying on it, you'd be a dead man right now.'

'I *was* lying on it,' said Julian, 'just before the roof caved in. I got up to answer the phone.'

'Saved by the bell, you might say. You're a lucky fellow. I'm awfully sorry about this, Mr Trask, but you know, an Act of God is what it is. I'm not liable.' He shook his head in bewilderment. 'It's peculiar. The rest of the inn wasn't hit nowhere near this bad. Hardly touched. Sure am glad you're not hurt. I'll move you to another room right away.'

'Thanks. That will be fine.'

When Jed had left, Julian pondered his words: 'An Act of God.' Was it? Or was it something closer to Henryk Stefanski's phrase, 'fearful and ungodly forces?'

His room was the only one that had suffered serious damage. Coincidence?

Fire, water, earth, and air . . .

Tim Galen had encountered a strange manifestation of

207

fire in his home. And now this nearly fatal quaking of the earth that seemed to have singled out Julian for persecution. Am I becoming paranoid? he asked himself.

Fire, then earth. What would be next? Where would it strike? Who would be the target?

# 37

TIM, SAID JULIAN to himself. He could be the next target. In fact – and the thought galvanically propelled him out the door – in fact, he might even now be lying dead in his room under a heap of rubble.

In moments, he reached Tim's room and flung open the unlocked door. Tim wasn't there.

As he walked back to his own room, he met Tim returning from an outing.

'Did you feel it?' Julian asked him.

'Feel what?'

'Quake is what Jed calls it.'

'Jennie and I felt a little something just as I was dropping her off at her home – we thought maybe it was a sonic boom from a jet.'

'For some reason,' said Julian, 'it was localized on the inn. Specifically, my room. Come with me, I'll show you something.'

Julian brought Tim back to his room and showed him the bed under its load of debris. 'Do you remember what I told you,' he said, 'about the elemental forces?'

'Yes.'

'They're being controlled,' said Julian, 'I'm convinced of it. Roiled and stirred up and whipped into a fury against us. That creature has gone mad with frustration. We've put obstacles in its path, kept it from what it feels to be its mission. And it's striking out . . . '

Tim backed away from Julian. The man's voice, his eyes, were fiery with conviction.

Now, Julian grew quieter. 'You,' he said softly. 'You hardly felt anything tonight, you say. "A little something."' Julian pointed suddenly at the ruined bed. 'Would you call *that* a little something?'

'No . . .'

'I was nearly *killed* tonight by a monstrous convulsion of the earth. And you felt almost nothing! *Why not?*'

Tim continued to back away from Julian. 'I don't know . . .'

'What makes *you* immune? Are you protected? Or are you the one who caused it?'

'Me? No!'

Julian seized Tim's shoulders. His eyes glared into Tim's. Pagan eyes, Julian thought. The eyes of Pan. The satyr, the sex god. *Great Pan is dead*, they said, but they were wrong. They mourned too soon. The sex god, the dawn god, the incubus, he's *alive* – alive and well and living in Galen, raping and killing and enlisting the aid of his old friends, the elements, against us . . .

Julian released Tim and leaned against the wall. 'Forgive me,' he said. 'The plain truth is, I'm scared to death.'

'That's all right,' said Tim. 'We're all scared.'

The telephone rang. Julian answered it.

'Mr Trask?'

'Yes.'

'This is Miss Rudden again. We were cut off.'

'Miss Rudden . . . yes . . .'

Tim, miming friendly leavetaking, quietly vacated the room.

'I'm afraid I have sad news,' said Miss Rudden.

Julian groaned. It could be only one thing. 'He's dead?'

'Yes, sir. Less than an hour ago. I knew you'd want to be informed.'

'Thank you.' Grief knifed Julian, stabbing his heart.

'The professor felt very close to you.'

'He was like a father.'

'And he was thinking of you at the very last,' she said. 'He

209

spoke your name, several times. Said he had to tell you something.'

'Do you know what it was?'

'Well, he wasn't very coherent at the end,' said Miss Rudden, 'and his voice was very weak, but he kept repeating a name . . .'

'My name, you mean?'

'He did that, too, but there was another name. Do you know anyone named Ware? Bill Ware?'

Julian searched his mind. 'Ware? I don't think so . . .'

'Of course, I may not have heard correctly. And the professor had a rather strong accent. It may have been more like Wahr. Does that sound familiar?'

'No,' said Julian, 'it doesn't. Did he say anything else? Please try to remember.'

'No, sir. It was very difficult for him to speak – I had to put my ear almost to his lips – and he just spoke your name, several times, and then he said, "Tell Julian . . . Bill Ware . . . Bill Ware . . ." At least that's what it sounded like to me. He repeated it a few times. Very emphatically, as if it were extremely important. Then he was gone.'

Julian sighed. 'Thank you, Miss Rudden,' he said. 'It was good of you to call.'

After he hung up, Julian walked numbly downstairs to the inn's bar. He had received two shocks in quick succession: a narrow brush with death, and now the loss of a beloved friend and colleague. He needed a drink. 'Vodka,' he said, 'straight up.'

It had been Stefanski's favorite potation, in the days when he still allowed himself an occasional taste of liquor. 'The Russians claim they invented it,' he had said, 'but they lie, Julian. It is Polonian!' He had always used that archaic word instead of the modern equivalent, 'Polish'. And he had proudly referred to himself as a *Polak*. 'Why not?' he would say. '*Polak* is just the Polonian word for "Pole".' When the glass of vodka was set before Julian, he tossed it down with one gulp, as Stefanski had taught him to do.

'Again,' he said.

As he sat at the bar, Julian made an effort to remember every man he knew whose first name was William. He then mentally scanned all the Williams he did not know personally but who had done work in his and Stefanski's field. None of them were surnamed Ware.

He recalled the first time he had met Stefanski. He saw the mane of straight, snowy hair, like a Kabuki lion's; and the old eyes sharp and lively behind the glasses. He had known the old man only through his books, at first, and on the basis of these he had written to him and made the trip to Boston to meet him.

'You are too young,' were the words with which Stefanski had greeted him. Julian had been taken aback, particularly because he was well into his thirties and considered himself stolidly middle-aged. 'The young are materialists, all. That is why always revolutionaries are young. They think they can solve the problems of the world by putting food into bellies, by taking money out of one bank account and putting it into another. Or they think of sex only, as if sex were a magic formula for happiness. They believe what they can see and touch, only. Try to talk to them about something beyond the senses, something above Nature or below it, and they laugh.'

Julian, his voice thin with nervousness, had replied, 'I think that's changing, sir. Today it's the young people who are looking beyond the material world, trying to find something more spiritual, transcendental.'

Stefanski had grunted. 'Answer me a question,' he said gruffly. 'What is a ghost?'

'I don't know,' said Julian.

'Good. Neither do I,' said Stefanski. And he laughed, putting Julian at ease. 'But do you believe in them?'

Julian thought carefully before replying. 'I don't deny their existence,' he said.

From that point on, the two men had become fast friends.

Now, as he sat at the bar, Julian had another thought. Perhaps Bill Ware wasn't a name at all? 'Bill' was also a word, with several meanings. The beak of a bird; a creditor's claim; a poster or circular; a piece of paper money; a menu, or bill of fare; a legal term – bill of indictment, bill of divorce, bill of rights. A bill was also a kind of broadsword, Julian recalled from historical studies. It also meant a promontory or headland. And what about 'bill and coo?' But none of these bypaths led anywhere. Julian tossed down his second vodka.

Who or what was Bill Ware? And why had Stefanski, with his dying breath, so desperately wanted to convey the information to Julian?

He ordered another vodka.

The night was humid. When Jennie returned home after her evening with Tim, she felt hot and sticky, in need of a shower. Quickly peeling off her clothes, she selected a fluffy fresh towel from her linen closet, and padded into the private bathroom that adjoined her bedroom. Placing the towel on a small metal stool, she stepped into the shower stall, sliding the thick glass door shut. She turned on the water, adjusting the mix of hot and cold until it was a comfortable temperature, and stood luxuriating under the invigorating spray for several moments before she began soaping. Then, with a fragrant patchouli-scented bar, she briskly soaped her entire body. That done, she rinsed herself thorougly from head to foot, and, her shower completed, turned the water handles to the Off position.

Nothing happened. The water continued to cascade down upon her. She tried the handles again, turning them back and forth, but they had absolutely no effect on the stream. If anything , the force of the water seemed to have increased – what had been a gentle spray was now a torrent.

Aware of a new difficulty, Jennie looked down at the tile floor of the shower stall. The drain was not working. Her feet were entirely covered by water. It was almost up to her ankles.

She tried the water handles again, still with no result. The force of the water grew stronger. Hearing a wrenching metallic sound above her head, she looked upward.

The power of the water had forced the spray-nozzle completely off. It fell to the floor with a clank and a splash.

The water, no longer hampered by the nozzle, erupted with fresh frenzy into the shower stall.

With a moan of annoyance, Jennie gave up and turned to leave the shower. This was a job for a plumber, she told herself. She tried to roll back the sliding glass door, but it was stuck. She tried harder. It refused to budge. She tugged at it frantically, but it was no use.

She was locked in.

Looking down, she saw that the water was now half-way between her ankles and knees, and rising rapidly.

'Help!' she shouted. 'Someone help!'

But she knew it was futile to shout. Three closed doors stood between her and the rest of the house: this shower door, the bathroom door, her bedroom door. And the water was making too much noise.

Again, she tried to slide back the shower door, and again her efforts were in vain. She pounded against the heavy glass with her fists.

'Help! *Help!*'

The water had reached her knees. She screamed as loud as she could, as it continued to gush down upon her, gallon after gallon. In desperation, nearing hysteria, she raised both hands to the nozzleless pipe and covered it, trying to stem the relentless flow with her hands.

For a moment, this seemed to work, but soon the water began to seep and trickle and spurt between her fingers, and then its pent-up power forced her hands away, and she was pounded with an iron-hard jet of water as furious as that from a firehose. It pushed her back against the opposite wall of the shower stall.

She felt the water rise until it lapped insidiously at her crotch. She screamed again. In what seemed no time at all, the water had risen to her waist.

And – did she only imagine it? the water was warmer.

By the time it had risen to touch her nipples, there was no doubt. It was not her imagination. The water was growing warmer by the second. It was getting hot, very hot. Hotter and hotter, and higher and higher.

When the scalding liquid had risen to her shoulders, she knew she was going to be boiled alive. Like those witches Tim had told her of – skinned, then boiled in a giant vat until they were dead.

She screamed again, in mortal terror. Nobody heard her. The water continued to rise.

## 38

*drink deep girl drink all thou wilt*

Tim abruptly awoke from the recurring dream and sat up in bed. His heart was pounding and he was drenched with sweat. He gasped for air, as if drowning.

There was something different about the dream this time. What was it? He rubbed his eyes and tried to remember, tried to pin it down before it vanished from his mind completely.

The dream had always been the same, like an old film shown over and over, every sound and movement, every face, every inflection identical to all the previous times.

Except tonight. Tonight it had been different. But in what way?

He closed his eyes again and tried to recapture it. The dungeon had been the same. And the same three men. The same questions, the same screams, the flickering torches set in sconces on the walls. The rack, the dipper of water, the girl gulping and gagging on it, *drink deep girl* . . .

The girl, that was it. The girl was different. Tonight, she was not the flame-haired one so familiar to him from endless repetitions. Tonight, she was familiar for another reason.

She was Jennie.

*drink deep girl*, and it was Jennie who gagged on the water.

It frightened him. Never before had the dream deviated

from its pattern in even the smallest detail. Some people believed dreams had hidden meaning, portents . . .

He told himself he was probably being foolish, but he turned on the light and reached for the phone.


Doc had been inspecting the trespasser's damage to the rec room door when the phone rang. He picked up the rec room extension. 'Dr Jenkins.'

'Is Jennie there?' Tim asked, without ceremony.

'Well, yes,' said Doc, 'but she may be asleep by now . . . '

'Will you check? I want to make sure she's all right.'

'You escorted her to the front door yourself, Tim . . . '

'Please! Now!'

The urgency in Tim's voice startled the doctor. 'All right,' he said. 'Hang on.'

Doc put down the phone and climbed the stairs to the master bedroom, where Martha was preparing to retire. 'Where's Jennie?' he asked. 'I thought we agreed she should sleep with you tonight because of that broken window in her bedroom and all.'

'Don't fuss, Sam,' Martha said. 'She's just taking a shower in her own bathroom.'

'That's Tim on the phone, wants to talk to her.'

'Well, she's probably through by now.'

Doc walked to Jennie's room and tapped on the door. 'Jennie?' Receiving no answer, he opened the door and peeped in. The sound of water from her bathroom satisfied him that she was still showering. He began to close the bedroom door again when he thought he heard a faint voice from the bathroom, over the roar of the water. It sounded something like 'Help.'

He rushed to the bathroom door and threw it open. Clouds of steam rolled out, stifling and blinding him. He just barely was able to see, through the translucent glass door of the shower stall, the pink silhouette of Jennie, thrashing helplessly in water over her chin. She was screaming.

Doc tugged at the shower door with all his strength, but could not open it. Wasting not another moment, he seized the small metal stool, and swung it.

The glass smashed into fragments, and the cataract of water that burst upon him, carrying his wet and naked daughter with it, threw him off his feet.

By the time that Tim arrived at the Jenkins house, Martha, responding to a frantic yell from Doc, had turned off the water at the main. Jennie and Doc were both wrapped in thick robes of absorbent terry cloth, and the flooded floors of Jennie's bathroom and bedroom were covered by layers of sodden towels. Jennie was suffering from the effects of a bad scare and minor cuts from the great guillotine blades of broken glass, but she had not been immersed in the hot water long enough to be burned.

'I still don't understand what happened,' she said, her voice trembling. She was sitting in a big chair now, with Tim and both of her parents standing over her.

Doc shook his head. 'Neither do I. From the look of it, I'd say something happened to the water turnoff *and* the drain *and* the shower door –'

'All at the same time?' said Tim.

'That's the part that's hard to credit,' Doc replied. 'Any one of them, by itself, would be a common householder's problem, and a pain in the neck, but not dangerous. But all three together . . . '

It could not be explained away as coincidence, Tim told himself. The fire in his own home, the quake that had nearly killed Julian, and now this. Fire, water, earth.

Jennie was saying, 'I don't think I'll ever take a shower again in my whole life.'

'Don't blame you,' said her mother. 'Tubs are safer.' The manner of Mary Lou's death had slipped her mind for the moment.

Doc said, 'I'll get someone out in the morning to give our plumbing the once-over. Meanwhile, I suggest we all get some sleep. Jennie, you go in with your mother. I'll sack out downstairs on the couch.'

It was only now that Tim noticed the broken window of Jennie's room. 'What happened here?' he asked, walking over to it.

'We had a visitor this evening,' said Doc, his voice grim. 'While I was out making my rounds and Jennie was with you at the movies. Mrs Jenkins scared him off with an air rifle. He must have entered through Jennie's window. You were right about that tree, Tim. The limb will have to go. I'll have it attended to in the morning.'

'Life is funny, isn't it?' murmured Jennie. They all looked at her. 'I mean,' she continued, 'Prue Keaton goes to the movies, and it kills her. I go to the movies, and it saves my life.'

Doc grunted. 'Saves it so you can be damn near drowned and parboiled in your own home.'

'Well, she's alive, Sam,' said Martha.

'Yes,' Doc said with feeling. 'She's alive.' Turning to Tim, he said, 'How did you get over here from the inn?'

'Ran,' Tim replied, 'all the way.'

'Come on, I'll drive you back.'

'No, don't go!' said Jennie. She hurtled herself out of the chair and embraced Tim. 'Please don't go! Hold me!'

Tim looked at her parents. 'Maybe I could bunk downstairs, too?'

Doc and Martha were about to agree to this suggestion, but Jennie said, fiercely, 'That's not what I mean. I want to *be* with you!'

Her candor, in the presence of her parents, embarrassed Tim, and he said, evasively, 'I'll be right downstairs, honey, under your own roof.'

'No, no, don't leave me,' she moaned.

Martha Jenkins, after a short inner struggle, said, 'Oh, for pity's sake, take her back to the inn with you, Tim.'

'Martha!' said Doc.

'Sam, they love each other and they want to be together. They won't be doing anything at the inn they haven't done already a dozen times. If you don't know that by now, you're a lot less smart than I think you are.'

'Damn it, she's a child!'

'I was younger than she is when you first played doctor with me.'

'That's a hell of a thing to say in front of the kids.'

'They're not kids and, besides, it's true.'

'But we knew we were going to get married.'

'So do they,' said Martha, and turned to the two young people. 'Or, if they don't, they'll have me to answer to. That's right, isn't it, Tim?'

Tim looked down at Jennie, snuggled in his arms. He kissed her forehead. 'I've known I was going to marry Jennie ever since I was twelve years old,' he said.

'Sam,' said Martha, 'all the terrible things that are going on . . . doesn't she have a right to a little happiness?'

Doc understood his wife's elliptic logic. But it wrenched him to think of his baby girl and Tim . . .

He threw up his hands. 'All right, all right,' he said. 'If you don't mind the gossips wagging their tongues, why should I? But you two aren't going to walk back to the inn this time of night with that rapist still on the loose. Here.' He handed Tim a set of keys. 'Take the car. And just be sure to have it back here tomorrow morning early.'

'Thanks, Dr Jenkins.'

Doc favored him with a lopsided grin. 'Might as well practice calling me Dad.'


Julian kept drinking vodka at the inn's bar until closing time, but it seemed to have little, if any, effect on him. 'Bill Ware, Bill Ware,' he occasionally muttered under his breath, hoping to evoke a flash of meaning from the name.

When he got to his feet to return to his room, he discovered that the vodka had been more potent than he'd realized. His step was unsteady as he began to climb slowly up the stairs. 'Bill Ware, Bill Ware,' he continued to mumble.

He tried other forms. 'Willy Ware. Billy Ware. Will Ware. Wilhelm von Ware . . . ' It was becoming silly. How about trying all the combinations again, substituting Wahr? Miss Rudden had said it might have been more like Wahr. But nothing clicked, even taking into account Stefanski's dying condition and heavy accent. 'William Wahr, Willy Wahr, Billy Wahr, Bill Wahr . . . '

Jullian froze, halfway up the stairs. Bill Wahr – of course! He ran the rest of the way to his room.

Tim and Jennie drove with the top down, because of the oppressive and unusual humidity of the air. She clung to his arm.

'Let's cut through the park,' he said, turning into the automobile path that divided the wooden preserve. 'There'll be more of a breeze there.'

'I can hardly breathe,' she said. 'Such awful weather. Do you think there's a storm brewing?'

'Could be,' said Tim. As he drove, he chuckled. 'You broads,' he said, in a tone of grudging admiration.

'What about us broads?'

'Pretty clever, the way you and your mother suckered me into a proposal of marriage.'

'We did not!'

'Oh, I don't mean to say it was planned or anything like that,' he was quick to add. 'Just that old feminine instinct at work. First you practically come right out and say you want to spend the night with me – in front of your parents. That was Step One. Then your mother tells me to carry you away, and she even talks your dad into it, and pretty soon they're both saying bless-you-my-children. Neat. Very neat.'

'You can back out any time you want.'

'Are you kidding? And face your mother with that air rifle she uses on rapists? Talk about shotgun weddings!'

Jennie stiffened and pulled away from him.

'What's wrong?' he said. 'I'm only joking.'

'How did you know about the air rifle and the rapist?' Jennie asked.

Tim braked the car. 'What?'

'How did you know?'

'I don't believe this,' he said. 'You're as bad as my aunt.'

'Tim, *tell* me!'

He turned off the ignition. The car stood in the center of the park. With the convertible top down, they could feel a stirring of the night air, but it was unrefreshing, like a

219

breeze in reverse, as if the air were being sucked away, leaving them in a silent, breathless vacuum.

'All right, I'll tell you,' said Tim. He laughed. 'You little nut. Just a few minutes ago, in your bedroom, your dad told me all about your mother scaring off the intruder with that gun. Don't you remember?'

She covered her face with her hand. 'I'm so frightened I'm beginning to suspect everybody. Even you. Can you ever forgive me?'

He took her hand away from her face and kissed her. 'Ask me again in forty or fifty years,' he said.

Something she saw over his shoulder caught her eye. 'What's that?'

He turned. A few fallen leaves were chasing each other in a circle on the ground, caught in a spiral of air. 'Just a little gust of wind stirring up the leaves,' he said.

'Tim, look.'

He turned again. The pinwheel of leaves had grown into a spinning top of air, a small furious funnel about a foot high that scattered dust as it moved in the direction of the car, with a hissing, whistling sound. As it drew closer, it swelled in size, becoming wider and taller.

'Like a miniature whirlwind,' said Tim. 'I think you may have been right about a storm brewing. We'd better get to the inn before it breaks.'

The whistling sound of the tiny tornado grew louder as it spun closer to them. Tim turned the ignition key. The car's engine wheezed asthmatically, but did not turn over. He tried again, with the same result.

'*Start*, damn it!' he growled.

The dark dervish of air was as tall as a man now, and its angry whirling threw clouds of gritty dust into the open car.

'*Start!*'

The engine was dead. 'Put the top up!' Jennie said, her eyes shut tight against the dust.

'No time – ' Tim started to say, as the twisting wind buffeted the car. 'Run for it!'

They flung open the doors and tumbled from the car.

'The trees!' yelled Tim. 'This way!' Grabbing her hand, he pulled her toward the most densely wooded area of the park.

As she ran, Jennie turned to look over her shoulder at the howling black funnel that now was close to eleven feet tall.

'Oh, God!' she cried in disbelief. *'It's following us!'*

# 39

WHEN JULIAN UNLOCKED the secret of Henryk Stefanski's dying words, and understood their full implication, he felt a thrill of enlightenment, coupled with anxiety and depression. For, although the old man had found a possible answer to one enigma, he had created a web of new complications, new problems, new suspects. Now – if Stefanski had been correct – there was even more cause for fear.

Alone in the new room to which he had been moved, Julian began to reconstruct the series of nightmares in his mind. One by one, he ticked them off, beginning with Gwen Morrissey and concluding with the hideous roadside death of Carrie Hunt. He did not yet know of the recent attempted attacks on Belinda Fellowes, Martha Jenkins, and Mona Garrett, or he would have included them, too. Each attack was examined carefully by Julian, every aspect of it turned over and over again. The longer he thought, the grimmer he grew, until at last, struck by the possibility of an insupportable horror, a groan escaped his lips.

He picked up the phone and called Laura's home. There was no answer. He called the *Signal* office. That number did not answer, either. Deep fear gripped Julian. He bolted from his room, ran downstairs, and left the inn. He had to find Laura before it was too late.

After Tim and Jennie had run for cover into the woods, the

leaves above them began to tremble with the approach of the pursuing whirlwind. The trees shook; leaves and small broken twigs rained down upon them as they ran; the whistling noise of the uncanny funnel built to a scream.

If Tim had ever entertained doubts about Julian's warnings, now they were completely dispelled. A whirlwind that spawned out of nowhere and hunted its prey with animal cunning – it was a thing to shatter sanity, and Tim knew it was the last of the elemental forces, marshaled against him and his beloved in retaliation and rage. Fire, water, earth, and now the very air was conscripted against them. The atmosphere, the breath of life, had become an instrument of doom, twisted into a weapon by powers older than Man.

They ran hand in hand, sometimes stumbling and falling but always rising again to flee the spinning wind that followed close behind. Jennie began to gasp and slow down. 'I ... can't ... go on,' she said.

'You've got to!' he shouted, and pulled her along roughly, deeper among the trees. She felt she could run no more – her heart was like an arrowhead in her chest – and then she said:

'Wait ... listen ...'

Tim listened. The sound had stopped. They turned and looked behind them. The living wind had vanished, as suddenly and mysteriously as it had appeared.

Tim sank to the ground, exhausted, and Jennie dropped beside him. For long moments, they could say nothing. At length, their breath returned.

'I thought we were goners,' said Tim.

'But what was it?'

He saw no need to alarm her further. 'A freak wind, that's all, what they call a dust-devil.' An uncomfortably apt name, Tim told himself.

'But it *followed* us!'

'It just seemed that way,' he said, believing none of his own words. 'Wind can't follow anybody.'

'Tim, I saw it! It came right at us and –'

'Shhh.' He covered her mouth with his hand, and whispered, 'Be very quiet. There's someone here. Among the trees.' He removed his hand and touched a fin[...]

Fearfully, Jennie looked around. She could[...] She looked back at Tim, quizzically. Again he pu[...] to his lips. And now she heard it: the soft crunch of [...] leaves underfoot, once, twice, coming closer.

A form stepped out from behind a tree. Jennie screamed. Tim spun around to look. It stood upright, like a man. Nothing else was certain, for in the dense foliage the moon cast little light.

'Who's there?' cried Tim.

The form advanced, one step, two, crunch, crunch.

'Get back!' Tim shouted. Jennie screamed again.

A strong arm shot out like a piston from the form, reaching for Jennie.

'*Run!*' Tim told her.

She scrambled to her feet and ran blindly, deeper into the trees, still screaming. The dark form ran after her with cheetah speed.

Now she felt its hand claw her shoulder, ripping her dress, but she pulled away and continued running. The top half of her dress hung away from her body and her bare breasts bobbed as she ran. She had packed a small overnight bag and dressed hastily before leaving the house, not taking the time to put on underclothes or stockings.

'Run, Jen! Run!' Tim called again.

Her pursuer assailed her like a football tackle, steel-hard arms encircling her waist and throwing her to the ground. She struggled mightily in its grip, shrieking, squirming, but her efforts were futile. She felt her dress ripped completely off her body, leaving her utterly naked. She was sprawled face down on the coarse carpet of dead leaves, her attacker's hands pinning her own hands to the ground, and it was in this awkward position that the molester now tried to take her. She screamed piercingly as she felt its stiffened flesh searching for the haven it craved.

Now Tim threw himself at the creature, tugging at its shoulders in an effort to dislodge it from Jennie's body. 'Stop it! Get away from her!' Tim cried. It was like fighting a thing of iron come alive, but Tim's frenzies were not in in, for the molester was distracted from its purpose and ose from its knees to dispose of this nuisance.

Using only one hand, it seized Tim by the throat and lifted him off his feet, held him dangling in the air at arm's length for a second, then flung him away as a man might fling away a dead rat by the tail. Tim hit the ground five yards away and lay very still, his neck broken.

Jennie had jumped to her feet and now was running again, naked, into the darkness, unaware of Tim's fate. In a moment, her attacker was in close pursuit.

From the inn, Julian drove immediately to Laura's house. Running up to the front door, he rang the bell and pounded loudly. 'Laura? Laura? You in there?' He forced the lock and yanked the door open. Snapping on lights, he ran quickly through the small house, looking into every room.

Failing to find her, he grabbed the phone and called Hank Walden. 'No time to explain,' he said, 'but we've *got* to find Laura Kincaid. She's not home, I'm calling from there. I'm going over to the newspaper office now. *Find* her, Hank! She could be anywhere!'

He hung up and dashed outside to his car. In seconds, the black Porsche was screeching away from the house.

After a time – it was impossible to know how long – Jennie stopped running and leaned against a tree, panting, her heart hammering, her bare bosom heaving with effort. She listened, but could not hear her pursuer's footsteps. Perhaps she had succeeded in eluding him, she thought. But she worried about Tim – where was he? What had happened to him?

When she had regained her breath, she pulled away from the supporting tree and began again, not running now, she had no more strength for that, but walking, plodding, leadenly putting one foot ahead of the other, her mind dulled by shock, vaguely wondering when she would ever get out of these woods, and slowly beginning to fear she had been traveling in circles.

Her fear was confirmed when she stumbled over a human form on the ground.

It was Tim. She dropped to her knees beside him, calling his name. He did not respond. A doctor's daughter, she knew where to feel in the neck for a pulse. She found it, throbbing faintly. He was alive, just barely, and her touch also told her that he had been gravely injured.

'Tim,' she said softly, *'Tim.'* But he was incapable of speech.

Ignoring her own vulnerability, she shouted as loudly as she was able: *'Help! Somebody, help!'*

Dead silence answered her. Kneeling naked beside her ominously still man, she began to sob. Her body shook with weeping, her eyes were squeezed shut, all the horror of the past weeks welled up and overflowed.

She sensed the reappearance of the molester before she saw or heard its presence. A tension in her blood told her, a tingle of lust pervading the air, a feeling that the world had grown suddenly very young and raw. She looked up and saw it standing over her, its monumental masculinity like an outstretched arm. She stared at it with the frozen fascination of a bird bewitched by a serpent.

On her knees, in the posture of prayer, she felt a strange sensation of worship, as if she were a priestess at creation's birth, making her obeisance to the sacred symbol of life, humble and awed before its power.

This is a dream, she told herself, a terrible dream. None of this is happening. I'll wake up soon, in my bed, in my parents' house, and the terror will vanish, and all the other terror that the other women felt – that will vanish, too, because it's all been a dream.

A hand grasping her hair jolted her back to reality. Her head was jerked back abruptly by the Shape that stood above her. In defense, she reached out and seized the thing that jutted in her face. It was like holding a column of warm, veined stone. She felt sick.

Her whole body was yanked backward by the hair, and she was thrown upon her back. Stepping over the fallen form of Tim, the molester dropped to its knees to mount her.

She fought with desperation, striking out, screaming, writhing, pushing the swollen member away from her loins. She tried to hold her legs together, but her assailant easily forced them apart. She screamed her help.

And now hope died, for Jennie felt the start of the awful entry that had killed so many others. The great slick bulb that topped the organ was the size of a grapefruit, and now she closed her eyes and screamed in pain and fury as this monstrous protuberance began to part the delicate petals of her body.

Suddenly it was withdrawn.

Jennie opened her eyes. She was still pinned under the creature's weight, but the attack had been interrupted. She saw Tim, his head grotesquely twisted to one side, but on his feet, striking again and again at the molester's back with a small, curved knife he had pulled out from under his shirt.

The attacker rose to its feet and turned toward Tim. Jennie could see blood streaming from its back. It struck out at Tim, its hand grazing his head. Tim stood his ground.

Again the skinning knife flashed out, this time slicing the rapist's stomach. The enraged creature dealt Tim a powerful blow on the side of the head, sending him reeling, making him scream with the pain of his already broken neck.

Yet Tim stayed on his feet, and advanced again. Swiftly, he darted forward, and plunged the knife deep into the molester's chest.

As the creature staggered backward, the knife remained in its body. It stood immobile for a moment, like a statue, then toppled forward on its face, forcing the blade even deeper into its heart.

Tim collapsed immediately after, and Jennie, overcome by the events of the night, sank into the protective comfort of a faint.

It was a bizarre tableau that met Julian as he entered the park a minute or so later: the nude girl, lying on her back, alive but unconscious; the lad, crumpled in a heap, his neck broken, his body still warm, but dead; and the naked Shape, dead too, lying on its face.

Julian turned the creature over on its back. He saw the legended organ, flaccid now but no less formidable. He saw the bulged layers of Herculean muscle that gave the creature its more-than-human strength. He saw the gashes on the stomach. He saw the ancient knife, blade sunken deep, blood still oozing dark and thick around the hilt, its handle protruding from between two soft globular female breasts.

Finally, he summoned the courage to raise his eyes to the face of the incubus. A long primitive wail was ripped from low inside Julian, a cry older than civilization, that spoke out angrily of his despair, and of the endless parched desert of his soul, and of his hopeless, dead, lost love. For it was as he had feared. The moon showed the face of the incubus to be ugly with rage and pain, and emptied even of these by death; and the staring eyes were plainly unhuman, saurian; yet beyond all question it was the face of Laura Kincaid.

## 40

JULIAN WAS NOT BY NATURE an early riser, but on those occasions when he had reason to awake with the birds and face the world at such an hour, he was always struck by the prettiness of it. A rosy-golden ambiance almost artificial, like a Maxfield Parrish painting.

This was one of those mornings, but Julian was in no state of mind to appreciate it. He had already packed his single large suitcase and stowed it in the trunk of his car. In it he had locked the copy of the *Artes Perditae* which had been deposited in Jed's safe, as well as Tim's incomplete edition. He would have felt uneasy about leaving behind even that relatively harmless version of the book. Technically, it was not his property – it belonged now to Tim's survivor, his aunt – but Julian felt no obligation to that point of law.

He wanted to be away from Galen as soon as possible, but

he had promised Dr Jenkins to meet him for breakfast in the inn's dining room before he left. Doc was late. Jed Purdy walked over to Julian's table and said, 'Doc Jenkins just phoned. Says he was detained by an emergency call, but he'll be here soon. Want some more coffee?'

'Thanks, Jed, yes.'

'I'll send the waitress over with a fresh pot.'

Julian was deeply depressed. All the recent devastating events, culminating in the ghastly disclosure about Laura, and her death, had blasted and shaken him. The death of his beloved colleague, Stefanski, had provided an additional dismal touch. But hanging over all was a pervading pall of impotence. He castigated himself for having done no useful deed in Galen; he told himself he had actually done harm. He had saved no one, he had prevented no tragedies. Jennie had been rescued from the wrathful water by her father; and Tim had saved her from rape and death, at the sacrifice of his own life. Julian felt directly responsible for Helen Keaton's death, and for the subsequent derangement of her husband's mind. If he had not suggested that all the women of Galen be sealed inside those dormitories, she might never have been attacked. He goaded himself with having been, as usual, an observer, a recorder, a scholar, a bookworm. A looker-on at life, not a doer. His one active idea, the dorms, had caused another death. What *good* was he? What purpose did he serve? For all his knowledge and expertise, all the books he had read and written, a scrubwoman served a more useful function than he. The fact that he had been right about the existence of an incubus in Galen was a matter of no importance. Thus, at least, ran his melancholy thoughts as he sat in the dining room of the inn.

That terrible night when he had discovered the dead bodies of Tim and Laura in the park – it seemed a year ago to him now, but less than a week had passed – Hank Walden had followed close behind. Between them, they had decided that the details should be shared with only one other person, Doc Jenkins. Hank put in an urgent call to him, via the patrol car radio, and the doctor met them in the park a few minutes later.

First, he satisfied himself that Jennie was all right; Julian had already covered her with his jacket. Then Doc turned to Laura's body. At the sight of it, every shred of his cynical shell peeled away. 'Dear *God*!' he cried. 'No, it can't be true, I don't believe it . . . ' He turned to Julian, as if pleading to be told his eyes had lied to him. 'It's just not possible! How can it be?' But there was no time for lengthy explanations – they could come later – and Doc was in no frame of mind to listen, anyway. He cried again and again, 'No, no,' shaking his head as if that could eradicate the body on the ground. His whole life had crumbled apart in an instant. His entire system of philosophy, his trust in the rational, his belief in logic, in science, in the hard realities of the material world: these had been stripped away by the thing he saw before him, leaving him naked in outer space, with no defense against the mad chaotic malice of the universe. This man, a physician who had looked without flinching on the ravages of cancer and the red remnants of mutilated flesh, now staggered behind a tree and violently vomited. Then, trembling, reeking, pale, he had rejoined Julian and the sheriff.

By common agreement, the three men fabricated a story in which there was a certain amount of literal truth. The rapist had attacked Laura in the park and killed her. He had attempted to rape Jennie, but Tim had fought him with a knife, wounding him severely and scaring him off – there were pints of blood on the ground, said Doc, and none of it was Tim's or Jennie's. Tim had been massively beaten by the rapist during the struggle. Jennie, they learned when she regained consciousness, had never seen the face of the molester. Doc secretly, surgically, altered the body of what had been Laura Kincaid and it was buried next to the graves of her parents, in the Galen churchyard. Tim was buried in the special section reserved for the Galen family, next to his mother, Kate. From the amount of blood lost by the rapist, Acting Coroner Samuel Jenkins declared, it was a safe assumption that, wherever he had fled, he would soon die. And, because no Galen men were missing, Doc was proved right in the conviction that he had held all along: the rapist was not a Galen man. Which also was the literal truth.

Doc arrived at the inn and joined Julian at his table. 'Thanks for waiting,' he said, and flagged the waitress. 'First off, get me some of that coffee,' he told her. 'Then put in an order for two eggs, over easy. A large o.j. Stack of buckwheats. Side order of pork sausages. Home-fried potatoes. Rye toast. Strawberry jam.' He glanced at Julian and said, apologetically, 'Got to keep up my strength.'

'And for you, Mr Trask?' asked the waitress, pencil poised.

'I'll just stay with the coffee,' Julian said.

'You know,' said Doc after the waitress had left, 'I'm a doctor, and I've saved and prolonged a lot of lives, as a doctor should. But I'll confess privately to you that I've never been a reverence-for-life buff. I've just never bought the package. I mean, this bleeding-heart idea that every morsel of life is sacred and has to be preserved at all costs. The "sanctity" of life, they call it, human life, animal life, birds, bugs, all that Albert Schweitzer stuff. I always thought it was a wishy-washy little-old-lady kind of thing, because Nature herself, or God if you want to use that word, has no reverence for life, human or otherwise. Plague and famine and flood wipe out more men, women, and children than all the wars and all the murderers the world has ever known. And look at the "reverence for life" in the insect world! Or the wholesale massacres under the sea! Or how about the shameful waste in the human reproductive process itself? All those eggs a woman flushes down the toilet every year, the millions and millions of spermatozoa sacrified in one ordinary male orgasm. Nature doesn't teach us reverence for life. The lesson of Nature is: life is cheap.'

Doc's coffee arrived, and he drank deeply of it. 'But lately,' he said, 'I've done an about-face. All these awful deaths here in town, youngsters with their lives ahead of them, dear people like Helen Keaton and Anita Grant. Slaughtered. "Wasted," as they say on those TV crime shows, and it's a good word because that's exactly what happened, those lives were wasted. I just don't want to see any more death for a while, although I know I won't be able to avoid it in my profession. I saw a spider on the bathroom wall this morning. One of these little yellow spiders we have around here. Used to be, I'd smash it and kill it without a second thought, like a reflex. But this morning I just let it be. Guess I must be getting soft in my old age.'

The doctor's Lucullan breakfast was brought to him by the waitress, and he began to dig in. 'Jesus, Trask,' he said, 'that coffee isn't going to be enough for you. You've got a long drive ahead. Eat a slice of my toast, at least. I'm on a diet, anyway.'

'Thanks,' said Julian, 'maybe I will.' He took a slice of the crisp rye toast and began to munch on it. 'Yes,' he said, 'there's been a surfeit of death. Nine, with Tim and Laura.'

'Ten,' said Doc, shoveling in home-fried potatoes. 'Agatha Galen's dead. Massive stroke. That's why I was late for breakfast. Last of the Galens. Last of 'em in Galen, at any rate. There may be a few others scattered around the country. I wouldn't know. I suppose you might say *she* died because of the rapist, too, indirectly. Tim's death may have been too much for her. She was too ill to make it to the funeral, you noticed. Well, she'd been ailing for a long time, and she'd had a long life. Here, have a couple of these buckwheats.'

'No, thanks,' said Julian. 'How's Jennie?'

'How would she be? She loved that boy. But I guess she'll get over it. People usually do, in time. At least that's what I keep telling Ben Keaton's son.'

'In a way, you could say there were eleven deaths,' said Julian. 'A wonderful old man, like a second father to me. And he was indirectly involved, too. He was helping me. In fact, the very last thing he did was provide the key.' Julian told Doc all about Stefanski, and his deathbed words.

'But who is this Bill Ware, or Wahr?' asked Doc.

'That's what I wondered,' said Julian, 'until it suddenly dawned on me that Stefanski was referring to Billuart.'

Doc shrugged, and popped a piece of sausage into his mouth. 'Never heard of him.'

'Actually, you have,' said Julian. 'He was one of the old writers I asked Stefanski to quote over the phone. Charles René Billuart. A French Dominican, wrote something called

*Tractatus de Angelis.* I read the quote to you one night in your home.' Julian took his notebook from his pocket. 'Funny,' he said as he turned the pages, 'it was right there in front of me all the time. In front of you, too.' Julian read the extract aloud: ' "The same evil spirit may serve as a succubus to a man and as an incubus serve a woman." In other words, the incubus is sexually interchangeable, able to switch from male to female and back again. One of its metamorphic attributes, like the ability to take on superior muscle strength.'

'Or that toughening of the skin,' Doc added, 'to withstand broken glass and whatnot.'

Julian put away the notebook and took another slice of the doctor's toast. 'When I finally realized that Stefanski had meant Billuart, I ran straight to these notes and read them. Suddenly the list of suspects *doubled* to include not only every man in Galen but every woman, too. My bright idea about the dormitories! We were locking the rapist *in*, not out. I began to make a mental list of all the remaining women in Galen, *ex*cluding Laura, of course, because she'd been a victim. But then I asked myself if I really *could* exclude her from the list of new suspects. She was Helen Keaton's roommate in the dorm, and she didn't have an alibi for the times the other women were killed, and we had only her word for it that she was attacked . . .'

Doc nodded and pulled a small object from his pocket. 'Hank showed me this last night. Found it in the drawer of Laura's desk at the *Signal* office.' It was a simple instrument with a handle and short metal claws.

'Some kind of gardening tool, isn't it?' Julian asked.

'That's right,' said Doc. 'It's called a cultivator. Hank found specimens of human skin and blood on the claws. It must have been what she used to make those scratches when she faked the attack. Which gives rise to a question. Was she aware, all the time, of what she was? After all, to fake an attack like that – it was an act of deliberate, planned deception.'

'Or,' said Julian, 'was it the single moment when her human and non-human personalities existed simultaneously?

Was it the *only* time they overlapped, human intelligence working together with non-human instinct, the instinct for self-preservation? When the moment passed, she herself may not have been aware of the deception. I don't think she was. Just as I think the identity of the molester was as deep a mystery to her as to everyone else. At least, that's what I prefer to believe.'

'So do I,' said Doc, pushing away his empty plate and pouring another cup of coffee. 'Because, you know, I'm going to miss her. There was something about her . . . '

'An aura,' said Julian. 'Sexuality incarnate. I felt it years ago, when she was a student of mine. It took all my will power to keep my hands off her then.'

'Yes, that's it, an aura,' said Doc. 'I felt it, too.' He was thinking of that morning in her bedroom when she had been deep in drugged sleep.

'Even Helen Keaton felt it,' Julian said. He told him of the incident in the dormitory showers. 'It was intersexual, that aura, it awakened desire in everyone. It's as if she were made out of the Primal Matter of old Greek myth, the basic stuff of creation, the prehistoric ooze life evolved from, a purely procreative substance, unthinking, radiating fertility, fecundity, the essence of male and female . . . or does that sound too fanciful?'

Doc replied, 'After the events of this summer, there's not much that'll ever sound too fanciful to me again.'

The two men sat silent for several moments. 'Well,' Doc said after a while, 'I'd better get going. I have a lot to do today. A long list of patients, complaining of everything from diarrhea to constipation, with a bit of bladder trouble thrown in just for variety. Revolting, hm? But that's a doctor's life. It's made me highly resistant to another wishy-washy little-old-lady idea, the one about the dignity of Man. Hell, there's no dignity in the way we live or the way we die. And there's certainly no dignity about the way we come into the world. Conception and birth are the most undignified procedures I can imagine. The old Church Fathers had it pegged: *Inter faeces et urinas nascimur.* Between shit and piss we're born. Not much dignity in that.

233

Come on, I'll walk you out to your car. Where are you bound for?'

'Eventually, I'll be flying to Boston,' Julian said, as they rose from the table and sauntered out of the inn. 'Stefanski's will makes me the executor of his unpublished papers, and I'll have to gather them together and bring them back to San Diego before school starts in the fall. But before I go to Boston, I think I may get in a few more weeks in Mexico. There's a very interesting old Indian down there, a *curandero* they call him. You'd like him. I think he has a lot more to teach me.'

'Just don't eat too many enchiladas. Bad for that uric acid condition of yours.'

'I'll be careful.'

As Doc watched Julian's black Porsche drive away from the inn, he thought of another death they hadn't counted. Number Twelve. Will Clemens. He felt, somehow, he didn't have the heart to return to his cracker barrel satirist role. Too much water had passed under the bridge. And, besides, where would he find another editor as receptive as Laura?

The bravado of his breakfast banter deserted him. The world rushed in upon him with all its multitude of horrors – the natural world and that other world of unexplainable malignancy. He felt empty and afraid and suddenly very old.

About an hour later, when Julian had left Galen far behind, and was riding the exhilarating curve of the coast highway, relishing the salty breeze that blew from the Pacific, he turned on his car radio. At the sound of the music, he smiled at an irony: it was the same Mahler symphony he had heard on his way to Galen.

He wondered if he would encounter a comely hitchhiker, with a tote bag and winking navel and pleading pout? If he did, he just might stop and pick her up.

He thought about Doc's parting comments regarding the dignity of Man. No riposte had occurred to him as they were sitting at the table. But if Stefanski had been there, *he* would

234

have come up with an answer. He probably would have said something like . . .

Julian felt a strange sensation. It was as if someone were sitting next to him in the car. He knew there was no one there, but he found himself unable to turn and visually confirm that fact. He felt, irrationally, that if he did, he would see bright eyes behind glinting spectacles and a mane of thick white hair. Nonsense, of course, purely subjective, a reaction to the onslaughts so recently suffered by his emotions. Even realizing this, he could not turn his head. And he could almost hear the phantom passenger speak, responding to Doc Jenkins:

'The miracle, dear Doctor Sam,' said the familiar Slavic voice, 'is that a creature such as Man, born *inter faeces* and such, in stench and slime, can measure the distance of the stars, and build the so sublime Sistine Chapel, and write *Hamlet*, and compose the *Missa Solemnis*. Or heal his fellow creatures, as you do. Or lay down his life for another, as the boy Tim. *That*, dear doctor friend, is the dignity of Man.'

The feeling that he was carrying a passenger passed from Julian. The Mahler symphony no longer pleased him. The turgid straining and striving of the music, the exquisite torment and despair, the romantic *Weltshmerz* were not what he needed now. He punched a button on the radio and got a weather report he didn't need, either – his own senses told him the weather was superb. He poked another button and received an earful of raucous rock. He sat back and enjoyed the simplistic mindlessness. It was exactly what he wanted. He sang along with it as he drove south, away from death and tears and ruined lives, back into the world of – what was that Warren G. Harding word? – normalcy.

The sun kindled blue fire in the flat eternal sapphire of the ocean.

I WAS BORN TONIGHT.

I think that in some other place or places I was born before and died and then was born again but none of that has meaning to me.

I only know that I was born tonight and that there is a thing that I was born to do.

And I will do it *now*.

... But lost arts, tempting tamperers, yet must unfailingly seal their doom — immutably, eternally.

*— Artes Perditae*

# THE HUMANOID TOUCH

## TOUCH

### Jack Williamson
### author of THE HUMANOIDS

More than thirty years ago Jack Williamson
created one of the finest science fiction novels of
all time – THE HUMANOIDS. In this new
novel he returns to his classic subject: the final
confrontation of man and machine. THE
HUMANOID TOUCH is a new peak for a
master of science fiction.

'Decades before the current headlines about
automaton, computers and robots, Jack
Williamson was examining the relationship
between humankind and machines in his stories
of the Humanoids. Now, in THE
HUMANOID TOUCH, the Grand Master of
Science Fiction carries that saga to its final,
irresistible step. This is science fiction at its best:
thoughtful, thought-provoking, and thoroughly
engrossing.' *Ben Bova*

SCIENCE FICTION   0 7221 9195 2   £1.75

Something has gone terribly wrong in the
charnel house of science . . . something that
must never see the light of day.

# CHIMERA

## Stephen Gallagher

Any government cover-up is news but this time journalist Peter Carson
knows he's onto something big. A top research laboratory on the
remote Cumbrian moors is cut off from all outside contact. Rumours of
an accident at the pioneering Jenner Clinic spread beyond the armed
roadblocks and seep through the massive official news blackout.

Dr Jenner's work matters to the government. It matters enough to have
a blank cheque, high security cover and the best technicians in the
country. But something has gone badly wrong. The project that has no
room for mistakes has produced a result so terrible that it must never
see the light of day. And now the evidence must be destroyed whatever
the cost . . .

ADVENTURE/THRILLER     0 7221 3757 5     £1.75

A selection of bestsellers from SPHERE

**FICTION**

| | | |
|---|---|---|
| REMEMBRANCE | Danielle Steel | £1.95 ☐ |
| BY THE GREEN OF THE SPRING | John Masters | £2.50 ☐ |
| MISSION | Patrick Tilley | £1.95 ☐ |
| DECEPTIONS | Judith Michael | £3.95 ☐ |
| THREE WOMEN | Nancy Thayer | £1.75 ☐ |

**FILM & TV TIE-INS**

| | | |
|---|---|---|
| E.T. THE EXTRA-TERRESTRIAL | William Kotzwinkle | £1.50 ☐ |
| FAME | Leonore Fleischer | £1.50 ☐ |
| CONAN THE BARBARIAN | L. Sprague de Camp & Lin Carter | £1.25 ☐ |
| THE SWORD AND THE SORCERER | Norman Winski | £1.50 ☐ |
| GREASE 2 | William Rotsler | £1.25 ☐ |

**NON-FICTION**

| | | |
|---|---|---|
| ONE CHILD | Torey L. Hayden | £1.75 ☐ |
| DAM-BURST OF DREAMS | Christopher Nolan | £1.75 ☐ |
| THE COUNTRYSIDE COOKBOOK | Gail Duff | £5.95 ☐ |
| GREAT RAILWAY JOURNEYS OF THE WORLD | | £5.95 ☐ |

All Sphere books are available at your local bookshop or newsagent, or can be ordered direct from the publisher. Just tick the titles you want and fill in the form below.

Name _____

Address _____

_____

Write to Sphere Books, Cash Sales Department, P.O. Box 11 Falmouth, Cornwall TR10 9EN
Please enclose a cheque or postal order to the value of the cover price plus:
UK: 45p for the first book, 20p for the second book and 14p per copy for each additional book ordered to a maximum charge of £1.63.
OVERSEAS: 75p for the first book and 21p for each additional book.
BFPO & EIRE: 45p for the first book, 20p for the second book plus 14p per copy for the next 7 books, thereafter 8p per book.

*Sphere Books reserve the right to show new retail prices on covers which may differ from those previously advertised in the text or elsewhere, and to increase postal rates in accordance with the PO.*